POLICE PROCEDURALS RESPECTED BY LAW ENFORCEMENT.™

"Usually it's hard for me to read cop books without picking them apart ...the way Carolyn wrote Madison describes me and the way I work and even my personal life to a t. I have never felt more connected to a character. Thank you for creating something so real."
— *Deputy Rebecca Hendrix, LeFlore County Sheriff's Department Poteau, Oklahoma, United States*

"Carolyn Arnold provides entertainment and accuracy."
—*Michael D. Scott, Patrolman (Ret.) Castroville, Texas, United States*

"Rich characters and a superb job of capturing the law enforcement partner relationship."
—*Kevin Johnson, Sergeant (Ret.) Minneapolis, Minnesota, United States*

ALSO BY CAROLYN ARNOLD

Ties that Bind
Justified
Sacrifice
Just Cause
Deadly Impulse
Life Sentence
Eleven
Silent Graves
The Defenseless
Blue Baby
The Day Job is Murder
Vacation is Murder
Money is Murder
Politics is Murder
Family is Murder
Shopping is Murder
Christmas is Murder
Valentine's Day is Murder
Coffee is Murder
Assassination of a Dignitary
Hart's Choice

FOUND INNOCENT

CAROLYN ARNOLD

HIBBERT & STILES
PUBLISHING INC.

Found Innocent (Book 4 in the Detective Madison Knight series)
Copyright © 2013 by Carolyn Arnold

Excerpt from *Just Cause* (Book 5 in the Detective Madison Knight series) copyright © 2014 by Carolyn Arnold

www.carolynarnold.net

2015 Hibbert & Stiles Publishing Inc. Edition

ISBN (e-book): 978-1-988064-17-8
ISBN (print): 978-1-988064-15-4

Cover design: WGA Designs

CHAPTER 1

"He didn't do it!"

The hysterical shouting pulled Madison's attention from her monitor to a woman rushing toward her.

The station was supposed to be quiet today. Sunday. She wasn't required to be there, and that made it the perfect day to dig into her cold case. She was so close to getting answers.

With one more longing look at her screen, Madison rose from her chair and held up her hands to stop the woman.

"Detective Knight." She stated this as if they had met before.

Officer Ranson, the female officer who manned the front desk, came up behind them. "Come on—"

Another officer brushed past Ranson and slipped his hands under the woman's arms. "Let's go."

He pulled on her, but she stayed still. Her eyes steadied on Madison.

"Please help me." She attempted to shake loose from the officer's grip.

Her frown lines were deep burrows, her eyes were sunken, and the flesh around them was puffy. She appeared to be rough-edged, but there was something desperate about her, and she didn't seem to be a threat to the lives of anyone here.

"I've got this," Madison said.

"All right, your call." The male officer let go of the woman, and he and Ranson left.

"I saw your face in the paper." The woman held up the Stiles Times. "It's you, isn't it?" Her lashes were caked with mascara, and she blinked slowly. Madison wondered if the cosmetic had sealed her eyes shut.

Madison passed a glance to the paper. It captured a moment she wished to forget. A day when she had been forced to speak in front of a crowd and to take pride in the job she had done. The thing was, though, a good cop couldn't care less about the recognition.

The woman sobbed, yet her tears didn't affect her makeup. "He wouldn't do this…"

Madison summoned patience. A list of envelope printing companies—which could prove to be a vital link in the chain of evidence against the Russians—would be on her monitor, right now.

She took a deep breath, passed another glance to her computer, and turned back to the woman. "Come with me."

Madison kept the woman to the side of her. Her first impression was the woman didn't pose a threat, but she still wasn't willing to sacrifice her back by leading the way into the room.

Inside, Madison gestured to a chair.

The woman dropped her red bag heavily on the table. It was large enough to serve as a duffel bag. She pulled off her jean jacket, folded it over the back of the chair, and revealed a pink sweater that displayed more cleavage than Madison could ever hope to see on herself. The woman went rooting through the duffel bag and she stuffed a stick of gum in her mouth. She worked at chopping it into a soft, pliable distraction. It snapped in her mouth.

"Let's start with your name—"

"Vilma with an 'i.' Vilma Thorne, well, it would have been. My God, Kev!" She raised her face upward as if calling out to a Greater Being. Her gum chewing paused only momentarily.

"Vilma—" Madison had to tune out the noise and the display of her open-mouth chewing. "Let's start at the beginning. Why are you here?"

Vilma stuck a finger through one of the large gold hoops dangling from her ears and leaned in.

Madison detected the blend of cheap perfume and cigarettes. Maybe—she inhaled deeper, trying not to be obvious—it wasn't perfume but whiskey. It was hard to discern. Her eyes appeared normal, except for the abuse of eye makeup. Besides the thick mascara, her lids were weighed with the color purple. Her pupils weren't dilated or pinpricks.

Still, she didn't respond to Madison's question.

"Okay, Vilma, if you need my help, I need you to talk to me."

Possibly this woman was on a new line of drug that disguised itself behind brilliant colors? Maybe this was a mistake and Madison should have let her get hauled away.

"My family is against what he did. But he didn't do it!" Her voice rose, tears flowed. She stopped chewing and, sniffling, went rooting in the duffel bag again. She came out with a bunched up tissue and wiped her nose.

Madison's tolerance level had almost reached its limit. "You keep saying he didn't do it. Do what?"

A tissue still pinched on the tip of her nose, Vilma said, "He didn't kill himself…someone killed him."

CHAPTER 2

SIXTEEN HOURS LATER, Madison still wondered why she had agreed to look into it. By all accounts, Vilma with an 'i' seemed to be either disillusioned or off her medications.

Madison had searched the database for Kevin Thorne. He had been twenty-seven. His cause of death was suicide. His body was released within the last week and his funeral was scheduled for today.

Vilma was having a hard time coming to grips with what her fiancé had done, and the fact their wedding was set for two days after his death wouldn't have helped the situation. Even with that aside, in suicide there was rarely an acceptable reason to justify the action.

She flicked a pen across her desk and thought about how the interaction had changed the direction of her day. She didn't get much accomplished with her cold case and it had kept her up most of the night. She knew who was behind the murder, but she had to prove who pulled the trigger.

The victim was a defense attorney who had been gunned down in his driveway after failing to come through for his client, Dimitre Petrov, a Russian mafia boss. He was sent away on a life sentence for a single murder, a joke when the man's hands were stained with blood. With him behind bars, she knew he wasn't physically involved, but she believed he'd ordered the hit. It was a matter of proving which of his right-hand men were responsible, and then this beyond a doubt to the DA and subsequent jury.

The bit of evidence she focused on these days came down to an envelope match—the infinity symbol was woven into the fiber of the paper.

A torn piece had been found next to the dead attorney and it was a comparative match to an envelope addressed to her from Petrov himself. The contents of the letter, however, she kept to herself. She never even told her partner, Terry, what it said.

Terry would mock her, asking what she expected to solve with an envelope.

Her thoughts on the matter were that small things pile up, and when there is enough, it builds a solid case. Just as a mountain is formed, one dirt particle at a time, she would gather indisputable evidence against all involved with the murder.

"So, what did I miss yesterday?" Terry came in holding two Starbucks. He smiled as he extended one to her.

She looked up at him, disappointed there weren't more hours in the day. She closed the Internet browser and, with it, a list of printing companies, but before she did, she sent the link to her home e-mail. "I take it you heard."

"Oh yeah." He started laughing. "I'd say eccentric, but everyone said she didn't appear to have any money." He spun his index finger around his right ear. "Cuckoo for Cocoa Puffs."

Madison laughed. "You have such a way with words."

"You're jealous of me." He pulled back his coffee for a quick sip and then put it on his desk. "Seriously, though. Clashing colors, screaming, 'He wouldn't do it.'" He steepled his hands. "What didn't he do? Spill it."

"Kill himself."

"Here I thought it was going to be so much better than that." He exhaled. "Disappointing."

"Disappointing?"

"Well, I thought maybe she was going to say the butler didn't do it. I don't know. I just expected something better."

"She says that her fiancé never would have killed himself."

"If I had a penny for every time I've heard that—"

She overlooked the cliché. "You've heard that before?"

"Nope, not really, just thought I'd bug you with a cliché. Too bad it didn't work." He pouted.

"Terry, I'm going to kill you." She rose and headed toward him.

He took his Starbucks and started into a slow jog away from her. "First you'll have to catch me."

She would catch him and she'd make him beg for a reprieve. At least that was her goal until Sergeant Winston came around a corner.

"Don't you two have work to do?"

Terry stopped moving. Madison caught up to where the Sergeant and Terry were.

"We're a little slow this morning," she said.

"As I can see. Well, now you're not. Remains have been found at nine twenty-three Weber Street."

"That's a residential neighborhood." Terry took a sip of coffee.

"Very good work, Sherlock. They were found in the backyard. Of a house." The sarge seemed to add the latter part for the purpose of mocking Terry. "Some poor sap thought it would be a good time to turn the dirt in his garden and came up with a finger on the point of his shovel."

It seemed a little early to start on a garden—it was March—but Madison focused on the victim. "Do we know if it's a male or female?"

"They were still working at uncovering it all, from what I know, but the finger indicates it is a female. Seriously, don't tell me you're both still standing here. You were moving quicker a moment ago."

"Leaving now."

"Damn right you better be."

"I call the driver's seat," Terry said.

Madison brushed past him. "You can call whatever you want. Still doesn't mean it's happening."

CHAPTER 3

THE ADDRESS OF 923 WEBER Street put them right in the middle of the popular east end—popular, at least, with drug users, prostitutes, and gang bangers. Narcotic detectives had recently shut down a meth lab on a nearby street, resulting in charges against three people. It was the type of neighborhood where people could slip away without being missed. It was also an area of contrasts. Some houses were well-tended to, showcasing people who took pride in what they could afford while other properties fell apart.

The houses they were passing right now were worn down. The paint was chipped off in large sections and some had broken front windows.

As Madison drove, Terry faced the window. "I wouldn't want my kid growing up here."

Terry's wife, Annabelle, was five months pregnant.

"Speaking of it—"

"It?" Terry turned to her from the passenger seat. "Nice." He laughed.

"Well." She didn't have a mothering instinct in her. "How else do you refer to *it* when you have no idea which sex it is?"

"As him. It's a he. I can feel it."

Her focus was on the road, but she heard the smile in his voice. "You sound pretty positive."

"A father knows these things."

"Yeah, what does Annabelle have to say?"

"Still staying on the topic of its sex? Because if we're going off topic, most of the time it's pick up a burger, or get me black cherry ice cream. The woman's got the strangest cravings. Last night you'll never believe what she had for dinner."

Madison smiled. "Amuse me."

"Canned salmon with a little dab of mayo and pickles. That's it. No bread, crackers, nothing else."

"Sounds healthy."

"Sounds like a boy." Terry flashed a goofy grin.

Madison parked in front of the house. Their light conversation faded as the eyes of onlookers fixed on them. They stood on the sidewalks, arms crossed, heads tilted, seeming happy the spotlight was on someone else. For now, whatever crimes they had committed would go undiscovered.

Cole Richards, the ME, was already there along with the Crime Scene Investigation Unit. Their vehicles were parked in front, on the road.

The house offered no driveway. The two stories of siding were pitted with dirt and the passage of time. The front yard was small and outlined by a four-foot high chain-link fence, but Madison could see down the side of the house that the backyard was long.

"Maybe there's more than one body. There would be room."

"You've always been a positive thinker."

"Well, it wouldn't be the first time. Right area for it."

Officer Higgins came to them.

"Hey, Chief." Madison addressed him like that sometimes. It made the man's face flush and his cheeks ball with a full smile. Higgins could have been the Chief if he'd aspired to be, but he preferred staying at a lower rank of officer. As Madison saw it, the man wasn't corrupt enough to be promoted to office.

"Not too nice around here." Higgins traced his fingers through the air directing their attention to the neighborhood, its implied reputation.

Madison looked back and noticed a pair of sneakers hanging by its laces over a hydro wire.

Higgins continued. "I've been called out on domestics to this house so many times, the car knows the route. I should have known it would be for the girl's death one day."

"Do we have an identity yet?"

He slowly shook his head. "Well, not a full anyway. You know how it is. Neighbors hear fighting and call it in, or the girl does, but when we get here, the guy's done nothing wrong. It was her fault. I can just remember a first name. Lacy."

"She never pressed charges?"

"Nope, and we can't make 'em. There's no ID on her. Richards said she hasn't been there too long. But I remember her face."

"Have the entire remains been excavated at this point?"

Higgins nodded. "The guy living here used her as his own punching bag. There was nothing I could do. The only time I got to haul his white ass downtown was when he answered the door with a .22. It wasn't registered." Higgins smiled. "But it didn't keep him behind bars long. He was back out to beat on her. That must have been ten weeks ago now. He got two months' probation. Speaking of which, I haven't been called out here since. Until now."

"What's his name?"

"Don't even need to consult the records for that one. Ralph Hennessey. We can't find him right now."

"Sounds like he's running." Madison glanced at Terry and gestured for him to start taking notes. He didn't make any move to.

"Had the woman lived here?" Terry asked.

Higgins shook his head. "I thought she did, but there's no sign of it inside, except for a package of prescribed allergy medication. Crime Scene found it under a couch. Unfortunately, the label was torn and her full name wasn't there. We just have Lacy, what we already knew. There isn't a script number either, but we have a partial logo and the pharmacy phone number. It might help. We'll also be getting out canvassing soon. If anything comes of it, we'll let you know."

"If Hennessey did kill her, he'd want to get rid of all the signs she was there. They could have even slipped out when he grabbed her purse to dispose of it," Terry said.

"It's possible," Madison said. "A lot of things are possible." She addressed Higgins. "How many apartments are in this house?"

"There are two rental properties. Hennessey lives on the main level, and a guy by the name of Elroy Bates rents the upstairs. He's got a record. B&E. Got out a year ago after serving three years. We've gone to pick him up. He works at a gas bar down on Bakker Street."

"Anyone contact the property owner?"

"No need. He's the one who called us."

"He's the green thumb who wanted to start the garden?" Terry asked.

"Donald Giles. He got a ride downtown. You can talk to him there."

Madison glanced at Terry, who tapped the names into his new phone. She rolled her eyes. He had discovered the technology age recently and it replaced his traditional notepad. Madison didn't put much faith in his new system. You could scribble something down so much faster.

"Terry."

"What?" He kept tapping on the screen.

Higgins smiled at Madison. The older guy knew her enough to know she wasn't the largest fan of electronic gadgets. Some things were better done the traditional way. She snapped her fingers. "By the time you're finished there, we'll have caught the killer."

"And the problem with that?" He smiled at her.

She narrowed her eyes.

"Fine." He snapped his phone back into its holder and pulled out a notepad. He held it tight to his chest, close to his face, a black pen poised over the lined sheet. She could picture him with small round reading glasses perched on the end of his nose.

"Yes, boss. What can I do for you?"

"Don't be a smartass." She smiled. "The names are Ralph Hennessey and Elroy Bates."

Terry wrote the names down.

"Does Richards know the cause of death?"

"Based on the hole in her head—"

"Gunshot wound?"

"Seems like it. Maybe even a .22. The .22 that had originally landed Hennessey behind bars was confiscated, but they're easy to get on the street."

"Hopefully there's still a bullet." Madison patted Higgins's arm on the way to the backyard.

"Keep safe out there, Maddy."

"You too, Chief."

Terry leaned into Madison, "What about me? He didn't tell me to be safe. Are you two involved and I don't know about it?"

"Seriously? The guy is the same age as my father. Now, if he were at least twenty years younger...maybe." She laughed.

The property seemed alive as Crime Scene crawled through every blade of grass. A barn-shaped shed was in a far corner. Mark Andrews, a CSI, was working through its contents.

The back door of the house opened and Cynthia Baxter came out. She stood there as if she were lost in thought. She pulled her sunglasses down from her forehead where they had been positioned. The regular studious eyeglasses may have been replaced by contacts today, which meant she must have had a good night's sleep.

Madison waved to her, but her friend's thoughts must have transported her focus. She didn't respond but walked back inside the house.

The shallow grave was in a garden that lined the property's perimeter. The remains were on a black tarp to the side of the hole. Richards was braced beside the vic's head.

Madison addressed him. "Higgins said it was a gunshot to the head that may be the cause of death."

Richards looked up at her long enough to communicate his disgust that an officer would make that judgment. "I haven't concluded yet."

Richards's personality usually accommodated for some small talk and lightheartedness. Today he didn't seem to be his normal self, although, Madison realized her approach could be what had changed the outcome. She had managed to insult his profession— something she had had no intention of doing.

"How long do you think she's been in there?" She remembered Higgins had mentioned Richards's assessment, but she would hear it firsthand.

Richards rose to his feet and squinted from the sunlight. "I'd say probably no longer than one month, but it's hard to pinpoint exactly."

"Which means we'll need to find last witnesses who saw her alive," Terry said.

Madison looked down at the woman. "First we need to figure out exactly who she is." There was dried blood caked with dirt around her mouth. "Gunshot to the mouth."

"Appears that way." Richards bent back down and opened the vic's jaw.

Madison looked inside her mouth. A few of the front teeth were broken off, likely from impact. "It looks like a small caliber. Like a .22."

"Possible."

"If that's the case, we probably won't have a bullet to trace. It would have fragmented in her brain, especially at such a close range." Madison noticed the muzzle burn around her mouth.

"Hopefully we can find the casing." Terry looked around the yard.

"First, we'll need the scene of the crime." Madison kept her eyes on the woman. She appeared anorexic. Her hipbones extruded from under her skin. She made an assessment based on the demographics of the area. "Drug addict?"

"My first thoughts on the matter, yes, but I didn't see any visible signs at first. Until…" Richards moved down the body and separated two of her toes to expose the center of them. There was a definite puncture mark. "This is where she shot up. I'll be requesting a tox panel on her to narrow in on exactly what she was into."

Madison noticed a rose tattoo on her ankle.

Richards pointed to abrasions on her knuckles. "It also looks like she may have been in a bit of a struggle. I don't typically like to speculate. I'd say it looks like a suicide, but—"

"So she killed herself." Madison glanced at the hole in the ground and back to Terry. "But how did she bury herself?"

CHAPTER 4

MADISON STEPPED INSIDE THE HOUSE WITH TERRY. She had expected it to be messy and unclean, based on the judgment of a lifestyle. "And we're sure she didn't live here?"

"Are you implying that only women can be clean freaks?"

"My thoughts were on their way of life. Drugs and domestic violence. Their minds are not organized. I'm surprised this place is. Seems out of character."

Terry walked toward the couch. "What are you thinking?"

"She could have been made to keep it clean and he's been gone since he buried her."

"Quite possible. We'll have to find out when he was last seen. Hopefully, the neighbors can help us out with that."

The house was boxy, with all the rooms being the same—square with small windows. Nothing was unique from an architectural standpoint. A small dinette table was to the right, with a galley-style kitchen. To the left, a couch was used as a separator between the living room and kitchen. A narrow walkway went between the two spaces, to a hallway that led to a bathroom and bedroom. The flooring was original hardwood and worn with age. The furniture was also old but kept clean.

Madison glanced at the kitchen sink. No dishes. She had the feeling her first assessment was right. Hennessey took off right after burying Lacy.

"Think my parents had a couch like this." Terry gestured to the tweed stripe. "Brings back memories." He moved through the room to the back corner. "There's some dust on this TV."

Madison moved into the area. The TV was a relic and rabbit ears protruded from the top of it.

"So far I don't see any traces of a woman living here at all, but he could have taken her clothing and other belongings and sold them for drug money," Terry said.

"There has to be more to this. What could she own worth selling? Why kill her?"

"You didn't see her fingernails when Richards held up her hands? They were manicured. I should know what that looks like—"

"Personal experience?" Madison laughed.

"Annabelle goes on and on about her day at the spa—when I let her go."

"When you let her?"

"Anyway, the paint on her nails wasn't that badly chipped."

Madison thought of the recoil. "Which means you don't think she fired the gun?"

"High-end polish and she likely had a manicure not long before she killed herself."

"We've got a woman buried in the backyard, a bullet to the brain, department store clothing, manicured nails, and a deadbeat boyfriend who is on the run. Why would she paint her nails to pull a trigger?"

Terry rubbed the back of his neck. "Good question but I'm thinking, based on this neighborhood, the girl had a sugar daddy."

"You're thinking a staged suicide? That could be motive."

"Yeah, looking at it either way. Hennessey didn't want anyone else to have her—"

"Or she holds leverage over her sugar daddy," Madison finished Terry's sentence.

Terry nodded. "Could be, or maybe he was just sick of her. She was always looking for a high. Most men can only enjoy a party for so long."

"You should have said can only keep up with it for so—" Madison stopped talking when Cynthia came up the hall.

"I found the scene of our crime." Cynthia held onto her camera even though it hung from a strap around her neck. "In the bedroom."

The room held a small dresser, a double-sized bed, a simple nightstand, and a wooden chair in the corner.

Cynthia pointed toward the chair. "Luminol showed positive for blood. She was shot sitting right there."

Madison nodded toward Cynthia's collection kit. "Won't any DNA be useless?"

Cynthia looked at Madison, insulted by the implication, as written in her expression. "We had no real idea where the vic was murdered. We only had the confines of this house being of primary interest. I started spraying higher plausible areas."

Her friend was in a mood this morning. Madison wasn't going to press why a chair in a bedroom would be a probable area.

Cynthia continued. "And, for the record, we use this new formula that does not alter the DNA, thereby allowing for genotyping. I've already collected some swabs. Hopefully, it connects us to the vic and we can confirm this as the primary."

"Lacy," Madison corrected.

"What?"

"That's what Higgins said her name was." Madison surveyed the bedroom. The bed was made in a fashion that would have made the military proud. Madison put on a pair of latex gloves and opened a drawer in the nightstand. "It's so clean in here I'm surprised there isn't a Bible."

The furnace kicked in and the ductwork rattled.

"Do you hear that?" Terry asked.

"It's an older house." Cynthia worked the strap and the camera over her head and put it in her collection case.

"I'm not talking about the standard rush of air. There's a ticking sound coming through the vents." Terry moved to a heat vent situated about four feet in front of the chair. "Cyn, take the grate off."

She looked at him as if to indicate she wasn't anyone's slave.

"You're already gloved up."

"Uh-huh." Cynthia bent down, took off the grate and reached inside.

"Feel anything?"

Cynthia pulled her hand up and looked at it. "Spotless house I give it that. Not one hair." She put her hand back down. The rattling continued. "There's got to be something—" She came out with her fingers pinched around something. Her face lit into a smile. "A shell casing and it's from a .22. I'll have to send it away to have it processed for prints. It may take a while."

"Send it away?" Madison moved closer.

"Well, there's a technique to reveal the impressions but it involves a special machine which passes high volts of electricity through the metal. It also utilizes a fine conducting powder. I won't get into the scientific details."

"Why should it be easy? And the bullet in her head's going to be useless for striations, but Sam could obtain grooves and impressions made from the firing pin on the casing to match a gun."

Samantha Reid worked in the lab and specialized in firearms and ballistics.

Cynthia held up the bullet casing as if it were a trophy. "Yes, she can."

CHAPTER 5

DONALD GILES SAT IN INTERROGATION room one looking like he had lost his dog. A cup, still full of coffee, sat in front of him. His balding round head came to a comical point at the base of his chin.

Madison and Terry were standing outside the room looking in with Officer Tendum, who had brought Giles in.

"His official statement is that he didn't do it and he never saw the girl before," Tendum said.

Madison kept her eyes on the older man behind the glass. "They all say that."

Tendum was still working through his probationary period but seemed to give the impression he should be exempt from it. Madison had run-ins with him before. She brushed past him. "Coming, Terry?"

"I had nothing to do with it. I told your man there." Giles pointed a finger toward the mirrorpane. "Did he tell you?"

Madison disregarded him and made the formal introductions. "You found the woman, correct?"

He nodded. "Yes."

"It's your property at nine twenty-three Weber Street, correct?"

His brows pressed downward. "I don't see—"

"You're legally responsible for your property, Mr. Giles."

"I never saw her before." He started shaking and wheezing. His one hand gripped at his chest.

Terry moved toward him, and the older man waved him off.

"Asthma, I'm used to it." Giles looked at Madison. "I'd have no reason to kill her. I don't even know who she is." He paused, heaving for breath and reached into a pocket to pull out an inhaler. "How could I anyway? My health is in the crapper."

"Not bad enough that you can't use a shovel. Isn't that how you found her?" Madison placed implication on the word *found*.

He glared at her and put the inhaler on the table. "This is entrapment."

"We're looking for the answers."

"I thought I'd do a garden this year and get an early start. Figures, with my luck." He inhaled from his puffer. "I couldn't beat her and bury her."

Madison glanced at Terry. She had picked up on a couple of things. One, either Giles didn't know how the girl had died or he had mentioned a beating to throw them off. And two, she remembered clearly what Higgins had said—Ralph Hennessey beat on her. Madison took a shot on the latter line of reasoning.

"You do know who she is."

"I—" He took another inhale from his puffer and caught his breath. "I assume."

Madison kept quiet and worked him over with steady eye contact. Sometimes silence was more powerful than words.

"All right, I saw a girl there before. At Ralph Hennessey's. I tried to overlook it."

"Why?"

His eyes fell downcast. "It doesn't matter. They paid the rent on time. Not many do these days."

Madison wasn't buying it. Giles was afraid of Hennessey. "We didn't find any evidence to show a woman lived there with him."

"Don't know what to tell ya then. She was there any time I came by to collect rent. Once she had a black eye. Said she fell. I knew better, but what am I supposed to do, ya know? Pretty girl. Too skinny, though."

Madison passed Terry a glance and they stepped into the observation room.

"So, she was covering for Hennessey. She loved him. She could have been manipulated into pulling the trigger." It sounded like a stretch of the imagination, but Madison verbalized it anyhow.

"And once she did, it was about getting rid of the evidence. Hennessey likely subscribed to the philosophy that if he couldn't have her, no one could."

"You're thinking of her nails?" Madison asked.

"Yeah. I think she had an upper-crust connection and wanted to move on with her life."

"Upper crust?"

"You're going to pick on my wording right now?"

Madison raised a shoulder.

"Anyway, Hennessey has a record. I think he found out about another man, told her she was worthless, maybe even dared her to pull the trigger on herself. Let's not forget the defensive wounds either."

"I agree. I'm beginning to think she may have pulled the trigger, but it wasn't her idea."

CHAPTER 6

THEY RELEASED DONALD GILES, who seemed more than eager to leave the station. He looked like he was longing for a drink and his eyes sagged with the stress of his day.

Madison and Terry entered the interrogation room where the upstairs tenant, Elroy Bates, sat wearing a black hoody. Bates was as black as night and had dreadlocks. The stereotypes became that for a reason—sometimes they held truth.

Bates slid his bottom lip through his teeth. "I don't understand why I was dragged down here. I ain't do nothing."

Madison noted that he wasn't very articulate and slipped into a chair opposite him. "A body was found in your backyard."

"It's not just my backyard, dawg." Bates balled a fist. "See RH yet?"

"RH?"

"Ralph Hennessey, the tenant from downstairs?" Bates rolled his eyes back hard enough Madison wondered if they'd return.

"We're looking for him. Until then, we're talking with you. Do you—"

"Talking *to* me, don't you mean? I know how all this shit works. Blame it on the black guy." He slapped his chest.

"Do you know where Hennessey is?" She had to ask the question, even though a full search for the man was under way.

"Nope."

"There was a woman who lived there with Hennessey."

Bates rubbed his chin across his shoulder. "I ain't saying."

"We don't need you to. The landlord told us she did."

"Can I go?"

Madison had to stifle her rising anger. "Did you know that Hennessey had a lady living with him?"

His eyes darted to the table before focusing behind them.

"When did you last see her?" Maybe she could fool him into disclosing something.

"How the hell should I know?"

Madison smiled. "You did know about her."

"I ain't sayin' that."

"We have all day." Madison put her hands on the table and rose to leave.

"Shit! Lady, I don't know."

She stopped walking and turned around. "Think hard."

"I dunno. A few weeks ago."

"This woman who lived with 'RH.' Describe her for us."

"She was a dirty blonde." He snorted a laugh, and when he realized he was the only one who found amusement in his statement, went serious again. "She was tiny. I like my woman with a better build." He stopped talking and eyed Madison as if she were candy. "A real woman, ya know."

If Madison cared what this creep thought of her, she might feel self-conscious about her size. She carried a few extra pounds but was more athletic build, than she was the bikini model. So far, the description, although vague, matched Lacy's physical description.

"Anything else?"

"She was popular with men friends."

"She slept around?"

"Not with me. Not sure if she put out with everyone but no one minded trying to git with her if you know what I mean."

"You tried?"

"Maybe I did, maybe I didn't." Bates extruded his lips and pulled them in.

Madison noted his demeanor. "You were close enough to know her name."

His eyes took in the room.

"Bates if you know, it's best you tell us. Are we going to find your prints on the shovel that buried—"

"Lacy. A'ight?" Bates splayed his hands on the table. "That's all I know. She's RH's girl."

"You don't know her last name?"

"Can't say I do."

MADISON SPOKE TO TERRY ON the other side of the glass. "No further ahead, except we have confirmation she lived there, at least in a roundabout way. And we can't hold him because of his skin color." She referred to their superiors' viewpoints on such matters. They would lock up any who appeared guilty based on a pre-set mold if they had their way.

"The sarge really isn't that bad."

"You're blind then. Every time someone is less advantaged or fits the stereotype, Winston narrows in on them."

"I think you should give the guy more credit."

"As soon as he gives me a reason to, how's that? And since when are you on his side?"

Terry didn't answer her, but she witnessed insecurity in her partner's eyes.

CHAPTER 7

TERRY PULLED UP THE INTERNET and did a telephone search for the partial phone number they got from the allergy medication. "Hopefully this brings us something."

"It should help, that's for sure. Too bad all we have is her first name to help us out."

Terry glanced at her and smiled. "You're always so skeptical. Here it is. Dixie's Pharmacy on Lexington."

Lexington was in the north end of the city, a particularly wealthy area.

"You're certain?"

"That's what came up with the four digits. Besides, the logo that was left matches up to theirs." He pointed to the screen.

Madison grabbed her coat. "Let's go then."

Sergeant Winston stopped her. "Whatcha got, Knight?"

And the play-by-play begins.

"We're close to getting a full ID for the girl."

He studied her eyes as if he suspected she knew more than she was telling them. "Fine, but keep me posted."

THE PHARMACIST STOOD BEHIND THE counter, both hands braced on it. The way he stood there, it was as if he looked down on them and viewed himself as superior. "Normally, I'd ask for a warrant."

"We're asking for your help with a suspicious death," Madison said.

He shrunk behind the counter. "It has nothing to do with our dispensing of drugs?"

"Not that we're aware of."

His face lit up. "Murder?"

What was wrong with society when the thought of someone's life being taken made their eyes widen with excitement? Madison blamed Hollywood for glamorizing evil and spreading the fever like an epidemic.

"Do you show a client with the first name of Lacy?"

He laughed. "You're going to need to give me more than that. An address? A prescription number?"

"Here." She showed him a picture of the package they recovered at the crime scene.

The pharmacist leaned over to look but said nothing. His eyes revealed that he recognized the packet.

Terry stepped closer to the counter. "Please just try the name Lacy in cross reference with this medication."

"I should get a warrant first."

"Don't you understand we don't have time for this? The longer you take, the farther away her killer could be," Madison said.

"You people don't give up."

"Just try the name—"

He held up a hand to stop her and started typing. "Lacy."

"Try it without an e."

"Yes, I got it."

"You found her?"

He looked up. "I mean I got it, as in I remember the name from—what?—less than twenty seconds ago." He looked back at the monitor. "Okay, let's see what we've got. All right, nothing there." He typed something else in.

"No Lacy?" Madison asked the pharmacist.

He exhaled loudly. "I'm working on this. Just give me a minute."

Madison rolled her eyes toward Terry.

"I show a Lacy." He flattened his hands on the counter and stared at them.

"Last name?"

"I'm not really sure if I should give that out." He leaned across the counter. "With the economy these days, everyone's replaceable."

"The woman's dead, she won't care. Her family, on the other hand, is probably looking for her." Madison had a feeling that wasn't the case. There was nothing in missing persons that had matched any identifiers on the vic. She kept eye contact with the man. He could be a father, possibly even a grandfather. "What if she was your child?"

"Oh no. Not playing that game."

"We won't release the source of how we came to ID her," Terry said.

The man scanned their eyes and let out a deep breath. "Last name is Rose."

Madison's mind went straight to the tattoo on Lacy's ankle. Her name was there all along.

"What address do you show? Is there a medical plan in place for her?"

"I will require a warrant for that. Now, if that will be all, I have prescriptions to fill." The pharmacist walked away.

She didn't expect him to answer the questions, but she studied his brief facial reaction and she would swear Lacy Rose had coverage. In the car, she asked Terry, "Did you see the flicker in his eyes?"

"Pretty clearly."

"Now we have to answer the question of what Lacy was doing with a guy like Hennessey in a cheap neighborhood when it seems likely she had a wealthy benefactor in the north end."

"And what was her relationship with her benefactor?"

Madison picked up her cell and dialed Sergeant Winston.

"Surprised to hear from you. Not used to this."

She ignored his attitude. "We've got a full ID on the vic. Lacy Rose. We've pulled the background and are headed over to notify next of kin now."

"How did you manage to get the ID?"

Madison told him and hung up.

"We promised that guy we wouldn't disclose who provided the full name," Terry said.

"Actually, you promised." She smiled at him and put the car into gear, but with speaking the word promise, two that she had made came to mind. First, the one made to herself to close her cold case, once and for all, and two, the one she had made to Vilma Thorne. But she didn't have time to deal with either right now.

CHAPTER 8

THE BACKGROUND CHECK ON LACY Rose showed the last known residence was located in the east end, only about a block from where she was found. The property had belonged to Patricia Rose, the deceased's mother, but she had died three years ago of a drug overdose.

The paternal name Patricia had stated for her daughter's birth record was Maurice Kendal. His address was in the north end of the city.

Madison stopped at the security gate for the neighborhood of Deer Glen. Bars prevented entry of any unwelcome visitor. It represented the line between the haves and have-nots.

"Please state who you're here to see." A man's voice came through the speaker beside the driver's-side window.

Madison held up her badge to the guardhouse where the small man hid behind the power of the uniform.

"Mr. Maurice Kendal, number six thirteen Fawn Avenue."

"Do you have an appointment with Mr. Kendal?"

"Police business. I can drive through the gate if you want."

"No need."

She heard the motor working and the arm lifted.

"You would have driven through it, wouldn't you?" Terry was laughing.

"Guess we'll never know now." She smiled.

A WOMAN IN A MAID'S uniform stood behind the door. "I'm sorry, but Mr. Kendal is not in." Her one hand steadied on the open door.

Madison heard talking in the background. Someone was there and by the tone, it wasn't more hired help. The man's voice held authority.

"We have bad news for Mr. Kendal." Madison flashed her badge.

The woman's posture slipped, and her Italian accent riddled into her speech. "I get him for you."

A large man, oddly resembling Daddy Warbucks of *Annie*, stood in front of them dressed in a Hawaiian shirt paired with khakis.

"What the hell is this?" His eyes surveyed both of them, one at a time, from their feet to their eyes. "I didn't receive a call from the gate notifying me of visitors." He turned and briskly clapped his hands. The maid picked up a phone on a nearby table and dialed a number. He twisted his wrist and looked at his watch. "I have a meeting to get to. What is it?"

A meeting in that get-up? Maybe his priorities would change when he heard what they had to say.

"Maurice Kendal?"

"Yes." The man nodded impatiently.

"This will only take a few minutes." Madison stepped through the door.

"By all means then, come in."

Luggage sat on the floor and would explain his tropical get up. Madison felt the "meeting" was more likely a vacation than a business affair.

"Don't have much time."

"Is there somewhere we could sit down?"

"Bad news is bad news, standing or sitting." He put his hands in his pockets.

Another man approached but kept back at a distance. His face reflected a warmness Kendal was sorely lacking.

"Your daughter, Lacy Rose, was found this morning and we believe she may have been murdered."

"I don't have a daughter. What is this?" Kendal looked around and Madison noticed the expression on the other man's face.

Madison continued. "We're sorry for your loss, and if there is any family we can call or anything we can do—"

"You can get out for one." He pointed a thick finger to the front door.

"You were listed as her father on the birth record."

"Doesn't mean anything. If, and I mean if, I had any connection with this girl, I would have been nothing more than a donor." He turned to the other man. "This is why you don't throw money away on the ten-dollar whores. They somehow sniff money and come back around. Stick to a reputable escort agency." Back to Madison. "Some girl came around a while ago. She claimed to be my daughter."

The man, who had been in the background, came closer. His breath was somewhat labored as if he debated whether to talk.

"You know her?" Madison asked him.

"I do." His voice cracked slightly. "I did."

Maybe it wasn't Daddy Warbucks supporting her, but rather, this man.

"And what's your relationship to Lacy?" Madison noticed Kendal's clenched jaw and the anger in his eyes.

"I'm not related." He glanced nervously at the homeowner. "And Mr. Kendal and I are business partners."

Madison addressed Kendal. "You mentioned Lacy came around. How long ago was that?"

"A few weeks ago." He turned to the other man, who nodded with the assessment. "She came begging for money and gave me all this talk about starting out in a new life. She rambled on about being found innocent." He nodded toward the other man. "Peter was here."

Madison noted the phrase "being found innocent." There was evidence that Lacy had shot drugs in her past. They would have to wait for toxicology results to see if she had stopped the habit more recently. And if she had stopped taking drugs to turn her life around, what had served as her motivation?

"Before that she never talked to you? She just showed up to ask for money and told you how she planned to change her life around?"

Kendal went to cross his arms but settled his hands on his hips.

"Essentially."

"That wasn't all there was to it?"

Peter eyed his business partner. "She wanted him to be her father."

Kendal's jaw tightened at Peter's statement, but Madison sensed Peter experienced more grief over Lacy's death than the father of record. Madison addressed Kendal. "But you told her to get lost?"

"When you've got money as I do, you get users."

"Users?"

"You know, the people who want to suck the life out of you, more importantly, drain your finances. They claim they want something more, something special." He dittoed his fingers when he said the word *special*.

Daddy Warbucks, or, as he was legally known, Maurice Kendal, wasn't a trusting person by any means. A puppy could likely approach him to be pet and he'd assume it wished to piss on his shoes.

Madison made special note of the other man's reaction. His eyes fell to the floor, if only for an instant. "Did you provide Lacy medical coverage?" she asked Kendal.

"You're not listening to me. I told her to get lost."

"All right." Madison and Terry backed away. "That will be all then. Sorry for your loss." The latter was added in the hope it would impress guilt upon a man Madison feared didn't have the ability to feel it.

CHAPTER 9

THEY SAT IN THE CAR outside of Kendal's house.

Madison grabbed a Hershey's bar from her jacket and took a large bite. "I think we should get on a warrant to release the information from Lacy's medical records, but I also believe this Peter guy has the answers we're looking for. Did you see his reaction to Lacy's death?"

Terry glanced down at her bar and then back to her full mouth. "I've told you how much I hate it when you do that."

"Lacy came around a few weeks back." She swallowed, took another bite. "A mother with a record, who dies, a father who disowns her, and a boyfriend who beats her. This girl had crappy luck. Drugs were probably her only escape. What made her change? Did she truly change?"

"I'd believe she killed herself if it wasn't for finding her in a hole. Someone else was around, and until we get an answer as to time line—"

"I know. It makes me wonder if she killed herself of her own volition. It seems she had a newfound hope in her life. We'll have to figure out what that was too." She gestured with her chocolate bar to the two vehicles in Kendal's driveway—a Jaguar and a BMW. Madison's eyes rested on the former. "I'd say Daddy Warbucks—"

"You thought he looked like that too?"

Madison laughed and nodded. She typed the plate of the BMW into the DMV database. "We only have Peter's first name, but his plate is going to give us the rest."

"Which car?"

She cast him a glance. "The Jag is more show and fun. Did you see Kendal's shirt?" She took another bite of her bar and tapped on the screen. "Peter Hargrove. Age fifty-eight. The file says he's married. The residence is located at twenty-one eighty Barber Avenue."

"That puts us at the same end of the city."

"Yep, Peter's got money too. Guess it makes sense with them being partners, and maybe when he saw Lacy, he thought he'd take advantage of a broken girl."

Terry lowered his chin and looked upward at her. "You don't know that."

"I don't *yet*." She felt pretty confident in her assessment. *What other purpose would a man have with a younger woman to whom he wasn't related?* "Also, Kendal told Peter to stick with the escort agency so he's probably not all that innocent."

THEIR FIRST THOUGHT WAS TO wait on Hargrove back at his house, but if he was involved, what would stop him from making a run for it after they left. Instead, after driving around the block to make the men think they had left the area, they had gone down a side street that afforded a clear view of Kendal's house. They would wait for Peter Hargrove to leave and follow him. The dusk of evening helped their cover.

"I hate stakeouts." Terry took a sip of his aging Starbucks.

"Yes, you have it so terribly hard." Madison laughed.

"I just want to be with Annabelle. We find out the baby's sex tomorrow morning. Only one more sleep."

"Don't be thinking you'll have some time off to go."

"Will be, Maddy, no question."

She smiled as she accomplished her purpose and got a reaction. She straightened up as she noticed Hargrove come out of Kendal's house and get into his BMW. "Here we go."

They followed him through a few subdivisions when they realized they knew where he was going. He wasn't making a run for it—he was going home.

"This could get interesting." Terry turned to face Madison. "That is if your feelings about Peter hold true."

"He wouldn't be the first cheating husband caught in the lie."

"It doesn't go with Lacy turning her life around. How would destroying a marriage figure in?"

"No one is innocent until proven such, in my opinion," Madison said.

"That's because you're such a positive person."

"Well, until tox comes back on her drug use, or lack thereof, I'm her advocate, but not necessarily a firm believer in her full transformation."

"Well, in support of her turning her life around, she had a fresh manicure and medical coverage."

Madison laughed, dispelling her partner's theory. "All that proves is someone—Hargrove possibly—was looking out for her. We have to get to the why. Were they sexually involved? Did Hargrove's wife find out about it?"

"You take everything and put such a dirty twist on it."

"How do you see it?" The truth was she couldn't look at it any other way. Blame it on the skepticism that came with the job. Her thought processes made her think about Vilma again—her large hoops, heavily painted eyelids, and her pleas to find her fiancé's killer. The report said it was suicide.

"How am I supposed to break it to her? Tell her to move on?" Her thought process gave audible birth.

"What?"

The comment would have come out of nowhere for him. "The crazy lady." She only used that description so that Terry would know to whom she referred.

He stared blankly at her. "You won't be telling her anything new."

"Then why do I feel like shit?"

"Because you made a promise you shouldn't have."

There could be no response for that. He was right. "She buried him today."

"It's sad, but it's not your fault."

She nodded. She knew it was the truth, but sometimes the truth sucked. "Maybe I'll go by in person tomorrow—"

"In the middle of an ongoing investigation?"

Her head turned to her partner, who was smiling. "Yeah, smartass." She punched him in the arm, nearly knocking his cup out of his hand.

"Careful. Ruin my Starbucks, I might kill you."

"Might? You're such a girl sometimes." Madison laughed. "You upset mine, you're—"

"I'm what?"

Her eyes fixed on Hargrove's BMW as it pulled into a driveway. "Looks like we're home."

The house was a two-story grandiose display. The entrance was two black doors adorned with polished brass hardware. Sidelight windows were to the left and right. Two ceramic urns sat in front of them and had small fir trees in them to suit the time of year. No doubt these would overflow with flowering plants in the summertime.

Lights on the front lawn shone on the house, encasing it in a warm glow as if it were a showpiece, and the chandelier in the alcove over the doors was bright enough to reach the road. A pair of matching fixtures, yet were smaller in scale, were attached at each end of the double-car garage. They were also on. Madison could only imagine how bright the house would be when decorated in holiday cheer.

Madison made all these observations as she walked up the driveway with Terry on her right.

"Peter Hargrove?"

He clicked his car's security system and it let out a soft chirp. "Detectives?" He slipped his keys into his pocket. If he was surprised that they were already aware of his last name, he didn't give that impression.

"We have a few questions for you. We can do it out here, or we could go inside."

"I have nothing to hide."

"What was your relationship with Lacy Rose?" Madison asked.

"If you're implying something improper, it wasn't like that." He paused as if waiting for Madison to object. "I felt for her when

Maurice sent her away."

"It didn't go beyond that?"

He let out a half-laugh. "Seriously? I'm a happily married man. I know it's hard to comprehend these days, but it's the truth."

Madison tried not to let it show that she bought into the fact that most marriages were doomed to failure. She picked up on where he took the direction of the conversation. "Why would you assume we thought that?"

"It's the look in your eyes. I see it every day. You're hungry." His eyes finished the statement with, *and I don't want you sinking your teeth into me.*

"I believe Lacy deserves justice."

"Please don't imply that I don't. If I could help you any more, I would." He made a move toward the house.

"Did you provide her medical coverage?" Madison asked.

He took a deep breath and passed a glance to Terry. He didn't answer the question.

"Did you do anything else for her?"

"I helped her out as much as I could. I'm grieved by her death."

Madison sensed, by the way his eyes softened along with his tone of voice, he felt somehow responsible for Kendal's rejection. "Does Mr. Kendal know what you've done for her?" She had to think his name through. She had almost said Daddy Warbucks.

"Heavens no. He's a controlling man and thinks he can tell everyone what to do."

She would come back around to what he referred to when he mentioned helping Lacy out as much as he could. For now, she would steer the questioning down another path. "Did Lacy say if she had problems with anyone?"

"You mean Ralph? All the time. She was going to leave him. I was helping her set up an apartment. I couldn't give her a position within our company, but I have contacts. She was willing to do whatever it took."

"Do you think Ralph knew she was leaving him?"

Hargrove sighed heavily. "Lacy had one weakness, she was a true person. She could never hide who she was. If she was angry, you knew. If she was sad, you knew."

Madison thought back to the limited evidence they had so far. "Was she depressed?"

"She went through a lot of misfortune in her short life. Her mother died three years ago, not that she was much of a mother when she was alive." He looked at them as if gauging their knowledge.

Madison noticed the corner of a curtain move inside the house. Hargrove's wife was watching them.

He followed where Madison was looking. "If that will be all."

"Actually, you mentioned setting up an apartment for Lacy. We're going to need its location and get a key."

Hargrove studied them.

"We're still looking for who did this. If this person knew about the apartment, he might be hiding there. Or, at the very least, we may find some other answers."

He nodded. "You just catch who did this to her. And if it's that no good Ralph kid, I might kill him myself." Hargrove's voice didn't fluctuate. They were sincere and he held no shame in them. He pulled out his keys and worked at twisting one off. "And for the record, I only have a key in case Lacy lost hers. I would never allow myself in without her permission."

Madison took the key from him, and he handed her a business card as well.

"It's apartment three-oh-five in the Luxor Complex." He started to walk toward the house, stopped and turned around. "If you find a small silver heart pendant on a silver chain, please bring it back to me. It was a gift I gave her."

"Of course." Madison looked at Terry. They both knew there was no sign of it where she was buried.

CHAPTER 10

MADISON PARKED THE DEPARTMENT'S CROWN Vic in the underground garage of the Luxor Apartment Complex. In a way, the pompous show of the building reminded her of a man she had recently parted ways with. She should have known it would never have worked out. He defended the guilty while she worked to convict them.

They loaded onto the elevator. Terry pressed the button for the lobby. "I know the sign says apartments, but it should read suites or condos. Lacy really lucked out with this Hargrove guy."

"Yeah, she lucked out all right. A shallow grave in a backyard."

"Well, we certainly took what should have been a light conversation somewhere dark." Terry's voice held a sulk.

"Guess that's life. In our world anyway."

"Wow, someone's mood has changed."

She wasn't going to get into her feelings with him. She didn't get into them with anyone. Most of the time she preferred to bury them and convince herself that she didn't care about anything. But if she were being honest, in a quick reflection, she would admit that she was thinking of Blake—even if its length was the blinking of an image. It had been her idea to end things, and for the most part, she accepted it, but she didn't fall easily, and when she did, she felt duped. The disappointment centered more on her than the failed relationship. She had to preserve herself and her emotions, but how far could she continue to stamp them down?

The elevator doors opened to the lobby, and it was decorated like a fancy hotel. Looking up, the floors curved with the exterior wall and overlooked the space below. A mahogany desk served as the concierge and reception area.

The man behind the counter eyed them with distaste as they approached. He wore a black suit with a brass nameplate over the left breast jacket pocket. It read ANTHONY.

Madison lifted her badge from under her jacket. She kept it on a chain today. "Mr. Hargrove's apartment, number three-oh-five."

He angled his head to the side. "Did something happen to—"

"This is a police matter." She held up the apartment key.

"Okay." Anthony gave them directions.

They took the elevator instead of walking around the spiraled tiers of the building.

Terry knocked on the door and held his head against it to see if he could hear anything inside. "I'd say it's clear."

"Last chance to answer the door. Stiles PD." No answer. Madison put the key in and unlocked it. She pulled out her gun and bobbed her head toward Terry to inquire if he was ready. If Hennessey were inside, he could be armed.

Terry drew his weapon as two women walked toward them laughing and talking about some guys they had met. When they saw the guns, their eyes widened.

"We're going to need you go to your apartments," Madison said. They hurried down the hall and went into a place a few doors down on the left. All talk of guys and overdrinking was forgotten.

Madison turned to Terry. "Ready?" She turned the handle and broke the seal on the door.

Terry went in first and covered her. She crept in behind him and surveyed the entry, taking advantage of the hallway lights. The front foyer had marble flooring, and two marble pillars that separated the dining room and sitting room. Madison closed the door and noticed that light from the moon and city lights seeped in through the windows on the other side of the room. It didn't do much more than a nightlight would.

She took in the high-end furniture and the decorative pieces that were showcased on tables and bookcases. Some art deco pieces hung on the walls. Large framed prints also accented the walls and complimented the colors of the apartment.

I take it back. She did luck out.

She kept her gun at the ready as they performed a sweep of the apartment.

There was a *thump*.

Both of them stopped walking. Madison's heart sped up. Nothing as a cop was routine. Each call was potentially fatal. If a trained officer forgot that in a lapse of poor judgment, it could be their last mistake. She swallowed hard, focused on her job, and tried not to dwell on her mortality.

Another *thump*.

She held her gun braced with one hand and made signals directing Terry to approach from the opposite side of the door. They'd go in together, backs covered with the wall as they slid around. She mouthed to him, "Ready."

He nodded.

The door opened to a small laundry room. The dryer was running and the clothes inside tossed noisily against the drum.

She holstered her gun. "We didn't miss him by much."

Terry slipped on a glove and opened the dryer. "Men's clothing."

Madison was sickened by the thought that a man who Lacy had cared for took over a life that was to be hers. But she was used to seeing this in the world around her. People cast aside as garbage when their usefulness expired. She would make sure Hennessey would pay for the crime. Her thoughts stalled there—if he were guilty. She was starting to think like her superiors—if the suspect fit a stereotype, he was the culprit.

They made their way into the bedroom. The bed was unmade and the sheets were strewn. Madison would guess it had been slept in recently. On the nightstand, Madison noticed a white residue and a small razor blade. She pointed it out to Terry.

"The guy seriously isn't that smart is he?"

They performed a sweep of the rest of the place. "Well, if Hennessey was here, he's not now," Madison said.

"But I'd place a bet he's coming back."

She smiled. "You have to bet on something all the time don't you?"

He shrugged.

"This time it won't work 'cause we'd be making the same bet. He wouldn't leave his score out there and—"

The apartment door opened and closed.

She pressed an index finger to her lips to silence Terry. He was already braced for action.

They made their way down the hallway. The front foyer light came on. They rounded the bend.

"Stiles PD! Put your hands up!" Both of them had their guns drawn.

There was a loud pitched scream. A young lady of about twenty stood there. Her foundation was heavily applied and a shade darker than her natural skin tone. Her greasy black hair was pulled back into a ponytail. She was pale and had a small, skeletal frame.

Madison and Terry placed their guns back in their holsters. Madison conducted a quick search of her.

"What's your name?" Madison asked.

The lady still had her arms in the air.

Madison motioned for her to relax.

"Rebecca Scheibe. Ralph said it would be all right for me to come here."

All Madison could think was his girlfriend wasn't even dead an entire month and he was onto another one. He probably slept with both women when Lacy was alive. And maybe there were more. It usually wasn't a very loyal world among the cockroaches.

"This is Ralph's place?" Madison played along with the girl.

Rebecca tucked a cheek into a shoulder and rubbed it there. "You're here. You tell me." The initial shock of running into cops had transformed into a defensive stance.

"How long have you known Ralph?"

"Met him this afternoon. He gave me this." She held up a brass key, fingered it, and slipped it back into a jean pocket.

"He's meeting up with you here?"

"Yeah. I guess so."

There was a knock on the door.

Rebecca turned as if she were going to answer it.

"Stop there," Madison said. "Don't open the door." Madison motioned her to the peephole. Rebecca glanced out, reaching it only by balancing on her tiptoes.

"Is it Ralph?" Madison asked.

She nodded.

Terry moved around in front of Rebecca and directed her away from the door. Terry needed to open the door in such a way that Hennessey wouldn't see them and bolt, or retaliate and put Rebecca's life in danger.

"Is someone in there with you, baby? You've got a surprise for me?"

Madison rounded the bend to the hallway. Terry opened the door and slipped behind it so Hennessey only saw Rebecca.

Hennessey moved toward her and Terry came up behind and grabbed both his arms, snapping the cuffs on him.

"What the fuck?" Hennessey pulled on his arms and his eyes fired rage at Rebecca. "You."

Terry riffled through Hennessey's pockets and pulled out a baggie of white powder. He dangled it in front of Hennessey's face, yet spoke to Madison. "Like I told you. Not too smart at all. We're taking this party downtown."

CHAPTER 11

THEY TOOK HENNESSEY AND REBECCA downtown and both were sitting in an interrogation room. The apartment at Luxor was cordoned off with an officer guarding the door. Crime Scene was called in for evidence collection in relation to drugs and anything that might confirm Hennessey's involvement with Lacy's death and burial—besides an opportunistic coincidence.

Hennessey sat back in the chair, one arm slung over a side of it. He had a thick chest and didn't carry any extra weight on his frame. "She made me do it."

"Rebecca made you kill and bury Lacy?" Madison asked the question, mocking his cavalier attitude.

Terry stood by the door with his arms crossed. He had that look where his jaw appeared tight and something in his eyes communicated not to mess with him.

"No. It has nothing to do with Rebecca." Hennessey straightened his posture. "I...we...didn't kill her."

"What did Rebecca make you do then?" Madison studied his body language—the way his fingers tapped on the side of the chair, the way his eyes took in the room without focusing on anything in particular. "Rebecca says you two just met."

Hennessey didn't say anything and avoided eye contact. Rebecca's statement was fact. When he'd said, "She made me do it," he was passing blame to Lacy.

"So, let's start with why you were at the apartment. It's not yours," Madison said.

He kept looking at a place behind her and remained silent.

"Can you explain what you were doing there?" Madison leaned across the table and laced her hands.

Hennessey dragged a hand down his face. Silence.

"The longer you screw us around, the longer you'll be here."

He gave no visual acknowledgment that he had heard her.

"When was the last time you saw Lacy Rose?" Five seconds of silence. Madison slapped the table. She raised her voice. "She was found in your backyard."

Terry walked over to Hennessey. "Answer the question. When?"

"I…I don't know. A few weeks ago." He looked between the two of them and his feet bounced under the table. The laces of his running shoes clicked against the floor.

"When exactly?" Terry put a firm hand on Hennessey's shoulder.

He looked at Terry's hand and then up to his face. Terry left his hand where it was positioned. Hennessey shifted. "Listen. I don't know, all right."

"You beat up on her, didn't you?"

Hennessey looked up at Terry again, back to Madison. "There are no charges for that. Check my record."

"We have an officer who tells us he was out there a lot."

"Means nothing."

"Means nothing that a sworn officer of the law testifies to being out there? It means nothing that there is a record of the calls?" Madison pulled out the report from a file folder. "Shows about twice a week. The last time being ten weeks ago."

"Doesn't mean anything."

Terry pulled back on Hennessey's chair and got in front of him. "It means you beat on her. She was afraid to press charges—"

"Did you shoot her to silence her? Stage it to look like she pulled the trigger on herself?"

Sometimes it was necessary to volley a suspect back and forth to make progress. The evidence seemed to indicate that Lacy pulled the trigger on herself. But Madison hesitated to accept that, based on two facts—people had said she was turning her life around and, the glaring obvious, that she couldn't have buried herself.

"You guys are crazy."

"You don't seem to understand what we're saying here." Madison stood. "We believe you're responsible for her death."

Terry stayed within the boundaries of Hennessey's personal space.

His leg kept bouncing. "You can't prove it." He wiped down his face again.

"How did you get the key to the condo?" Madison leaned farther forward. "You killed her, buried her and took it."

"No…no…Lacy and I would go there."

"You expect me to believe that?"

"It's the truth. Swear." Hennessey glanced up at Terry. "She liked the finer things. She said her daddy got the place to help set her right."

"Her daddy?"

"Yeah, that's what she said. I'm just telling you what she said."

"Lacy's father wasn't in her life."

Hennessey sank into his chair. "That's what she said."

Madison knew Maurice Kendal had been telling the truth when he said he expelled Lacy from his life. It was clear in his eyes—the hatred for a young woman he never really got to know.

"Did Lacy sleep with other men?"

A steady pulse tapped in Hennessey's cheek.

"The condo was paid for by an older man, but it wasn't Lacy's father." Madison poked at the underlying fire.

His eyes went to hers.

Madison cocked her head and spoke to Terry. "When she said Daddy maybe what she really meant was sugar daddy."

Hennessey sat straight, formed a fist with his right hand, and slammed it into his left palm.

"You knew about him," Madison said calmly.

He sat staring at his fist. "I guessed. I mean, how else could she afford that place?"

"And you killed her for it." Madison pulled back in her seat. "You killed her because no one else was allowed to have her."

"I didn't say that."

"But it's the truth, isn't it? When did you find out she was sleeping, well, not really sleeping, but having sex, with another man?"

Hennessey harbored a lot of pride; she would continue to beat him where it hurt—his ego. He glared at her.

"Jealousy is one of the greatest motives for murder. There's nothing new about it." Madison addressed Terry again. "Not even original."

"I didn't kill her." He clenched his teeth.

Madison rose to her feet and paced the room. As she neared Hennessey, Terry stepped back to make room for her. She leaned in next to Hennessey's ear. "Where did you get the key?"

He hit the table with his fists. "I told you we'd go there together—"

"Lacy is dead. She didn't let you in. In fact, I don't think you were there together. She was trying to get away from you. I'll ask the question again—where did you get the key?"

Anger tapped in his cheeks, and he clenched his fists.

Madison continued to speak in his ear. "You stole it from her purse. You took her clothes, her jewelry—" Madison thought back on the chain Peter had said he'd given her. "You sold them for drug money. You killed Lacy and then profited from her death." She was close enough to Hennessey she felt her warm breath swirl back at her.

Hennessey's hands stopped moving and he slowly turned to face her. Their noses were less than an inch apart. "Prove it."

She made sure to look him in the eyes. "Don't worry, we will."

Hennessey's fists continued to pump, but he diverted his gaze from her and faced forward. "Am I free to go now?"

Madison straightened out, laughed, and addressed Terry. "He thinks he's free to go."

Terry smirked.

"Are you for real? You were in possession of cocaine—"

"It's not my apartment—"

Madison studied his face, picking up on the contradiction in his words. "You can't have it both ways. First Lacy basically told you it was also your apartment, and now it's not yours. Which is it?"

Hennessey slammed his fist onto the table.

She had him. Now she needed the solid evidence to place him behind bars for what happened to Lacy.

"And you must be forgetting we took two ounces off your person. Let's just put it this way, you won't be going anywhere for a while." Madison opened the door and Alex Commons from narcotics walked in.

"What? Who is—" Hennessey stood to his feet and made an effort to leave. Terry pinned him against the back wall. The narcotics detective put cuffs on him.

"You have the right to remain silent," the detective began.

Madison and Terry left the room.

"Do you think he did it?" Terry asked the question and stood to one side of the open door.

"I think we got lucky we can hold him for something else. It also gives us room to deal."

"What? Take a murder charge to lessen a drug one?"

Madison smiled at Terry. "As you said, the guy isn't very bright."

Chapter 12

Rebecca sat in interrogation room two. She had her arms wrapped around herself and rocked back and forth. She straightened when Madison and Terry entered the room.

"We have some questions for you." Madison slid a file folder on the table as she took a seat. Terry braced against a side wall.

Rebecca nodded and as the fluorescent lights hit her cheeks, it became obvious they were damp from crying.

"You said you just met Ralph?"

"Yes." She bobbed her head as if it would add proof to her verbal answer.

"Where did you meet?"

Her eyes went between them. "At a club on Forty-Six. He came up to me."

"You normally get together with guys you just met?"

Rebecca's eyes went downward. There was more hidden there than a rendezvous.

"Why did you arrange to meet Ralph Hennessey?" Madison asked even though she was aware of the likely answer.

Her voice seemed shrunken. "For sex."

"The way your eyes divert and the way your tone lowered tell me there's more to it."

"I'm not lying to you!" She shifted her position and clasped her hands, letting them rest on the table.

It was with this movement Madison noticed a silver chain around her neck. The base of it was hidden under the collar of the sweater she wore. She did her best to look at the young girl's chest area without being obvious.

Madison relaxed her posture and settled into her chair despite her obsession over the necklace. She decided she would play this straightforward.

"The main purpose was to score cocaine wasn't it?"

Rebecca fidgeted. The necklace moved with apparent weight, like that caused by a pendant. With Rebecca sitting the way she was now, Madison could make out a small indent under her sweater.

"I want a lawyer."

It was the meekest demand for legal representation Madison had ever heard. Rebecca was new to the game—her young face not even etched with the hardness of the lifestyle.

"We'll get you a lawyer." Terry headed to the door while Madison stayed seated.

The girl had requested a lawyer when it came to the drug allegations.

Madison leaned across the table. "Nice necklace."

The girl's brows tightened with confusion before her fingers went to it. She pulled the necklace up and the pendant was exposed. Rebecca seemed to admire the silver whale before looking up at Madison. "Thank you."

Madison had her answer—this hadn't been Lacy's necklace. She went straight to the point. "Hennessey is being investigated for the murder and burial of a young woman."

Rebecca gasped. "Oh my God! I never should have…oh my God!"

"Now, you say you just met him, but you can probably see why we want to make sure you're telling us the truth."

A slow nod as she pinched the pendant in her fingers.

Madison placed a photo of Lacy Rose on the table. "Did you know this girl?"

Rebecca picked it up and looked at it.

"I don't. I'm sorry."

TERRY LAUGHED OUTSIDE THE INTERROGATION ROOM. "You really thought it would be that easy?"

He must have known what she was getting at with the necklace and the pendant. Instead of a whale, she was hoping that a small silver heart would emerge from the sweater collar. "Hey, sometimes we get lucky."

"We do? Name once."

His direct inquiry caused her mind to go vacant. "Okay, nothing's coming to mind."

"That's because there's nothing to come to m—"

"Hey watch it." She smiled at him.

Chapter 13

MADISON AND TERRY MADE THEIR way through the lobby of the Luxor apartment complex. The man at the front desk was the same one as earlier in the evening. His jaw tightened at the sight of them. He was probably the one facing all the questions from management about what was going on.

An officer stood outside of Lacy's apartment with a hand above his holster, giving the impression he stood vigil, but his eyes gave him away.

It was only ten at night—the new recruit would never make it if he didn't learn how to function without sleep. Madison should know.

Madison found Cynthia processing the bedroom. Terry went off in another direction.

"Find anything?" Madison asked.

Cynthia looked up from where she was hunched at the closet doors dusting for prints. "You mean besides the few ounces of cocaine?"

Madison nodded.

"Not much."

Madison moved closer to the closet and noticed it was empty. *The thieving, murderous bastard sold pretty much everything.*

"No clothes that belong to a woman?"

Cynthia shook her head as she lifted a print, sealed it for evidence, and rose to her feet. "If our vic ever lived here, there's not much sign of it."

Madison's mind fixed on Cynthia's words. "You said that there was 'not much sign of it.' Is there something to prove a woman lived here?"

"There was a tube of lipstick in the bathroom medicine cabinet and did you see the artwork? My guess is it's a woman's taste. Now whether that woman was our vic—"

"Lacy Rose." Madison had let the first generic reference go.

Cynthia let out an exhale. Madison knew what her friend was thinking—she hated that Madison would get personal with the deceased at times, giving preference to referring to them by name rather than the label of victim. Madison wasn't going to feel sorry for who she was.

"You mentioned the artwork? Peter Hargrove likely would have picked it out for her or took her shopping with him," Madison said.

"Do you think he's involved with her death?"

"My main question is what makes a man do all this for a woman if he isn't having sex with her? He would deserve the Good Samaritan of the Year Award. Maybe even of the century."

"The big word in there being if. These condos go for half a mil each. What would make someone do that for a girl he just met? And for nothing in exchange?" Disbelief danced in her friend's eyes.

"When Terry and I spoke to him he said he felt bad for her. She had reached out to her biological father and he had turned his back on her—"

Peter had said he was a happily married man and would never touch the girl, yet Maurice Kendal had told him this is what you get when you sleep with ten-dollar whores. The two thoughts were contradictory. They needed to do more digging into Hargrove's world.

Then the revelation hit her.

"Holy shit."

"Maddy?"

"The man who set Lacy up in this apartment, Hargrove, told us that he only met her a few weeks ago." She thought on that for a second. Did he say that, or was it inferred from the conversation with Kendal? She shook her head. "How is that possible when her time of death was pegged at a few weeks ago? If Kendal, her father of record, had his dates right that would mean Hargrove knew her before that. We need to figure out who had the most to lose—the boyfriend or her benefactor." She looked at Cynthia. "We still need a motive for Hargrove and why he'd want Lacy dead, but he's not off to a good start with misleading us."

"Might be a good question to ask—"

"You're taking over my turf now?" Preston Marsh, a narcotics detective, stood in the doorway. He was all of five-foot-five but housed a lot of power in his small frame. His chest and arm muscles tugged on his shirt. He had thick dark hair, a trimmed mustache that suited him, and an award-winning smile.

"Hey, murder trumps drugs," Madison said.

"In your mind." He smiled at her.

"Well, if you had this city under control with the drugs, maybe we'd see fewer murders." Madison raised her eyebrows at him.

"Whenever you Major Crimes Detectives can pass the buck." Marsh walked around to the end of the bed, moving closer to Madison.

"You want to play this game? I specifically remember a case a few years back when—"

"There's no need to go there."

"Come on. Let's." Madison passed a glance to Cynthia. "They booked this guy for drug possession, but the chain of evidence was broken."

"Rookie. Don't go there." Marsh's shoulders sagged. "Knight, I'm begging you."

"Anyway," Madison picked up the story again, a smile tugging at her lips, "the charges didn't stick, and the guy was back on the streets within twenty-four. He was picked up four hours later and charged with the attempted murder of a seventeen-year-old boy."

"Everything worked out in the end."

"Eventually, but it wasn't because of the Narcotics Division. It was Major Crimes."

"Toot your own horn much."

"Hey, who would have thought that newbie would have

amounted to anything? Yet here you are."

Marsh smiled at Madison. "Are you finished with story time?"

"I'm sure I could pull out more."

Marsh held up a hand. "Save it for a drink with me sometime."

"We'll see, big boy." Madison smiled at him and went to look at Cynthia, but she had packed up and was headed out of the bedroom.

Madison had gotten to know Marsh when a few cases intersected with narcotics. Marsh was easily five years younger and had the reputation of a being a lady's man. What he lacked in height he made up for in charisma. Although, for Madison, there was never any real chemistry between them.

"I heard you're single," he said.

"Keep it in your pants, Rookie."

"Hey, I'm not a rookie anymore."

"That's not what I hear."

"Ah, Knight. You can be cruel."

She smiled and turned her back on him then left the room. Terry nearly bumped into her.

"Look what Mark found." Terry held up a sealed evidence bag with a package of unopened allergy medication.

Mark Andrews was a member of the forensics team who specialized in trace evidence.

"They were under the mattress in the second bedroom. The prescription reads for Lacy Rose."

Madison read the prescription. It had been filled by Dixie's Pharmacy, the same one they had visited earlier in the day.

"Guess that gives us the evidence we were looking for. Lacy was here. This should also give us enough for a warrant so we can find out the name of the healthcare provider," Madison said walking toward the kitchen. Terry came with her. "And from there we can track the policy to its holder."

Terry nodded. "Tomorrow."

She glanced at the clock on the stove. 11:55 PM.

"Yes, tomorrow, Terry."

"And don't forget I'll be catching up with you a little later tomorrow. I've got the—"

"Yes, the appointment with the doctor, with Annabelle." She smiled.

"All right then. I'll catch up with you in the morning. Probably about eleven or so."

"Sure."

Mark walked by and Terry handed the evidence bag back to him.

"Tomorrow then." Terry turned to leave.

"Terry," Madison called out to him.

He turned around. "Yeah."

"Hope everything goes good. Let me know what you find out." Terry smiled. "Will do."

With him gone, somehow the apartment felt empty. It was as if she could hear her thoughts clearer, despite all the activity with Crime Scene eagerly working their way around.

MADISON LEFT THE CONDO BUILDING and headed home. The thought of touching her fingers to Hershey's soft ears made the day melt away. Dare she even admit that Terry had a point when it came to dogs? They not only had a way of loving unconditionally, but they also had a healing capability.

She leashed Hershey and took him outside. The air was chilly, but the harshness of it had lessened from prior weeks. The hint of spring was carried in the air.

As she waited for her canine companion, she remembered when she had come home late one night to find Blake waiting there for her. There was no chance that would be happening again, and, really, it was for the best. They were on different paths in life— parallel lines that would never meet.

Hershey did his business then sat at her feet.

"Come on, buddy." She tapped her thighs excitedly. "It's time to go to bed."

When she had arrived home, the time in the car had read shortly after two in the morning. It must have been creeping closer to three at this point. Her body sagged from exhaustion, but her mind kept firing scenarios in the case.

There were a few people who could have wanted Lacy Rose to die, but they were all hinged on suspicion at this point, with nothing solid to convict any of them. She had to will her brain to sleep. Morning was technically already here.

CHAPTER 14

"You're wanting a warrant issued in regards to the allergy medication?" Sergeant Winston sat behind his desk, fortressed behind mounds of paperwork that never seemed to shrink, but instead only grew.

"Yes, for the purpose of tracing back to the Medicare provider and the policyholder." Madison was used to defending everything she did. She tagged it on being a woman in a career field dominated by men. Men were always right, even when they were wrong. At least that was the theory they subscribed to.

"She had a wealthy male friend from the north end who'd set her up in a luxury condo and took care of her. He was working on getting her a real job. Again, this is only what we know so far. What Hargrove has told us—"

"You don't believe he's telling you the truth?"

"I don't believe anyone. I've seen too much." The confession took her breath. She couldn't connect eyes with her superior. "I get the job done." She shifted in her seat and made herself look at him. "I subscribe to guilty until proven innocent."

The Sergeant had his eyes trained on her. She swore she saw a spark in them, a flicker of pride in his detective.

"And you think Medicare will lead back to this man," Winston rolled his hand, "from the north end."

"Yes, I do. And if it does—"

"If it does, how much further ahead are we? You already know the man takes care of her. What's his motivation? Tap into that."

Madison exhaled. "If we can prove that he set her up with

health care and a doctor to prescribe medication, we have cause to seriously question his relationship with Lacy. Right now it's his word against our suspicions."

Winston seemed to consider what she had said as he studied her eyes, yet he didn't say anything for seconds. He picked up about an inch of paper from the stack on his left and put it in front of him. His pen was poised over the sheet. "Okay, we'll get your warrant in the works, but may I also remind you that you have two other suspects behind bars already."

"Really only one. The girl was let go. Hennessey's being booked for drug possession. The truth of the matter is, from my standpoint, not only am I doing my job in trying to solve a murder, but I took a drug addict off the street, possibly a dealer." She noticed the corner of his mouth begin to lift. "Maybe I should look into a transfer." She smiled at her superior.

"Don't get all cocky on me, Knight. There's no room for an ego in the equation."

She winked at him as she rose to her feet. The occasions were few when they got along.

"Where is Terry this morning?" Winston asked.

"At the doctor's with his wife."

"His baby all right?"

"As far as I know. They're finding out its sex." She pushed the chair she had been in closer to the Sergeant's desk.

She had made it to the door before he asked, "When are you having kids, Knight?"

She kept walking, trying not to choke when she swallowed. Somehow, whenever she had a glimmer that she had gained his respect, it was inevitably followed by a backward landslide.

CHAPTER 15

SHE OPENED THE MORGUE DOORS. Cole Richards stood over the body of Lacy Rose. He held the woman's heart in his hand. He put it on the scale and noticed Madison at the same time.

Madison's earlier coffee came up the back of her throat.

"The victim's heart weighs eight-point-five ounces," Richards said, not for her, but for the recording device on a side table. He gave her a look that said, *I'll be with you shortly.*

"The time is seven of ten on Tuesday morning. Taking a pause from the autopsy now." He pulled his gloves off, paused the recorder, and looked up at her. "Something I can do for you?"

"Have anything for me?" She smiled, hoping it would melt his mood and work to dislodge the growing heave in her throat. It failed on both counts. Most wouldn't understand her distaste for the sight of blood, and she wasn't going to volunteer her aversion to it.

"I always tell you when I do." He clasped his hands in front of his bloodstained smock.

"I know you do." Madison took a step toward the body, but her legs weakened and planted her feet to the floor four feet away.

The blood.

"First, the easy news. Blood genotyping that Cynthia collected from the bedroom was a match to the victim and confirmed the bedroom as the scene of the crime. Now, onto the cause of death. Preliminary COD was damage to the frontal and parietal lobe. In layman's terms, a bullet to the brain." He pointed toward the dissected brain matter and to the small bottle that held bullet fragments. "As for her condition at the time of death and her drug abuse history, appropriate samples will be sent to the lab for a full tox panel."

"A person who knew Lacy said that she was turning her life around. The tox panel should also tell us how long she used, and the last time."

Richards nodded. "Yes, it should at least provide us with an approximate picture." His eyes went to the table, to the body, and his interrupted autopsy.

Madison's eyes were on the multiple bottles and items pulled for the forensic lab.

Richards walked around the body to Madison. "I pulled trace from her nails, and her hands were tested for gunshot residue and came back positive. I believe I told you that latter part at the crime scene." He glanced at the body. "The strange part about all of this is it looks like a suicide, in that she pulled the trigger. I did pull trace of GSR on her hands, and the angle on her broken teeth seems to indicate this. Besides the fact she couldn't bury herself, we can't dismiss the struggle she had with someone prior to her death." He pointed to her scraped knuckles.

Madison took a deep breath, and with the inhale came the potent scent of death—blood, tissue, and decomp. She swallowed hard. "The boyfriend had a history of beating up on her, although no charges were filed. Higgins told me he saw the girl when she was alive—beaten up, but alive. She never wanted to press charges, so, besides a record of calls taking them to the area, and officer's notes, nothing else substantiates that. We have to figure out if the defensive wounds were from that abuse or related to her death."

"A sad fact when it comes to the victims of domestic abuse— very rarely do they fight back. They may hold up a hand or arm instinctively, to block blows, but one is usually too beaten down mentally to fight back physically. They don't believe they are worth defending."

"Very good point." Madison couldn't believe she had missed thinking that. It would coincide with what Hargrove told them about Lacy trying to get her life together, about Kendal's claim she wanted to be found innocent. "She didn't want to die."

Richards slowly shook his head. "It doesn't seem that way to me. Now, you know I don't like to speculate, but I think she was coerced into pulling the trigger, or someone made it look like she did."

"You are talking possibilities?" Madison asked.

Richards's dark skin pinched around his eyes. "I'm trying to play along today. I see you're down your partner."

Madison smiled at him. Her relationship with Richards would return to the way it was before the last case before she took things too far and pried into his personal history.

"He's off finding out the sex of his baby."

"Well, good for him."

Richards was a married man. He and his wife never had children, but it wasn't for the lack of trying.

An awkward type of silence filled the space. If Lacy couldn't control her life, maybe she thought she'd take the power over how she'd exit. Or maybe it was as Richards had suggested, someone made it look like she had pulled the trigger.

"What would make Lacy shoot herself? Did someone threaten to kill her if she didn't kill herself?"

"Now that is a question worth asking."

Her cell rang and she answered. "Knight… Okay, I'll be right up." She hung up and looked at Richards. "I'll let you get back to her."

"Thank you." He smiled at her, close to showcasing his white teeth, but not quite.

CHAPTER 16

"Ranson." Madison addressed the female officer at the front desk. Today her hair was brown with blonde highlights—she had a thing for experimenting with hair dye. Ranson had been the one to call her when she was in the morgue with Richards. She told her a young lady was here looking for Hennessey.

"She's over there," Ranson said.

Madison peeked around the corner to see a Hispanic woman sitting on the bench. She sat bent forward, doubled in half, her fingers laced through her shoulder-length dark hair.

"Did she give you a name?"

Ranson shook her head. "She said she needed Hennessey now."

"Her dealer." Madison tapped the counter and headed to the young woman. "You're looking for Hennessey?"

No response.

Madison got closer to her. "Hennessey?"

Slowly, the girl siphoned her fingers from her hair and then straightened up to look at Madison. Her eyes were half-mast and vacant. Her gaze went to Madison.

"Who are you?" she asked.

"Detective Knight. Why are you looking for Hennessey?"

"He's my man. I heard he was here."

"You heard correctly."

"I need to see him." Her eyes were still on Madison, but her focus seemed to trail behind.

"Let's go somewhere and talk."

The girl let out a loud sigh. "I need Henn-e-ssey." She dragged the name out.

"I'll take you to him after we talk."

"Whatev."

Madison directed her to interrogation room three, where she had the girl sit across from her. "First off, what is your name?"

The girl leaned on the table with her elbows bent, her fingers fanning through her hair again. She stared at the tips of her hair. "Why do you need to know?"

"You want to see Hennessey, you start talking to me."

A dramatic deep exhale. "Sahara Noel."

"Very pretty name."

Sahara's eyes connected with Madison's. "He used to call me Christmas Morning."

"Used to?"

Sahara snorted. "Yeah."

"But he doesn't anymore." Madison pushed her.

"That's what I said bit—" She stopped there. She must have received the message in Madison's eyes.

"When did he stop?"

"When he met her." Her words were slurred.

"Met her, who?"

Defiance sparked in her eyes. "Lacy."

"You didn't like her."

"I had no reason to like her."

"So you hated her? She stole your man."

"It's not like that, it's—"

"Just what?" Madison tapped the table to realign Sahara's focus.

"Okay, yes I hated her! I found him fucking her like a dog on the damn couch." Instead of tears of heartbreak, anger and hatred marred her expression.

Madison pulled back and studied the girl in front of her. *Would she be capable of forcing Lacy to pull the trigger on herself?*

"Can I see him now?"

Madison played the power of silence. She heard Sahara's foot tap off at least thirty of them.

"I need to see him." Sahara wrapped her arms around herself as tremors shook her body.

"Here's the thing, Lacy's dead."

Sahara's eyes shot upward from the table she had become focused on. "I didn't—"

"You hated her. You said that."

"It doesn't mean I—"

"She was found buried in Hennessey's backyard. Did you have access to his apartment?"

"I...no...yes..."

"Which is it? You said you found them on the couch. You got in somehow."

"Yes."

"You had a reason to want her gone. She came in, took your man. Christmas Morning was over."

Sahara ran the back of a hand under her nose. Tears fell now, but Madison sensed they were out of self-preservation, not remorse or grief.

"Why did you do it? Did you make her kill herself?" Madison asked.

"She killed herself?" Sahara straightened out.

"Well, she had a bullet to the brain."

Sahara scrunched up her face.

"She was found buried, and she didn't put herself in the ground."

"But you can't prove anyone made her do it...pull the trigger."

Sahara had stated the plain truth—this would be a difficult case to close unless they could prove it was a staged suicide. "How was your relationship with Hennessey? Did he beat you?"

Silence.

"We know that he beat Lacy."

"Whatev."

"But he never beat you?" Madison rose to her feet and paced around the table. "I find that hard to believe. Normally if a guy is a beater, he doesn't change. The truth is, if he beat Lacy, he likely beat you."

Sahara didn't follow Madison's movements around the room, but instead, kept facing forward.

"If you and Hennessey went separate ways, why are you here to see him?" Madison moved beside Sahara, close enough to smell her pharmacy store perfume—strongly floral with a metallic edge.

"He's still good to me."

Her voice wavered, and Madison picked up on an underlying connotation. "How long has he been pimping you out?"

Sahara faced Madison.

"That's why you're here. You have nowhere else to go. He hooked you on drugs, and you're one of his girls now. One of many."

Sahara spit. Madison moved out of the way just in time.

"Stand up!"

"I'm sor—"

"Stand up! Hands behind your back."

"No, please."

Madison grabbed the girl's shoulder and pulled her upward.

"I want to see Hennessey."

"You might get a cell right next to him." Madison snapped cuffs on her.

"No!"

"You assaulted an officer. You gave me enough reason to hold you."

CHAPTER 17

MADISON WAS AT HER DESK, her mind full of thoughts. Hennessey was not only an abusive boyfriend, but he was also a pimp. He lured the girls in, got them addicted to drugs, and then started hooking them up with other men. He owned them, and when they diverted from his course, he beat them into alignment. Nothing new in the world, but nonetheless disturbing.

Terry draped his coat over the back of his chair. "Did I miss anything?"

Madison massaged her left temple. "You first. What is it?"

Terry sat down across from her. "Don't know." The two words came out as a deflated balloon.

"What do you mean you don't know?"

"Just that. His back was turned. There wasn't a clear—"

Madison laughed.

"What's so funny?"

"You. You get all worked up about this appointment and tell me everything you're going to teach your son. I tell you it doesn't really matter which sex you have, you tell me it does. And now here, it's camera shy."

"Not it, he."

"It could be a she."

Terry flicked his computer monitor on, signaling the end of the personal conversation. She filled him in on her morning and Sahara Noel.

"I would have loved to have seen her spit on you," Terry said.

"I tell you everything she told me about Hennessey and her hate for Lacy, and your response is you would have liked to see her spit on me? And she missed by the way."

"I can only imagine how angry you got. Were your earlobes red?"

"You're a kid sometimes, you know that?"

"You take yourself too seriously sometimes."

"She tried to spit on an officer—"

"But she missed. You pointed that out."

"That doesn't matter."

The smirk lingered.

Madison let out a deep sigh. "I need a new partner."

"Same old conversation. What would you do without me?"

"Sometimes, I think I'm willing to find out." She narrowed her eyes.

"What else have you been doing besides eating chocolate bars and getting spit on?"

Madison scanned her desk and noticed the Hershey's wrapper. She bunched it in her hand, swept it across the surface, and under her desk to the garbage can.

"What happened to this diet you're on?"

"I'm not on a diet."

"Apparently."

"Seriously, Terry, I'm going to wipe that smirk off your face."

DIET WAS A WORD PEOPLE invented to give themselves a name to define deprivation and sacrifice. Diets were what approximately seventeen percent incorporated into their New Year's resolutions, yet statistically broke within the first week. Madison didn't diet. Diets took commitment—the one word that scared Madison more than anything.

"I'm just watching what I'm eating."

"Yeah, a diet."

"It's not a diet, Terry." Her cell phone rang and she let it go for a few rings. She spent the time glaring at her partner, giving him a silent reprimand. "Knight." She kept her eyes on him. "Hey, Cyn… whatcha got…okay…I know Richards has some samples coming to the lab too…I know you're only one person…yes, and mine isn't the only case…bye."

"Let me guess, the lab's not moving fast enough for little Maddy."

"Oh shut up." She scrunched up a piece of blank notepaper and threw it at him.

Terry caught it. "At least it wasn't an elastic this time."

"You're still whining about that? That was months ago." Madison rose to her feet.

"You got me right in the meaty part of the arm."

Madison walked away and Terry followed her.

"Hey, where are you going?" he asked.

"We're going to speak with Bates."

"But you let him walk."

"We had nothing to hold him. It doesn't mean he may not prove more useful."

CHAPTER 18

MADISON PULLED THE DEPARTMENT-ISSUED sedan to the curb in front of 923 Weber Street. Yellow tape blew in the breeze across the gate to the backyard as a silent reminder of what had transpired here. They had released the scene early that morning.

She filled her partner in on Cynthia Baxter's findings on their way over.

She climbed the stairs to the upper landing and knocked on the apartment door. A blanket served as curtains in the large window that overlooked the backyard. It was draped askew, exposing a peephole of sorts. She paced the small balcony and pressed her face to the window where the blanket was open. She held a hand over her forehead to cut out the glare from the sun.

"He's in there." She rapped her knuckles on the glass, slow at first, then louder and more persistent. Eventually, he moved from the recliner he had been sleeping in. He noticed her in the window, and she saw him flail his hands in the air as he rose to his feet.

The door cracked open the width of a chain. "What do ya'll want?" He rubbed a hand over his right eye.

"We need to talk to you."

"I said everyt'ing the other day."

"You didn't tell us you knew about Lacy's sugar daddy."

"Huh, lady? Sugar what?"

"Her older boyfriend."

Bates's hand dropped to his side and his eyes squinted. "She didn't have a—"

"She did actually. We'd like to come in and talk about him."

"I didn't do it." He sniffed back hard. "Lacy was a sweet girl."

"Let us inside, or we can drag your ass back downtown—your choice."

The door closed, the chain released, and the door was opened wide.

"By all means. Yous ain't leavin' me alone. I'm the black guy so I must've done it. I know how you cops think."

"Your record isn't clean." Madison recalled the B&E charges.

"That's in the past."

"There's a saying that a leopard can't change its spots."

"Why are ya here?"

Bates didn't offer them a place to sit. They stood inside the door. The place was tiny and messy. The kitchen was straight ahead and was simply some counter space on either side of a single sink. The fridge was a pale green and the stove a burnt almond. Dishes were piled on every surface.

"Did you know about Lacy's older boyfriend?"

His head shook rapidly, his dreadlocks swaying with the motion.

"But you did know about her fancy condo."

She saw the flicker, the small spark of light flash in his eyes.

"What do you know about it?" she asked.

"I ain't said I know about it."

"Your eyes gave you away. Your prints were found there. Did you work with Hennessey to pimp Lacy and the other girls out?"

Bates's face hardened.

"Can you explain why your prints were there?"

"I don't have to answer to you poleece."

"You do actually." Madison placed a hand over her holster, careful not to make any contact with it.

"You threatening me now? You gonna shoot me if I don't answer the way you like?" Bates's arms were restless and moved pointlessly. His thumbs went to latch onto his jean pockets but released as quickly as they touched them.

Terry stepped closer to Bates. "You help sell her stuff to buy drugs? She was money to you. She wasn't making it anymore. She was trying to get her life straightened around."

Bates laughed. "That girl was bad news."

"You said Lacy was a sweet girl." Madison reminded him of his earlier words.

His eyes went between her and Terry. "I don't wanna say anyt'ing more."

"You don't have to, but we can also drag your ass downtown—" Madison looked to Terry. "I actually think that's a good idea. Let's do it."

CHAPTER 19

"LET'S START WITH YOU EXPLAINING why you were in Lacy's condo."

They were back at the station and Bates sat across from them in interrogation room one.

"I never was."

"Your prints put you there."

A hand flailed forward, pawing at the air. "Someone is settin' me up."

"You're going to have to do a lot better than that," Terry said.

"But I ain't do it, man." Bates sucked in on his bottom lip and sank farther into his chair.

"You work with us and we'll work with you."

"You tryin' to set me up." Bates looked from Terry to Madison.

"Your prints were found in many places throughout the condo."

"I'm tellin' you—"

"And why? Tell us why someone wants you to take the fall. Your prints wouldn't magically appear."

"Dunno." Bates rubbed a hand on his thigh.

"Did he know about you and Lacy?"

Bates made eye contact.

"It would explain a lot. He got jealous and killed Lacy because of it." Madison glanced at Terry, who braced against the wall behind Bates. "Your prints were all over. You were sleeping together."

"No." A flicker shone in his eyes.

Madison rose to her feet. "You're going to start talking, or I'm going to throw you into holding. It will remind you of what's at stake."

"Looks to me, you's the one who's hostile."

"Were you sleeping with Lacy? Yes or no?"

"It wasn't—"

"Yes or no?" Madison held eye contact with Bates until he turned away.

"Okay. I was at the apartment."

"Hooking up?"

"No." Bates shook his head, his dreads going with the motion again.

"You're going to let a *sweet* girl go without justice?"

Bates lifted his palms off the table. His eyes misted over.

"Listen, I can tell you cared about her."

"I didn't kill her. I tell ya that."

"Did Hennessey?"

Silence.

Madison smacked the table and repeated her question. "Did Hennessey?"

Bates covered his face with his hands. Madison and Terry shared a look as Madison took a seat again.

"Listen, if you give us your sworn oath that Hennessey is the one who killed Lacy, if you're privy to convincing evidence—"

"I ain't saying the man did it." Bates's hands lowered.

Madison pointed a finger at him. "But you know who did."

MADISON AND TERRY STOOD OUTSIDE the room and looked in on Bates.

"There's no way he's going to hand over his friend," Madison said.

"He said that Hennessey didn't do it."

Madison faced her partner. "And you believe that?"

"Until we have more to go on."

They walked back into the interrogation room. Terry sat while Madison paced around the table. Bates sat with his head bowed.

"Hennessey knew about the condo and the healthcare and—"

Bates looked her in the eyes. Something about the way they glazed over had Madison questioning the man's complete innocence.

"He didn't like the attention Lacy was getting from this other man." Madison moved in close to him. "Did he?"

Silence.

"Was she trying to straighten out her life, come off his leash?"

Bates didn't respond.

"Yes, we know about the pimping."

"She wasn't into all that anymore. She wanted a new life."

"You sound sad about that. This man who set her up with a condo, was she sleeping with him?"

"No."

"That was a quick response."

His eyes shifted from hers for a brief moment. "I know he wasn't her type."

Madison straightened up. "What would make you say that? He took care of her, set her up in a condo, bought her nice things—"

"He wasn't the one, a'ight."

"Who was?"

"Lace was a pretty girl. Everybody wanted to get up with 'er, but she no be spreadin' her legs for anyone."

"Hennessey pimped her out."

The dreads shook rapidly. "Not her idea."

"Is that why Hennessey killed her? She refused to keep doing it?"

"I said he didn't, a'ight."

Terry stretched out in the chair, extended his legs, and slipped his hands into his pockets. He jingled the change there. It warranted a glance from Bates.

"I'm sure you can understand why we can't take your word for it," Madison said.

Bates let out a large sigh. "What do you people want from me?"

"Who was this other man?"

Bates's eyes flickered. "I never said—"

"Listen, the truth of the matter is, your friend's looking pretty good for this, so unless you give us—"

"I think the guy's name was Andy." Bates's jaw tightened and shifted askew for an instant before realigning. His eyes remained unfocused.

Chapter 20

"A FIRST NAME. That's all he could give us." Madison pressed her forehead against the cool glass of the mirrorpane and looked in on Bates.

"Did you want his social too?" Terry asked.

Madison gave him a cool look. "Yes, Terry, actually, I'd love that." She paused a few beats. "The way he came back with Andy so quickly, I even wonder if he just made him up."

They headed back into the room with Bates. They had been questioning him for hours but didn't seem to be getting far.

Madison sat across from him. She didn't believe Bates when he had said the name Andy; maybe it had to do with his facial language.

"Do you own a gun?"

Bates's eyes skirted from the table to her eyes, to Terry, to the wall, to the window behind them.

"I'll take that as a yes. There's none registered to you."

"Why are you looking at me? I gave yous a name."

"We need to be certain. You had motive too. You saw Lacy with two other men, possibly three." She referred to Hargrove, who set her up in the condo, Hennessey, and perhaps an Andy. "And you didn't like it. You made her shoot herself—"

"She shot herself?" Bates slid his bottom lip through his teeth.

"Seems like it," Madison stated casually, coolly.

"She would never."

"Would Hennessey?" Madison pushed him hard, hoping he would eventually give up his friend.

"You're confusing me."

"Someone either made her pull the trigger, or made it look like she did. And she didn't put herself in the ground."

Bates avoided eye contact.

Madison wanted to ask if he had helped put her there, but she knew she would lose him. She clasped her hands. "I'll ask again. Do you own a gun?"

"No."

"We didn't find one when we searched your place—"

"Then—"

"Doesn't mean we won't find one now." Madison glanced at her partner, back at Bates. "Are you opposed to us searching again?"

Bates sat quietly, his eyes settling on nothing as they darted around the room. He eventually drew them up to meet with Madison's. "Go ahead."

CHAPTER 21

THEY COULD HAVE SEARCHED BATES'S residence when they went to ask him some questions about his fingerprints being found at the condo, but Madison knew they wouldn't get anything out of the man. As it was, they never got a straight answer on why he was at the condo. It seemed Hennessey had as much control over Bates as he did over the women he pimped out.

"We never found anything the first time," Terry said as he walked up the stairs behind her. "You really think he was stupid enough to bring it back here?"

"I guess we'll find out. Like we've talked about. Criminals can be stupid."

Madison unlocked the door and they stepped inside. The interior had a faint smell of garbage she hadn't picked up on when they were there earlier.

"I have a feeling we're going to find it this time."

"There's that gut feeling."

Madison smirked at her partner, and would have jabbed him in the shoulder if he were within range, but he headed left, toward the bedroom, while she went to the living area.

Bates had a gaming console sitting in the middle of the floor, the cords haphazardly streaming across to a flat screen television of approximately forty-two inches. Two of the gaming controllers sat on a suede ottoman that ran the length of the loveseat. Four game cases looked like they were tossed beside the controllers.

Madison looked at the game covers. "Our guy likes to play shoot 'em up," she called out to Terry. "And it looks like he plays with someone else. Two controllers are out."

She kept looking around the room, taking in the clutter that occupied the second-floor apartment. She had to think like Bates. After spending hours with him in a single room, she had an idea as to how his mind worked. If she were him, she'd hide something in plain view, thinking no one would assume to look there.

Her cell phone rang. "Knight."

"Have you found my husband's killer yet?"

It took Madison a moment to connect the out-of-context question to the caller. "Vilma?"

"Yes, who else would it be?" The woman sniffled on the other end.

"I actually—"

"You haven't done anything." Sobs filled the line.

"Listen, Miss—"

"Mrs. Thorne."

"Mrs. Thorne." Madison played along, knowing that technically she had been his fiancée at the time of his death. "I haven't been able to find out anything new in your fiancé's case. It was actually closed already—suicide."

More sobs, but she spoke through them. "You...you said you'd look into it again. You'd reopen the case."

"I said I'd see if I can find anything."

"But you haven't even tried, have you." It was an accusation, not an inquiry.

Madison focused on the television and the ottoman. *Plain sight.*

"I will contact you as soon as I find out anything."

"Do you promise?"

Madison heard a clicking noise from Vilma's receiver and pictured her wiping her face with her hand, her ring hitting the phone.

"Yes, I promise." Madison didn't wait for a response but hung up instead. Everyone else was right about the woman. She was in denial and a tad—maybe even more than a tad—crazy. For less than a second, Madison reprimanded herself for making a promise to the woman again, but as her eyes settled on the ottoman, her guilt lifted as fog in the sunshine.

The ottoman was hinged. She put on a pair of gloves and worked at clearing the top of it, transferring the gaming accessories to the couch. She lifted the ottoman open.

The inside was full of clutter, delivery menus, more game cases, batteries, music CDs, and a few DVDs. She moved the items around cautiously until she found what she was after.

"Terry, you can stop looking." She lifted the gun and checked to ensure the safety was on and then looked to see if it was loaded.

Terry walked into the room.

"And there are even a couple bullets in it. We'll have Cynthia's team run ballistics testing on the gun. Maybe they'll be able to connect it to the one that killed Lacy."

CHAPTER 22

MADISON DROPPED THE BAGGED GUN on the table. "Does this look familiar to you?"

Bates leaned back into the chair and stretched his legs out.

"We found this in your apartment," she continued.

"Doesn't prove I did anything."

"What it does prove is you had access to the murder weapon." Madison knew she stretched the truth—the tests still needed to be run and the facts confirmed. She paced around him. "I can tell the way you're sitting there, you're not surprised we found it and you're not surprised that it was used in the murder of Lacy Rose—"

"I don't know nothin' about that."

Madison continued walking around the table. "We believe you do."

"You said she killed herself."

"That is still being confirmed. We know she didn't bury herself."

Bates's eyes flickered from Madison to Terry, to the clock on the wall. For about thirty seconds, the ticking echoed in the silence of the room.

"The tests will come back on the gun. Will they find your prints on it, Bates? I'm not really a betting woman" she shot a glance at Terry then smiled at the line, "but I believe I'd win in this case." Madison stopped beside Bates and angled over to look into his face. "You were there when she was shot."

Bates's eyes filled with tears, and he shook his head; it was almost in slow motion.

"Did Hennessey make her pull the trigger?"

"I dunno...I dunno." Bates sucked in on his bottom lip, a mannerism Madison recognized as his trademark. His eyes focused on nothing.

Madison stretched her neck side to side. "You said she had an older boyfriend named Andy. Are you certain that was his name?" She walked around the table and sat across from him.

She let the clock sound off the seconds in the room. It was shy of a minute before Bates spoke.

"It's Peter. Can I go now?"

"No," Madison said as she opened the door.

Bates's head dropped as an officer came in, put him in cuffs, and escorted him to holding.

MADISON'S MOUTH CURVED UPWARD INTO a full smile; she pointed a finger at Terry. "I knew it. There's no way that guy would set her up with healthcare and a condo and not expect anything in return."

"You're assuming the Peter he mentioned is the Peter we—"

"Hargrove. Let's make a bet."

Terry jacked a thumb toward the room. "You said in there you're not a gambler."

She narrowed her eyes. "Here's the wager."

"I'm listening." Terry's eyes sparkled with mischievousness.

"I say that this Hargrove guy figures into all this."

"More specifically."

"Maybe he paid Hennessey to get rid of her."

"Why?"

"Lacy and Peter were sleeping together and she threatened to take it to his wife. Peter approached Hennessey, maybe paid him to take care of her. But then you have Bates who loved her from a supposed distance." She wrapped finger quotes around the word *supposed*.

"You say supposed?"

"Until we can prove the two got together."

Terry smiled. "You're waiting for the verbal confession?"

Madison narrowed her eyes, jabbed his shoulder and smiled. "I'm not convinced Bates never hooked up with her. So, supposing

Hargrove had Hennessey and Bates kill Lacy, maybe they couldn't do it and that's why they made her pull the trigger on herself? Or maybe they staged the suicide?"

"Complicated."

"Very, but when is a case ever straightforward? Lacy must have been high, or threatened somehow, to make her go through with it. But why respond to threats when either alternative results in death?" She widened her eyes to drive home the point. "She had defensive wounds, so she fought back at first, but then stopped and took her life? It doesn't make sense."

"Maybe, because of her lifestyle and past, she didn't figure hers was one worth fighting for. Maybe whoever it was that made her pull the trigger laid out all her past sins, to the point she broke," Terry countered.

"Maybe she wanted control over how she exited this world, feeling as if she'd had none while alive. Or, it's just as likely, someone wanted us to think this way. One thing that stuck out to me was the inconsistency with Hargrove."

"Inconsistency?"

"Well, he led us to believe he met Lacy a few weeks ago. I made a call to the Luxor apartment building and was told that Hargrove purchased the unit two months ago."

"Interesting." Terry took his jacket off the back of his chair.

"Where are you going?"

"Home."

"Home? You just got here and we need to talk to Hargrove."

"I was only a couple hours late this morning and it's after six now."

"Seriously?" This was her partner, always trying to get on with his personal life.

He slipped his coat on. "We can go talk to Hargrove in the morning."

She held eye contact with him. "You want to push off talking to a murder suspect?"

"He's probably eating dinner right now."

"So we'd get him at home." She cocked her head to the side. The man's dinner wasn't her concern. She could tell by the expression on her partner's face, he was set to leave.

"First thing in the morning." Terry pulled his keys from a pocket. "The terms of the bet…you say Hargrove's involved somehow."

"He paid the kids to make it happen."

"I say he had nothing to do with it."

She was fuming. *How could he leave at a time like this?*

Terry extended his hand to shake on their deal. "Easiest twenty I've ever made."

Her partner walked away, and she dropped into her chair. Her thoughts were intermingled and shot off in different directions. It seemed obvious that Bates covered for Hennessey, and, despite his affection for Lacy, wasn't willing to hand him over. The question that needed an answer was why.

Maybe she should look to Bates. He knew about Lacy's older man too. Jealousy could have pushed him, despite his protests their relationship was simply platonic. After all, the gun was found in his apartment, and Madison had no doubts it would tie back to the casing found in the bedroom.

The thought of the gun brought her back to the phone call from Vilma and the promise she had made to the woman again. She typed the name Kevin Thorne into her computer. Richards's autopsy report filled the screen.

The gist was Thorne had slit both his wrists on the vertical and died due to blood loss.

She continued reading the report. Toxicology showed twice the legal alcohol limit in his system, plus a cocktail of drugs.

Richards had made a note beside this that no other tests proved that Thorne was a drug addict. In fact, results revealed no proof that Thorne had ever previously touched drugs.

Madison picked up the phone and dialed down to Richards, who answered on the third ring. "Do you remember Kevin Thorne?"

"Yes, I do. He killed himself. Exsanguination, I believe."

"I'm reading your re—"

"Then I'm not sure why you're—"

"There are some contradictory findings." The line went silent and she knew she had offended her colleague. "I didn't mean—"

"What do you think you found?"

She took a deep breath, longing for the time when she and Richards were close. She had crossed a line, and it seemed like she'd never get back into a good standing with the man. She had been motivated by a caring curiosity into his background, but she realized the error of her way. Richards was her colleague and friend. She should have gone to him if she had questions about his past, not the records.

"The report says he cut both wrists," she said.

"Suicide victims are motivated by self-hate, hence the infliction of pain. He didn't want to fail."

"Most also have a record of past attempts. Did he?"

"Not that was visible on his body, nothing noted in his health records. Family and friends were certain he never attempted in the past."

"That didn't stand out to you?" She asked the question and instantly wished she could reel it back. "What I mean is you concluded his death the result of suicide, but I'm seeing question marks."

"Detective Knight."

Him calling her by her official title and surname confirmed the fact the wound in their relationship had yet to scab over.

"I take all facts into consideration. Mr. Thorne lost his job and his fiancée was expecting a baby."

Madison thought back to Vilma, surprised she hadn't mentioned this. If Vilma was pregnant, she wasn't far along. Madison pictured her, thinking of what she had worn. It was a large sweater, and Madison remembered her heaving bosom.

Richards continued. "He had alcohol in his system, and drugs. This was unusual for him, as you likely have noted from the report, but it doesn't mean he didn't take drugs to help him take his life. There was no evidence to indicate that he died of any other means besides self-infliction."

"There was no trace evidence or fibers found that linked to another person?"

"He killed himself in a motel room. Of course, foreign DNA contributors were found. You can find this in the investigative report. You would have to see the lead detective on the case." He stopped speaking for a few minutes. "Why are you asking me all this anyhow? The case was closed."

"I made a promise to his fiancée."

She heard Richards exhale on the other end.

"It's not that I don't trust you. You know I have the utmost respect—" She was going to finish by saying, *for you.* But it would leave way for the contradictory thought to arise, respect for him, yet not for his privacy. "I know you would have considered all the facts."

She scrolled down the screen looking for the investigating detective. When the cause of death was unknown, it was approached suspiciously until it was ruled. She almost swore aloud when she saw the name.

"I really don't think you're going to find anything contrary to my conclusion," he said.

"Thanks, Richards."

"Of course."

He hung up and she was left staring at the name on her screen. Toby Sovereign.

CHAPTER 23

CERTAIN ASPECTS OF LIFE REALLY translated to unfair. For one, falling in love with a fellow student in the academy, to the point she had let her guard down and had accepted a marriage proposal.

Stupid.

It made her think of a man they had in their interrogation room not long ago. He had said love was for the weak.

She had made that mistake once, and almost had a repeat occurrence more recently, but she saw the clearing before she committed—thank God. Either way, to think that not only had the first man broken her heart, but he had taken away her ability to fully love again. She refused to be the one who got hurt. She would end things in any relationship before they got serious and started to hold power over her.

She left the station after seeing his name on the screen. She had made a promise to a woman, and now it would put her in direct company with Sovereign. Not that she would let that stop her from getting the truth, but she wasn't in the mood to deal with it now.

For one, she was starving. This new thing of watching what she was eating and striving to be more active didn't entirely suit her. She was used to driving through a fast food joint or ordering in a pizza. Those dinners were convenient, and with her working all hours, it suited a purpose.

The clock on the car dash read 7:20 PM.

Her stomach tightened and rumbled. The last thing she ate was a Hershey's bar, which she had snuck in mid-afternoon when Terry wasn't around.

Apparently, one needed more than chocolate to satisfy their appetite. She thought of where she could grab something quick that would also be healthy and went through a McDonald's drive-thru. They had salads, not that she ever had one of theirs, but maybe it would be a good time to try it.

She put the window down to place the order and the wafting smell of greasy food tempted her. For seconds, she had an internal struggle. She pictured herself stuffing fries into her mouth in rapid succession. But when the teenager operating the drive-thru came over the speaker, Madison took a deep inhale and ordered a salad.

There better be a lot of protein in this thing, she thought.

Struggling to balance the plastic container, and avoid a spill of lettuce on the interior of her car, she drove slower than normal. She had one more stop she wanted to make before heading home.

CANINE COUNTRY RETREAT BOARDING WAS located on the outskirts of the city, on a country road. A farm house was next to it, and another house sat right on the property and belonged to the owners of the kennel. The gravel crunched beneath her tires as she drove in.

Madison had dropped Hershey off there in the morning, knowing she might keep him there for a few days while working on the case, but she missed him and figured she could drop him off again tomorrow.

The door chimed as she opened it. A lady in her early twenties was smiling at her from behind the counter.

"Miss him?"

"Yeah, I guess I did." Madison returned the woman's smile.

"Well, he's doing great." She picked up a walkie-talkie and spoke into it. "Please bring up Hershey, kennel number three-B."

Madison tapped the counter and looked at the girl, passing minutes in awkward silence. This was new to her, all of it. The uncomfortable feeling associated with this and the caring for a canine companion. It wasn't something she had envisioned for her life, but it was starting to come together. At least Terry kept assuring her it would.

The boarding during the day had been his idea too, and he

and Annabelle were paying for half of it—for the first six months anyhow. She had decided to only bring him here when a case took over her life.

Terry said that it was advantageous to get Hershey used to being around other dogs sooner rather than later. Sometimes, the entire scenario had Madison shaking her head, hoping she'd wake up from a dream.

"He was out there playing with this poodle-cross we board. He likes her," the woman said, breaking through Madison's thoughts.

Madison smiled at the woman, her words bringing up another responsibility she would need to take care of—getting him fixed. This dog was going to break her. *Some Christmas gift.* "I'll bring him back tomorrow morning and he may have to stay for a few days."

"Sure, that's—"

Hershey came through the doorway, trailing a woman behind him, by his leash. His little body pulled her along, and his tail wagged wildly when he saw Madison. For a trace of an instant, Madison imagined his fur under her hands, and soon after it was a reality.

"Guess we'll see you again tomorrow, Hershey." The lady who brought him up rubbed the top of his head in a quick yet affectionate manner, much the same as a father does to his son. She passed Madison a smile and handed over the leash before going back to the kennels.

"See you tomorrow."

The woman behind the counter waved good-bye, and Madison wondered if she liked Hershey more than her, not that it mattered.

"Yes, we will." Madison directed Hershey to sit, something behavioral canine training was instilling in her. They had been to one class so far, but Madison already knew she was to be the boss and not let the dog think he was. The training instilled the fine line of being in charge—afford the dog dignity and respect its intelligence.

She waited for Hershey to sit, and when he calmed down, she took the first step. He took five. She stopped again, making him sit and wait for her command to move. She put on a good show in front of the lady, but inside, she boiled with impatience. What seemed like five minutes later, they reached the door, which was only about fifteen feet from the counter.

AFTER HAULING HERSHEY HOME AND taking him for a twenty-minute walk, more for herself than him, she settled in. The salad she had eaten was long ago metabolized and she was ready to eat again. She was never going to make it with this new healthy way of living. Maybe she should accept herself as being a little overweight and somewhat out of shape. So what if she couldn't keep up with Terry in a running pursuit, or make it up a long staircase without heaving for a solid breath.

Hershey settled on the floor at her feet and chewed on a rawhide bone she had picked up for him a few days ago. His oversized paws held a solid grip on it, and with the chomping of his jaw, Madison was thankful her arm wasn't the bone.

She brought up the results she had been working on at the station in regards to her cold case. She had e-mailed the list of printing companies home the other day, figuring after hours was likely the only time she'd have to dig into them.

She spent the next hour or so e-mailing them to inquire about envelope stock with the infinity symbol woven into the fibers of the paper. This would be step one.

After she received responses from them, she'd take it from there and ask for their customer lists. She was specifically interested in their business clients, hoping she'd find the connection to Dimitre Petrov, the Russian mafia boss and the piece of an envelope found beside the murdered attorney.

Satisfied, she dropped onto her couch, stretching out. She did her best to ignore the hunger pangs and turned on the TV. She wasn't really paying attention to what was happening on the screen and fell asleep with Hershey curled up behind her legs.

Chapter 24

She arrived at the station at five after eight. Terry raised a Starbucks cup to her as a greeting. He received a mumble in response as she pressed her lips to the edge of her own coffee.

Her neck ached enough it felt like dandelion head. She thought of the childhood song *Mama Had a Baby and His Head Popped Off.*

She had awakened on her side, with her arms tucked under her head. Seconds of convincing her back to move, she straightened out, but the residual effects of sleeping curled on the couch would be with her all day.

She pulled a plastic-wrapped muffin from her coat pocket and tossed it on her desk.

"I hope it's bran, otherwise—"

He stopped talking when her eyes narrowed to slits and she took a bite of the muffin, clearing off most of the top in one mouthful.

"Oh no."

"What, Terry?" With her mouth full, the only one that could have understood her would have been a dentist.

Terry's face contorted. "At least it's not a chocolate bar."

She swallowed hard, more of the muffin going down than was necessarily advisable. "I work with my father?"

"Call me a concerned citizen."

"You're a cop." She tore off another piece of the muffin with her fingers and stuffed it into her mouth. The salad from last night was long gone, and she wondered why anyone ate lettuce as a meal in the first place. *Did they want to become rabbits?*

"Concerned cop then." Terry took a drag on his Starbucks. "If you keep eating bars and muffins for breakfast you're going to—"

"What? End up fifty pounds overweight?" She paused for a sip of her caffeine to wash the lodge of muffin down. "Do you forget I rarely eat and I'm running around all day?"

"If you were running around all day you could have kept up in the chase."

"You really want to go there." She gave him a look that dared him to continue.

"Someone needs more food and sleep. It's gonna be a great day." He swiveled his chair, Starbucks cup firmly in hand.

"I'm going to pretend I never heard what you said, or the implication." Her mind was fully on business now. "We need to push Hennessey hard again today, show him a picture of the weapon we found and study his reaction. Hopefully, Cynthia can get us some forensic findings today."

Terry watched her rip off pieces of the muffin, smaller now, and pop them into her mouth.

"We also need to go see Hargrove."

"You remember we found the gun in Bates's apartment," Terry said.

She cocked her head to the side and put the wrapping from the muffin into the garbage. "I also know it hasn't been confirmed as the murder weapon."

"Do I sense a trust for other people?"

His question silenced her. *Was she getting weak?* She dismissed the doubt as quickly as it arose. "We have him in holding. He's not going anywhere. This Hargrove guy, I'd like to press him more about his relationship with Lacy, find out if his wife knows about the arrangement."

"You still think he's involved somehow."

"Yes, Terry." She recalled their bet yesterday. "And I'm going to make twenty off it." She smiled.

PETER HARGROVE WAS BUSINESS PARTNERS with Daddy Warbucks, Maurice Kendal, for a company called Solarpanel Energy. Their beginning was humble, but government funding had upgraded their accommodations to a warehouse in an industrial part of town. Now, company stock was traded. Cheap, ecological power was a hot commodity, and when that service offered dividends in return, there was nothing to lose.

The front desk was made of granite and easily fifteen feet long. Trays were stacked on both ends. Two ladies sat behind the desk, both with wireless headsets. One spoke into hers, and the other lady looked at them and offered a sincere smile.

"Welcome to Solarpanel Energy. What can I do for you today?"

Madison held out her badge. She noticed the lady on the phone glance at her before turning away. She spoke to the one who had greeted them. "We're here to speak with Peter Hargrove."

Her mascara coated lashes dropped heavily, only to open wide again. Piercing green eyes studied her. "Do you have an appointment?"

"Nope, but we have badges." Madison held hers up again. "I would think that trumps an appointment."

"I'll see what I can do." She pressed a button on the phone in front of her. After a few seconds, she spoke. "Peter, I have a—"

She pivoted her chair slightly to the right as if seeking privacy to identify his visitors. "They are cops…yes…okay. Thank you." She pushed a button on the headset. "He said to have a seat and he'll be out soon."

Fifteen minutes passed and they were still waiting. Madison glanced at Terry as she stood up. "This is ridic—"

"Detectives, I'm not really sure what more you want from me. Did you find the necklace?"

"Do you have somewhere private we can talk?" Madison asked.

"I do, but—"

"We could talk about everything here in the lobby if you wish." She looked into his eyes.

"This way." Hargrove led them to a large conference room with a marker board mounted to the wall on one end. A projection television box was secured to the ceiling at the other end, directed at it. The table was granite and the chairs surrounding it were plush leather. He gestured for them to sit across from him.

They both sat down and Hargrove looked at them as if doing his best to read the purpose of the visit. "Have you found her killer?"

Madison noticed how his eyes widened with the question. She had a hard time determining guilt or innocence, but her suspicions led her to side with the former. "You tell us."

"What is this, a game to you?" His brows furled downward into a V.

"Does your wife know—"

"Know what? That I set a young lady up in a nice place and helped turn her life around."

"You make her sound like a charity."

"I don't like your implications."

"I'm not implying anything. The facts are that rarely does a man provide all these things for nothing in return."

"So you're saying I must have been sleeping with her."

Madison let Hargrove's statement dry in the air, established eye contact with him, and sank back into the leather, letting it embrace her.

"This is ludicrous." He let out a puff of air as he rose to his feet. He paced a few steps. "Why can't someone do something out of the goodness of their heart? Why is that so hard for you to understand?" His questions were stamped with the rhetorical as he passed glances at them. "A job hazard?" He pointed a finger at her. "It's your job to prove I did something to the girl, and you can't. You won't be able to."

"Are you saying there should be something to prove? Does your wife know? Why not answer that question?"

Hargrove swiped a hand across his forehead and flexed his fingers on his temple. "She doesn't agree with it."

"Can we talk to her?"

Silence.

"If you have nothing to hide, it shouldn't be an issue."

"Fine."

"But one thing before we go. You told us you met Lacy a few weeks ago, but the apartment was purchased by you two months ago."

Hargrove let out a laugh. "I never said I met her three weeks ago. You assumed that."

CHAPTER 25

HARGROVE DIRECTED THEM TO HIS residence where he said his wife, Beverly, would be at this time of day. He had consulted his watch and had added that she would probably be home from her yoga class.

His statement prompted Madison to think how much easier it would be to schedule in exercise if she didn't have to work. From there, her thought process made a leap to Maurice Kendal, the luggage he had on his floor, and the Hawaiian shirt he wore. How long had his trip been planned? Was it a coincidence that he was leaving the country around the same time that Lacy's body was discovered? Then again, how could he have predicted her discovery?

"Here's another line of thought, what if it was Daddy Warbucks?"

"Daddy Warbucks?"

"You know, Maurice Kendal."

"Right."

"Seems like a convenient time to take off on a holiday, doesn't it?"

"Possible coincidence."

"You know I don't—"

"I know you don't believe in it. But it doesn't mean it doesn't happen."

"What if he were the one who—"

Terry let out a laugh.

She looked over at him from the driver's seat. "What's funny?"

"Just you. You put a bet in favor of Hargrove, and now you're flipping over to the biological father."

Madison looked back to the road. "A good detective needs to follow all leads and exhaust all potential suspects. Right now all we have is a bunch of loose ends." She noticed the clichéd phrase as soon as it slipped out, but it was too late for recovery.

"And you bug me about clichés."

"I blame my mother." She looked at him. "What are you smirking about?"

"The best part of being a man. The kid never says it's his dad's fault; it's always the mother's. And the phrase, son of a—" Terry waved his hand to fill in the expletive. He hated swear words.

"See, being a woman isn't easy." Her mind went right back to business. "Kendal said to Hargrove not to spend any more money on ten-dollar whores. Remember?" She didn't wait for an answer. "He has no respect for women and figured Lacy had turned up to take his money. She didn't hold any value to him."

"Still, why go to the trouble of killing her? If she meant nothing to him, why risk prison?" Terry looked at her blankly, but it got the point across.

Madison pulled the car into the driveway of Hargrove's house. They rang the doorbell and it seemed to echo off the interior of the expansive home before seeping through the door to them.

"What's it like to have all this money?" Terry tried to look through the sidelights into the interior of the house, but the glass was etched and patterned.

"Wouldn't know."

She remembered a time when she had a received a taste of the finer things.

Terry looked at her and his eyes read, *do you miss him?*

How did he know what she was thinking? She averted eye contact and pressed the doorbell again.

Footsteps came toward the door and it opened to a woman with long brown hair. It swept over her shoulders in soft curls and complimented her round face. Her eyes trained up and down on both of them. Smugness filled her expression. Madison didn't sense its source came from wealth, but rather from a readiness to defend herself and her husband.

"He said you would be coming." Beverly held one hand on the door, barring their passage through. She had stood there for a bit before she opened the door wider to allow them in, and Madison felt it was simply out of compliance with law enforcement. They were intrusions, not guests.

Inside the front doors, the ceiling was at least thirty feet high. Above them, an upper-floor balcony traced the perimeter of the second floor. A dark-framed mirror, the size of an average dining room table, hung on the wall over a fireplace. A formal sitting area was laid out in front of it. Oversized accent pieces were everywhere. A large vase sat on the floor and pieces of greenery tucked into it bowed gracefully over its edges.

Beverly directed them to two brown leather chairs that sat across from a matching couch.

There was a young boy of about ten playing a video game. He didn't even acknowledge them.

"Pete's nephew Kenny," Beverly explained as she straightened her posture and crossed her legs. "Kenny." The boy didn't respond. Beverly raised her voice. "Kenny! Go into the back room for a bit." Her directions were met with a moan, but the kid obeyed her.

Beverly reached for a mug from the side table and blew on it before she took a sip.

Madison gave the formal introductions.

"I understand why you're here. You detect there must be something immoral about my Peter." She blinked slowly, judgmentally. "You don't believe it possible that a man of his position in life is capable of a platonic relationship with a young woman."

"Mrs. Hargrove." Madison used the formal address, assuming this was how she was used to being handled. Beverly possessed the ability to look through them and down on them in equal balance. She had always had money. "Your husband is a good man for—"

"You are completely correct. I'm not really sure what this visit is about."

"You obviously knew about Lacy Rose."

Beverly blinked deliberately, her lashes touching beneath her eyes. She reopened them as if they were heavy.

"What did you think about your husband showing a 'young woman' attention?"

Beverly put the mug back on the table. "I believe it was very noble of him. The girl's own father rejected her."

"We met Mr. Kendal."

"He's a horrendous man."

The way she stated it and tightened her arms had Madison envisioning a shiver running through Beverly.

"He's your husband's business partner," Madison said.

Beverly passed Terry a glance but focused on Madison. "It doesn't mean I have to like him."

"How do you feel about Lacy's death?"

The question had hung in silence before she answered. "It's a shame."

"It is." Madison sensed sincerity in Beverly's inflection and studied her eyes. There was more beneath the surface. "What did you really think about your husband's charity toward Lacy?"

A spark fired, Beverly's eyes were now a blazing blue. "His charity, his compassion toward other people less fortunate, defines him. Lacy really was no different than the rest of them."

"The rest of them?"

Beverly dismissed the question with a wave of her hand. "All of the charities, the benefits, the campaigns to raise money for local funding. My husband has a large heart."

"But this is the first time he brought in a stray."

Beverly's eyes snapped to Madison's.

"He took things a little too far for you."

She licked her lips, her tongue barely parting them to do so. "I didn't necessarily agree, no." She took a deep breath. "But he is my husband and I support him." Beverly paused, and then continued. "He had me do things to help her out too."

"Do you know why your husband felt so compelled to help her?"

The woman's jaw tightened and her eyes read, *not for the tabloid reason.* "He just said he felt he had to."

Madison rose to her feet, warranting a questionable blinking from Beverly. Madison smiled at her. "Thank you for your time."

"Of course."

CHAPTER 26

MADISON MANAGED TO MAKE IT to the car before she said anything. She sensed the woman watching them from the front window. She slipped behind the wheel.

"This is the first time her husband took his charity to this extent and he felt he had to? Why? There is no way this was a platonic relationship. There has to be something we can find that will prove it."

"If there's something there to—"

"You still don't suspect anything?" She reversed out of the driveway and made her way through the subdivision.

"I haven't made my mind up yet."

"Well, you better have a twenty ready for me because I'll be winning another bet."

"Oh no, don't think—"

Her phone rang, bringing an abrupt ending to their conversation. She pressed the button and continued to drive. "Knight...all right." She glanced over at Terry and smiled faintly. "Thanks." She turned to Terry. "You'll never believe this—"

"That you're breaking the law again."

Her brows furled downward. His statement lost her.

His finger pointed to her phone. "On the cell while driving, in a department car no less. The new bylaw says it's a no-no."

"A no-no?" Madison laughed. "What are you, a ten-year-old?"

"Practicing my parental skills."

"Keep practicing." She dragged her eyes from him back to the road. "You hate it when I don't have both hands on the wheel. You don't care about that law. My driving makes you nervous."

"Too many close calls for me. Speaking of—" His sentence died there, the tail-end hanging with an enclosed question.

Her smirk gave full birth. "We know who paid for Lacy's healthcare."

"And?"

"My suspicions have been confirmed—Peter Hargrove. And we also have the name of the doctor who prescribed Lacy's allergy medication, but I'm not even sure he's worth talking to at this point. Maybe if things change."

THEY UPDATED THE SERGEANT OF their visit to Hargrove's wife. He was the one who had called with the result of the warrant. He also told them that Higgins and the other officers made no headway with their door-to-door canvassing. After that, they had Hennessey dragged into interrogation room one.

Madison slipped into the chair across from him. Terry walked behind Hennessey.

Hennessey looked over a shoulder, and Terry waved. As Hennessey turned back to face Madison, his eyes were still returning to a normal state from an eye roll.

Madison pulled a photo of the gun retrieved from Bates's apartment and flicked it across the table to Hennessey. Hennessey didn't reach for it, but his eyes settled on it.

"Recognize that?" Madison asked.

His eyes never left the photo. He said nothing.

"This was found in your neighbor's apartment."

Hennessey looked up, now, relief emanating from him. "He killed—"

"You're going to let him hang for this?" Madison asked.

"I don't kn—"

"I believe you do. What if I told you your fingerprints were pulled," Madison lied, hoping it would make him open up.

Hennessey's focus drifted over the room, settling on nothing in particular.

"You're thinking of a comeback to that? Your finger—"

"Okay, so I touched the gun. It doesn't mean I killed her. You check her hands?"

Madison settled back in the chair. "GSR was found on her hands."

"She shot herself. So why are you looking at me?"

"That's the thing about GSR, it gets everywhere."

Hennessey straightened in his chair.

"Do you have anything to say about that? We think it was staged to look like a suicide. You beat on her. You got her addicted to drugs. You hooked other girls on drugs. You pimp Lacy out too?"

A pulse tapped in his cheek.

"You didn't think we knew about that, did you." Madison rose to her feet. "We had one of your girls come in to visit with you. She's in holding now and about to face charges for assaulting an officer." Madison added the latter part, although, she would probably end up letting it go—the girl did miss in her attempt to spit on her.

"Don't know what you're talking about." The index finger of his left hand made circles on the table.

"You're choosing to play stupid." Madison walked over to him. Terry stepped to the side. "That's really how you want to play this? We have cops who testify to being called out to your residence on numerous occasions."

"We had disagreements. There were no charges ever—"

"Doesn't mean the beatings didn't happen. It means Lacy was afraid of you. She didn't want to see how angry you would get if you were put in jail and let go."

"No." He stopped tracing circles on the table.

"The gun was yours. Bates hid it for you. Did you kill Lacy together? You pressure her into pulling the trigger on herself or did you do it?"

"We couldn't—"

"She didn't bury herself."

His eyes flashed up to meet hers and drew back to the table. "She...we found her."

"We? We who?"

"Bates and me. She had popped one into her head before we

came home."

Madison took a few more steps. "So, she shot herself and you found her dead. You decide to bury her instead of calling the police." Madison put herself at his face level. "You sold her belongings and buried your girlfriend in a garden." Her eyes scanned his. He looked like he wanted to break the eye contact but couldn't seem to.

"It's not like—"

"It is what it looks like...based on evidence. What we want to know is why. Why did you bury her? You see, we think you made her pull the trigger. You knew about the other man. There was a struggle."

The pulse in his cheek steadied. "Other man?"

Madison straightened up and rested her hands on her hips. She glanced at Terry and jacked a thumb toward Hennessey. "We're back to playing stupid again."

"K, fine, I knew about him."

"How did that make you feel? Did you want to teach her a lesson? Did you?"

His head shook back and forth in small jerky movements.

"You didn't come home to find her that way."

"I can't go to jail."

Madison laughed. "You already are, on charges of drug possession. If we get your other girlfriend to testify, we'll be adding heading up a prostitution ring as well."

"I didn't kill Lace."

"You ever hear of the phrase 'broken record.'" Madison sat back across from him again. She tapped a hand on the photo of the gun. "You do recognize this."

Hennessey's eyes looked through her. "Yeah."

Madison clasped her hands and leaned back into the chair. "All right, now we're getting somewhere."

CHAPTER 27

THE NEXT FEW HOURS WERE spent questioning Hennessey. He stuck to his story that he showed up afterward to find Lacy dead. He said he panicked and called Bates to let him know what happened. He swore it was Bates's idea to bury her. Neither of them wanted to go back to jail.

"It's an entire case of he said, he said." Madison stood in the observation room with Terry. "We really need some forensic evidence tying them to the murder. Right now, all we have is one guy confessing to burying her. He'll be charged with indignity to a human body, but that's not good enough for me. None of this is sitting well."

"And why confess to something like burying her? Why not keep quiet? We still need to prove it beyond his confession."

"The guy's not that bright. We know that."

"Wonder what his friend would think about being sold out," Terry said.

Madison tapped her finger over her holster. "That's the other part. Bates seems to really care about the girl."

"Fear can be a strong motivator, though. Both have been in jail before."

"Hey, guys." Cynthia came up to them holding a beige folder. She extended it to Madison. "It's not a lot, but it's something. There's a lot to process in this case."

Madison opened the folder and scanned down its contents. "Fingerprints?" She looked up at Cynthia.

"Yes, there were prints found on the gun you took from Bates's apartment. They came back a match to Hennessey and the vic."

Madison glanced at Terry. "So, we're still faced with the question of who fired the gun. It could have been placed in Lacy's hands. Also, it seems Hennessey hid it in Bates's apartment."

"Or Bates used gloves to make sure not to leave his prints behind while Hennessey didn't think of it," Terry said.

Madison shook her head. "Why would an innocent person hide the gun? Especially since he's been locked up before. Why risk it? Unless Bates likes his three squares a day." She brainstormed aloud. "Guilt over burying her could have moved him to hide the gun. But it wasn't in Bates's apartment when we first searched it."

"Where did it come from?" Terry asked.

Thirty seconds of silence passed with the three of them passing glances at each other.

"Bates had to be involved, even if as an accessory after the fact. He must've hidden the gun for Hennessey somewhere off the property, and once we finished the search brought it back to his apartment," Madison said.

"But why his and not Hennessey's?"

The answer to the riddle sparked in Madison's mind. "The guys were really close. Neither wanted to go to prison or be charged with the murder—"

"You're thinking Lacy committed suicide and they panicked?" Cynthia asked.

"Not entirely sure. We need more to base it on. The history of Hennessey beating on her doesn't sit well with me either."

Terry rubbed the back of his neck. "And he sold all her belongings, took over living in the condo."

"The condo...that's where they put the gun afterward. They knew we'd never go there, or at the very least get there in time."

"The guy was a cockroach," Cynthia said, warranting a look from Madison and Terry. "They're both drug addicts. From what I hear, rumor is Hennessey was also a pimp. They're money hungry. It wouldn't matter. Say, if he did love her, this instinct would take over, just like cockroaches that eat their dead."

Madison scrunched up her face.

"Well, it's true. To Hennessey, this would have meant opportunity. He likely knew it wouldn't last forever and that's why he moved quickly to remove any trace of the vic—"

"Lacy," Madison corrected her.

"Yes, Maddy, Lacy."

"Okay, so we know that the two of them worked together, at least in some capacity. We can place Bates and Hennessey at the condo. We can place Hennessey's prints on the gun, but not Bates's. But it was found in his apartment. What am I missing?"

"We have yet to run ballistic testing on the gun to see if it's a match to the casing and fragments pulled from the—Lacy. We could be getting a little ahead of ourselves."

"When do—"

"Sam's working on it."

Madison nodded.

Cynthia pointed to the folder. "You will notice, I have results from the vaginal swab, and Lacy did have a sexual encounter within twenty-four hours before death."

"DNA?"

"There was. It came back a match to one in the system. It wasn't Hennessey or Bates."

Madison looked at Terry wondering if it was going to be Peter Hargrove. She still needed to pull his background.

Cynthia continued. "The guy actually died a month ago." Cynthia bent over the top of the folder and pointed a finger to the sheet. Madison's eyes followed where she directed.

"Kevin Thorne," Madison read the name aloud. Any passing thought she had to Lacy being involved with a john evaporated with this finding. Johns always wear condoms.

"Yeah, he apparently killed—"

"Yes, in a motel room, slits to both wrists. Ruled a suicide."

"Maddy?" Cynthia sought an explanation.

Madison closed the folder and looked at her partner. "That is the case I told that woman I'd look into." Madison's eyes went to her colleague and friend. "This woman showed up here on Sunday and asked me to look into the case involving her fiancé."

"Case? But it's closed with the ruling of suicide," Cynthia said.

"I know what the file says."

Cynthia enlarged her eyes toward Terry.

"What was that for?" Madison asked.

"Just you. You doubt the findings."

Madison adjusted her stance, jutting her hip to the right and placing one hand there while the other held the closed folder. "Maybe I'm the only one finding this odd, but the guy cuts both wrists to kill himself. His fiancée claims he never would have done that. Richards mentioned she was pregnant and that Kevin had recently lost his job—"

"It could have pushed him over the edge," Cynthia said.

"But all this combined with your recent findings. He had sex with our victim."

"Lacy," Cynthia's smile was subtle and barely curved her lips.

Madison waved a dismissive hand at her. Her mind was trying to discern the connection between everyone. How did Kevin Thorne factor into Lacy's death? Was his death actually a suicide or was it murder, as his fiancée had claimed?

"I've got to go." She took a few steps and heard Cynthia call out to her, but she didn't turn back. She knew what she had to do now. She waved a hand over her head. "Thanks, Cyn."

CHAPTER 28

MADISON WENT TO THE EVIDENCE storage locker and Terry came with her. She told the officer behind the counter what she wanted and he told her "two minutes."

Terry stood beside her with a ham sandwich he had grabbed on the way down. He took a bite and swallowed the mouthful before speaking. "So, now you don't think the guy killed himself? You doubt Richards's ruling on the cause of death? Thought you guys were friends. His favorite detective, he says."

"He used to—"

Terry tore another mouthful from his lunch. Meat dangled from the edge of the bread, taunting her, begging her to come back to the life where she could eat what she wanted, when she wanted. Terry didn't miss it.

"You're eating right?"

"Don't worry about me."

"Come on, you need someone to." He smirked.

She balled up a fist and punched his right shoulder. As she retracted her arm, she dwelled on his words about needing someone to care for her. She was the job. She had limited friends, a pretty much non-existent social life, and now tension with coworkers. Somehow, things would return to normal between her and Richards—maybe. At least she hoped so. She'd stand a better chance if she weren't now forced to question his ruling. She considered her options and, given the situation, would rather upset the balance in another relationship first, a relationship which didn't really matter to her anymore and was already beyond repair.

"We'll need to talk to Sovereign."

"I guess Hargrove's not the older man after all. I win the bet."

"I say we need to talk to Sovereign, and you say that?"

Terry bobbed his head.

"No bets are settled until charges are laid. Those are the rules."

"Why delay the inevitable?" Terry's eyes flashed with a revelation. "Suppose I'll have more time to bask in the vi—"

"There isn't any victory until—"

"Here ya go." The officer placed a box on the counter. "Case evidence for Thorne, Kevin. Sign here." He extended a log sheet toward her along with a pen that had been tucked behind an ear.

"Only the one?"

"Yes, ma'am." His eyes were bright.

"All right then." She scribbled her name and badge number, with a pen she had on her, and then looked up and smiled at the officer.

Madison grabbed the box, bending at the knees, anticipating it to be heavy, but it was light. "They must not have gotten much."

She didn't say what else she was thinking, but for an instant, she doubted her colleagues. Had they gathered all the evidence? Was something left behind—something that would confirm Thorne's death was a murder, not a suicide?

MADISON AND TERRY TOOK THE evidence box to an interrogation room and rummaged through it. The contents were easily spread on the table with room to spare. She fanned the crime scene photos out and studied them.

It was a standard cheap motel room. A tube television sat on a long dresser, opposite the bed. The artwork on the walls dated back to the seventies. The comforter on the bed matched the carpeting and had faded in equal harmony with it over the years.

"He was found here." Madison pointed to the bloodstained tub. "This photo was one taken after Thorne was removed. Tox showed two times the legal limit of alcohol in his system, and there was also a cocktail of drugs in his bloodstream." Madison looked up from the photo to her partner. "There was no physical evidence to support he used drugs regularly. The razor was on the tub ledge and only had Thorne's prints."

"And the fact he had no history of drug use wasn't found suspicious?"

"Guess not enough so."

Terry picked up the photo. "There are no alcohol bottles next to the tub. One would think he would have brought those in with him before doing the deed."

"Good point. Once a person is heavily intoxicated, a switch goes off. They wouldn't let their drink from their sight."

She looked back at the photo of the motel room and pointed at a bottle on the nightstand. She read the crime scene report. "An empty bottle of tequila was found. It was dusted for prints and it only showed Thorne's."

"Any mention of where they found the drugs he consumed? Any specifics on the drugs?" Terry asked.

Madison braced both her hands on the table and stretched out her back. Her focus stayed on the report. "It seemed to be a blend of drugs—meth, coke, and heroin."

She turned the sheet to Detective Sovereign's notes. She read some of it aloud. "No trace of cocaine or meth, or any other drug, was found in the motel room, despite confirmation drugs were found in the victim's system. As noted by Cole Richards, Medical Examiner, the victim was not a habitual user."

Madison looked at Terry, who gestured for her to continue.

"A puncture hole was found between two of his toes. It's figured that the cocktail he was on was in liquid form."

Madison stopped reading. "What's saying someone else didn't shoot this guy up and then kill him? No record of drug abuse, why did he start now?"

"He was under a lot of pressure right. Think about it, Thorne lost his job, had a pregnant fiancée, and an upcoming marriage that was a sham to start."

"Still, to turn to drugs—hardcore drugs? It seems a stretch to me," Madison said. "Most people who haven't used drugs just turn to alcohol and get wasted."

"Well, did they find any evidence connecting his death to anyone? Was there any trace drawing back to another person?"

"I talked to Richards about this—"

"You did?"

She read his eyes, his concern about questioning the ME's findings. "I wasn't confronting him. I asked if he remembered. I should have known he would, as he remembers every one that comes to his table. Anyway, his response was the body was pulled from a motel room, so there was trace, but nothing that could lead them anywhere."

Terry read from the report he had taken from her hand. "Sovereign says no one had reason to harm Thorne. He had no enemies. Maybe this guy did take care of himself?"

With the evidence presented, or the lack thereof, she could see why the case had been concluded suicide—it was the simple solution. She hated that realization. She hated it even more so because she had been with the man who, out of eagerness to move on to the next case, was willing to shut his eyes to what still needed to be uncovered.

"Do we have any witness testimony?"

Terry went through the folder and found the one labeled by the same wordage. He opened it and started reading.

"Are you going to share it with me?" Madison asked.

"They interviewed the motel manager, the housekeeper, the people renting out the room beside Thorne's. Here." He handed her the folder and dropped into a chair. She pulled one over near him and sat down.

"Who found him?" She went back to Sovereign's notes, skimmed them, and answered her own question. "Sheila Bolton, the housekeeper. It says here her shift started at eight in the morning that day. She got to Thorne's room around ten."

Terry went through the folders and found the interview with Bolton. Seconds after looking at the contents, he lifted his eyes to match hers.

"Nothing useful. I mean she basically described the scene exactly as they found it." Terry put his hands over the spread of photos.

"She didn't see anyone? Hear anything?"

"Like you said, her shift didn't start until eight. TOD was pinned at between two and three."

Madison looked over the table at the bagged evidence of which there was very little. She looked at the evidence report list. "Condoms, unused." Madison glanced at Terry. "That would explain how his DNA got into our girl."

"Our girl?" Terry raised his brows.

"You know what I mean. Lacy."

"It is okay to say vic, Maddy."

Her eyes narrowed slightly. "Let's assume he met up with Lacy at this motel, why did she leave? And is it a coincidence that our only potential witness to help us get closer to the truth is also dead?"

"There were also the people in the neighboring room," Terry said.

"Their statement was they were sleeping and heard nothing. We could always do a follow-up call on them, though, and see if their memories have been sparked."

"Their home address is two hours from the city. You're approaching this as a homicide." Concern swept over his face.

"Well, it's definitely suspi—"

"Hennessey or Bates could look good for this, but what if the fiancée found out about our vic, the other lady?"

Madison could tell by the flash in his eyes that he had used the label to refer to Lacy to make a jab at her. She didn't acknowledge it. "She came to me claiming her fiancé would never kill himself because—"

"Yeah, because she knew he wouldn't, because she did. If she's in our face, we would never suspect her."

"But why bring it up? The case was closed." She waved a hand in the air, gesturing in the direction of the holding cells. "Wait a minute, there are too many possibilities here. We have two guys who loved her, in their own way, mind you. One said she was a sweet girl. However, both of them knew about an older man. Obviously they knew about the condo and that Lacy was being taken care of, but maybe they had the wrong guy." She stopped talking, the revelation smacking her. "What if they found out about her sleeping with Thorne? What if they killed him but made it look like a suicide? They had access to drugs."

"I believe it seems more likely than Vilma, Thorne's fiancée. Aren't you always saying women know when their man is sleeping around?"

Madison felt her lashes touch her skin, as she blinked slowly. Still, years later, she felt the stab to her heart when her past betrayal resurfaced. She hadn't known before she'd walked in on her fiancé with the other woman.

"I do say that."

She hated being made a fool of so it was a secret she chose to carry. It wasn't the truth, sometimes no matter how much one thinks they know someone, it doesn't make their opinions of them gospel.

"You don't sound convincing."

"Listen, it's this woman, all right. She was hysterical. There was something in her eyes, helplessness."

"I'd be hysterical if I killed someone too. What's to say she didn't want to—"

"But what sense would it make for her to have us look at the case again? She was off, free and clear."

"Point taken," Terry said.

She saw it in her partner's eyes. The case had been closed and she was supposed to let it go. "I can't just walk away."

"This is going to create a real mess, you do know that?"

"What I know is that I have one body in the morgue, one six feet under, and neither of them should be where they are."

"You're going to reopen the case? Treat Thorne as a suspicious death, not suicide?" Terry asked.

Madison tossed the file on the table. "I don't see what other choice we have."

CHAPTER 29

THEY SPENT THE NEXT FEW hours sorting through the evidence, the interviews, and the forensic findings. To see all the DNA contributors pulled from the motel room, Madison's stomach tossed. Motels were a breeding ground for bacteria and infection.

"There was evidence of sexual intercourse in the bed. Semen and vaginal fluid were pulled and tested." Madison's face contorted. "There were two dominant donors and five other exemplars. Not dominant enough to pull DNA strands from, but identifiable as coming from other sources." She looked at her partner. "Do they not wash the sheets in hot water? Gives me shivers to think about it. Maybe that's why I never go anywhere."

"You don't go anywhere because you'd have to actually take off work. A holiday? You might want to try it at some point before you're eighty."

"I'll relax once I'm retired."

Terry let out a deep breath and shook his head.

"Come on. Let's not talk about this now."

"Okay. But we should talk about it."

"Terry."

He held up his hands. "All right. So we know that Lacy had sex with Thorne."

"We need to prove it was the night he died." Madison pressed a fingertip on the photo of the motel room, rose from the table, and pulled her phone to her ear. "Cynthia, I need you to cross-reference something for me."

"So, you want me to reopen a closed case?" Sergeant Winston clasped his hands and rested them on his paunch. "Richards ruled it a suicide. Sovereign didn't turn up any evidence to indicate—"

"Then they were both wrong." From her peripheral, she noticed Terry turn to face her.

They were both in the Sergeant's office sitting across from him.

"Two of my best were wrong, and you're right?"

The way his eyes trailed from her eyes to her mouth and back, to make eye contact—he assessed her in seconds. Now wasn't the time to argue that she would also be considered one of his best.

"Convince me." He swiveled slightly, picked up a pen from the desk and tapped its end on the surface.

She ran through the evidence as they saw it, presenting the list of possible people who would have wanted Thorne dead.

"Everyone was after this guy?" He moved his chair closer to his desk, dropped the pen, and clasped his hands again.

"I'm not saying every—"

"You're not even sure and you want the case reopened? Why even come to me at this point? Investigate it on your own. You normally make your own rules."

Madison took a deep breath. Maybe she deserved that. She had recently gone against direction and almost lost her job for it. The one thing that steadied her was that her actions had been justified.

"Okay, listen—"

"I have been listening, Knight. He slept with the young girl. So what? It doesn't mean he was killed for it."

"If you saw this guy—Hennessey—you would know that he was possessive of her. Hell, Higgins had been out to her place."

"Please don't swear in here."

"You've got to be kidding me. The truth of the matter is, everything is too coincidental. I don't—"

"I know, you don't like coincidences."

"Even you have to agree with me. It seems highly plausible our guy may not have killed himself." Madison was slowly losing the Sergeant's attention. "Evidence may lean toward Lacy pulling the trigger on herself, but she didn't bury herself. The evidence also shows a struggle. This guy Thorne appears to have committed suicide, but he may have been helped along too."

She watched, as her argument sunk into her superior's mind. His eyes met hers after a quick glance at Terry.

"It looks bad on the department to make one conclusion and then reopen."

Leave it to Winston to be worried about how the media may spin things.

"Isn't it more important to get to the truth? And people do it all the time."

"Here we don't." He paused. "If I recall correctly, wasn't there also a note?"

"There was an e-mail that was taken as such."

"Taken as such?"

"That's what I said." She noticed the Sergeant's brow lower from the attitude she served back to him. "Yeah, an e-mail. Suicides are usually decided at the moment. Even if planned, it doesn't mean one will go through with it. Execution to go ahead is statistically a quick decision."

"Continue."

"Even if Thorne had rented the room for the purpose of taking his life that night, it didn't mean he would follow through."

"What are you saying to me? Plain English."

She fought to suppress the anger she felt beneath the surface— the anger that came as the result of not being deemed vital to the department. The mistrust that seemed to originate from the fact that she wore a bra.

"In plain English, the e-mail taken as a suicide note was written the day before. But its wording has room for interpretation. It was an e-mail from Thorne to his fiancée saying he was stressed out and couldn't take it anymore." Madison gripped the arm of the chair. "I've been in that place before, not able to take it anymore, but it didn't mean I was going to kill myself. And the fact is that the e-mail came from Thorne's work account. Get this. One of the motivations that helped support the conclusion of suicide was the fact Thorne was stressed out because he lost his job and was getting married. He wasn't fired until the next day."

"He sensed it coming," Winston said.

"Listen, boss, you know it's too thin to be taken as a suicide note, and the entire thing is too coincidental. I can see it in your eyes."

"Should have known that you would analyze me too."

Why? Because it's my job to analyze people? She restrained herself from verbalizing the thought.

"Here's the thing, I authorize your looking deeper into this." He looked at Terry. "And I can see merit in doing so."

Madison straightened in her chair, drawing the Sergeant's eyes back to her.

"But until you get me more than the fact they had sex and they both happen to be dead a month later, the case remains closed. You hear me?"

Madison smiled. "Yes. Of course."

"Now, get to work." The Sergeant gave them both a once over and dismissed them with a brush of the hand.

CHAPTER 30

PARADISE MOTEL WAS ON THE main strip in the east end. The street was lined with motels whose décor all dated back decades. Swimming pools were outlined by chain-link fences and sat in the middle of most properties. The one where Thorne had met his death didn't have a pool. At quick count, twenty rooms squared off the parking lot. The huge sign out front read HONEYMOON ROOM WITH A HEART-SHAPED BED AVAILABLE.

They went in and asked for Sheila Bolton, the housekeeper who found Thorne, and were told that her shift ended hours ago.

"The maids clean from eight to one." The guy behind the counter didn't seem to fit in here. He wore high-end clothing and his hair was cut in a modern style. "It doesn't take them too long."

"What about Lance Ringwood?" Madison asked. He was the manager of record.

"Oh no, you won't find him around here. He runs this place from a distance." The guy leaned on the counter. "He actually owns several properties, and this one, let's just say, isn't his pride and joy."

"All right, then. What's your name?"

"Trevor." It took sustained eye contact, but he eventually volunteered his last name. "Trevor Whitmore."

"You do know that a body was found in one of your rooms?" Madison assessed his reaction to the news. What she expected and what she received were two different things. His eyes widened and he stood straight.

"A body? When? I didn't hear…" He shook his head. "A body?"

He looked back at her.

"How long have you worked here?"

"Two months. When did this—the body—when was it found?"

He swallowed audibly.

Madison gave him the specific date and then summed it up. "About one month ago."

"I had no idea. Someone killed someone? Here?"

The latter of his statement gave way to a latent excitement.

Trust me, in real life, murder isn't what it's like on TV.

"You've been working here for two months but never heard of this." Madison studied his eyes, beneath them his arms, looking for track marks, any way to connect him visually to the wrong crowd, the group Lacy had been a part of. He looked clean. The other thought on her mind was why he hadn't been questioned before now. Even if he weren't on shift the day Thorne was found, all staff should have been contacted and questioned. Madison pulled out a picture of Thorne. "Do you recognize him?"

The guy took the photo from her and nodded. "Yeah, I do." His hand shook. "This is the guy? This is the body that was—"

"Yes."

He looked at her, his eyes clearly marked with disbelief. "Kevin Thorne."

Madison and Terry shared a look.

"You were on a first and last name basis?" Madison asked.

"The guy was a regular. Every Thursday night, since I started working here anyway."

The body was found on Friday morning. "Did he meet up with anyone on these nights?"

"Yeah, all the time. She was a pretty thing. Really skinny. She had bones popping out of everywhere."

Madison pulled out a photo of Lacy and placed it on the counter. "Was it her?"

The guy exchanged photos, leaving the one of Thorne on the counter.

"Yeah, that's her."

"Did you know her?"

"Did? She's dead too?"

Madison gave a slow nod.

"Oh my God!" One hand went to his mouth. Tears formed at the corners of his eyes.

"You were close?"

"No...no." He attempted to compose himself with a shaking of the head. He dropped his hand from his mouth and crossed his arms. This time he also rubbed his arms.

"You seem to be awfully upset about this for not knowing her."

"She was always," he choked back on saliva, "happy."

"Happy has you this upset?"

He walked out from behind the counter and dropped into one of two sofa chairs that served as the lobby.

"We talked a few times. She had things rough, she said, but they were getting better. People were starting to believe in her again."

"She told all this to you, a stranger?"

"Yeah." His eyes read, *I don't care if you believe me.*

"Continue."

"Well, that's about it. She said she had a boyfriend who didn't treat her right, but she was trying to get out of it. But there was something about the way she said it, you know. Like she wanted to believe it but didn't really. Almost as if by saying it, it would make it a reality."

Madison asked him where he was the night of Thorne's death.

"You think I killed him?"

"His death was actually ruled a suicide."

His shoulders relaxed. "I was off that entire week and didn't come back 'til the following Monday. My baby sister was getting married. It was a big deal. It was five hours from here. A whole week of listening to 'No, no, I love you more.' Some couples make me sick."

It was possible that this guy never heard of the dead body, but Madison found it strange that the rumor hadn't circulated back to him when he had returned. "We'll have to check out what you're saying—"

"What, like it's an alibi, like I have something to hide?"

"Well, if you don't, it shouldn't be a problem."
"I'll get you her number."

CHAPTER 31

AFTER SPEAKING WITH TREVOR WHITMORE, they gained access to
room five, where Thorne had been found. The room wasn't rented
out so they struck it lucky, as the clerk had said.

"I find it hard to believe he never heard about this." Her line of
thought changed when she put the key in the door and gave the
handle a twist. "They haven't even upgraded to swipe locks here."

"It's like the dino era."

Madison looked over at her partner.

"What?"

She smiled at him and opened the door. It looked like it had in
the photos less the horror of the crime scene.

"At least if the guy did off himself, he was kind enough to do so
in the tub." Terry ran a hand along the dresser.

"Seriously."

"Well."

"Trace pulled a lot of evidence—hair, fibers, fingerprints—but
nothing came back to a match in the system. The evidence was
dismissed as circumstantial based on the location of the crime
scene."

"I can see that."

"Really? The suicide note isn't even what I would call a suicide
note. It was written a day before. There are people who would have
wanted Thorne dead."

"Yes, and that's why we're here. Sometimes it's easier to see
backward than it is ahead."

"You're getting philosophical on me now?" Madison asked.

"No, I'm just saying is all. Now we have another body tied back to this one, it casts more light on the shadows of the case."

"Shadows."

"Please don't pick on my word choice right now."

She held up a hand as if to say, *fine.*

Terry continued. "When the investigation first opened, there wasn't any connection to people other than—"

"Other than Vilma," she said. "We both know she was questioned at length about Kevin, their relationship, why he would have been at the motel."

"And her answer was she didn't know."

"Didn't know, or wouldn't say."

"You think she killed her fiancé?" Terry asked.

"Not sure yet, but it's possible."

"There's nothing showing in her background for drug use—"

"There wasn't anything in Thorne's either."

"But we know that Lacy used. We know that her pimp boyfriend, Hennessey, did and likely dealt."

Terry rubbed the back of his neck.

"You're still not convinced this was anything more than a suicide, are you? Sometimes I wonder if you disagree with me just for the sake of disagreeing." Madison walked around, Terry trailing behind her. She took in the space, breathing in the smell of cleaning chemicals, envisioning Thorne in the room.

The TV was on.

The sheets had evidence of a sexual encounter.

"Cynthia had noted the television was on the weather channel," Madison said while pointing at the TV. "He had sex beforehand. We still need to know, for certain, with whom. Cynthia's going to run—" Her thoughts shifted direction. "He didn't come here to kill himself. Why have sex? Why have someone else here?"

"One last time before—"

"No, it's not that. There's more here."

She noticed her partner roll his eyes but ignored it.

"Okay," Terry said, "so the guy shows up here intent on killing himself. At least that's the plan, if I'm playing along."

"He sets up a meeting, say with Lacy. Every Thursday night as the front desk guy said."

"Still following."

"She comes in and has sex with him. Then where does she go?"

"Back home before Hennessey has a clue?"

"Possible." She dipped her head left to right.

"I don't know what you expect to uncover. Thorne had lost everything and he was under a lot of stress. He had a new baby on the way, had to balance a fiancée, and apparently a lover on the side."

"He hadn't lost his job at the time of the e-mail. And he couldn't have been too down, though, or why meet up with a woman? Why meet up with Lacy? When I'm down, I prefer to be alone."

"You get down?" Terry asked.

"Listen, you're missing the point. What if Lacy showed up here as she did every Thursday night. Hennessey and Bates knew she had an older man. Maybe they had no idea about Hargrove? Maybe they assumed Thorne was the older man taking care of her. What if they followed her and killed him? Huh?"

"TOD for Lacy was put at a week after Thorne."

"An approximate timeline. And who knows, maybe they didn't kill her right away. Hennessey was more interested in reclaiming his property," Madison elaborated.

"Lacy could have threatened to go to the authorities about what they did to Thorne."

"Exactly. They killed her to silence her about Thorne's murder and then staged her death to look like a suicide too."

Terry looked around the room. "Now we just have to prove it."

CHAPTER 32

THEY SPENT THE NEXT THIRTY MINUTES examining the motel room and trying to relive the last night of Thorne's life.

"So, the guy was watching the weather channel," Madison said.

"They had questioned the fiancée about it and she said he was probably looking at it for their wedding date, which was that weekend."

"Another thing that doesn't make sense. If he was looking at the weather for that purpose, he had something he was looking forward to in life. It doesn't fit with a suicidal person. And when Vilma was questioned about whether she had sex in the motel with Thorne, she said she never did. She was certain he never would have cheated on her either. She said the lab must have been mistaken. She tried to say it was poor cleaning, even when they told her it had been confirmed as Thorne's DNA." Madison touched the comforter and pulled her hand back. She looked at her partner. "You never met this woman. She's kind of crazy, but not in the killer type of way, just crazy—in her own way."

"Clarify."

"She was in denial about a lot of things: Thorne sleeping with someone else. Thorne killing himself."

"What if she did it? I know we mentioned it in passing already, but—"

Madison shook her head. "I don't buy it."

"Just because you don't buy it doesn't mean it isn't the truth."

"Let's revisit the interviews with the motel staff."

THE INTERVIEW WITH SCOTT CLOUSE, a motel employee, showed a man who had everything together. Sovereign made a notation that he was calm and rational. He had attributed it to shock. She played the tape from one of the recorded interviews.

"You didn't see anything unusual?" Sovereign asked.

"You mean besides some kids I had to ask to leave the property? No. Just like every other night."

"Was Mr. Thorne a regular there?"

"That's his name? He paid cash."

"You ever see him before?"

"Nope," Clouse said.

"Never?"

"Never."

"All right, then, continue from the top and run me through your night."

Clouse continued to say how he had passed most of the night watching the television in the lobby. He said his usual shift wasn't Thursday, but he got suckered into it. The regular employee, a kid name Trevor Whitmore, was off for his sister's wedding.

Madison and Terry shared a look as the tape continued to play on screen.

Clouse added that he preferred to work the start of the week, when couples would rendezvous. *"To see all those people who live double lives. They are going for what they want in life."*

That opinion grated on Madison. She passed a glance at her partner, who was intently listening to the interview.

"The girl that came for his room was fine."

Madison paused the tape. "There is evidence right there. Sovereign should have followed this up. This guy is confirming a person went into that room with Thorne."

She hit play before Terry could respond. She was seething angry with Sovereign for rushing the case to a conclusion.

"Describe her for us," Sovereign said.

"Blonde, thin, real thin, pretty face."

"Did you get her name?"

The man laughed. *"Rarely do we get names here."*

"*Continue, what happened next?*"

"*She showed up and...well, she showed up and went into his room. I noticed because I saw a cab's headlights pulling in and got up to look. That's how I saw her and knew she was fine.*"

"*You could tell all this from across a parking lot?*"

"*I know what I saw.*"

"*Then what?*"

"*I went back to my television show.*"

"*Nothing else after that? Name of the cab company?*"

"*Nope, and I have no idea.*" There was a pause. "*Well, a couple cars came in after that and parked in front of other rented rooms. I never thought anything of it.*"

"*You saw the cars earlier in the day when they rented the rooms?*" Sovereign asked.

"*No, I'm not saying that. Shift started at seven.*"

"*You don't know if those cars belonged to the other rented rooms? There's no record of license plates when people check in?*"

"*I assumed. No...wait a minute, am I a suspect here?*"

"*We're trying to find out what happened to—*"

"*Well, it had nothing to do with me.*"

"*What were the makes and models of the cars?*"

"*I don't know. I'm sorry, but I didn't look that close. I'm pretty sure one was older. It was large and boxy. But the other was smaller, compact.*"

Madison hit the stop button. "Neither Hennessey nor Bates has a car registered to them."

"It could have been a friend's."

"What if they came in the cab, although, Clouse made it sound as if Lacy did."

"This is a mess."

"What about Vilma? What car does she drive?" Madison asked.

"I'll be right back." Terry rose and left the room, headed for his computer.

Madison sat looking at the crime scene photos. Sovereign hadn't checked out all the angles, yet Winston had termed him as one of his best. She didn't find any follow-up notes made on the "large and boxy" or "compact" cars.

Knuckles rapped on the door.

She expected to see Winston checking in on their progress with the case. It was Sovereign. She turned back around to face the table. Her next exhale of breath was stymied.

"I hear you're looking into my closed case."

She heard his footsteps coming closer and felt his confident arrogance sweep across the room.

"You think I missed something?"

She faced him. When their eyes met, she felt the familiar tap in her chest. "Yeah, I do."

"What exactly? You think the guy was murdered?" He pulled out a chair opposite her, flipped it around, and straddled it backward.

"It doesn't matter what I think." She pulled a sheet out of a file. Her mind wasn't on the words; it was on her discomfort. "You have a job to do? A case to work on?" Her eyes looked into his. She refused to let him see how their past still affected her. She hated to accept it herself.

"There's always a case." His eyes scanned her face, paused at her mouth, and traveled back to her eyes. "You still hate me."

Her eyes narrowed. "To hate you would imply that I care."

"Thorne had a crappy hand dealt to him. He didn't have a reason to live. His e-mail said he couldn't deal with it anymore."

"There are a lot of holes."

"You think that Richards called it wrong too? COD wasn't self-inflicted? Have you run this by him to see what he thinks of your superior point of view?"

"Don't be like—"

"Like what, Knight? Right?" He rose and turned the chair around, tucking it back into the table before leaving the room.

Madison's hand balled into a fist on the table.

CHAPTER 33

TERRY FOUND OUT VILMA DROVE a car which could be described as a compact.

"I can't see her doing it." Madison stuffed photos into folders and then put them into the box.

"Because you can't see it happening doesn't mean it didn't."

They took the evidence back to lock-up and headed out to see Vilma at her home in the east end. The house was a two-story brick, turn-of-the-century home. The front garden looked in need of tending, but would wait until the new season. The front patch of grass was brown from the snow and winter thaw.

Vilma answered after their first knock. It was about seven in the evening and nightfall was imminent. At least the days were getting a little longer.

"Detective Knight." Vilma opened the door for them to enter her home. Her wild curls were pulled back into a clip, except for a few strands that dangled over her ears. Large hoops adorned her ears, like the ones she wore the first time they had met, and her eyelids were painted teal today. She wore tight blue jeans and a black sweater that reached the middle of her thigh in length. She burrowed beneath it and stuffed one hand into a pocket. "Have you found out anything?"

They had decided not to confront her on the witness's note of a compact vehicle. This visit was simply to derive more background into her relationship with the deceased.

Madison introduced Terry, and then Vilma led them to her kitchen table.

Vilma studied Terry's face before turning to Madison.

"We're here because we're looking into things," Madison said.

Vilma's mouth curved into a small smile.

"We don't want you to get your hopes built up too much."

"Hopes are what give me breath, Detective. Without them, why bother?" She glanced at Terry again. "Yes, hope and dreams are what keep this planet turning."

"While I believe hope is important, I want you to realize it's still early on in the investigation." Madison regretted saying what she had the second it came out.

"Oh, thank god!"

Madison tapped her hand on Vilma's forearm a couple times.

"Don't get my hopes up," she mumbled, repeating Madison.

Madison nodded slowly.

They had decided not to get into the fact that Thorne's case had been connected to another one. Everything had to be executed perfectly to obtain anything from her that may prove useful—something that may have been overlooked by Sovereign. She was out to confirm that the man was wrong now. She hated that it took Richards down with him.

"Your fiancé died in a motel room."

"Paradise Motel."

"Correct." Madison took a deep breath, her patience level breaching the surface already. "There was evidence that he had company that night."

"Nope, I do not believe it." Her face was stoic.

"Well, I'm going by what the file said."

"The same file that said he killed himself? You may want to find a new file. I told the original detective that came here—what was his name? Trim, blond hair, nice looking."

Madison's jaw tightened. "Detective Sovereign."

"Yes, that's it. I told him that there must have been a mistake. He'd never do that me. My Kev and I were in love—real love."

Love was a fabrication to make one feel better, like they belonged in the world, like they had a purpose. Madison's thought made her remember a man she had met during a previous investigation.

"There are people who don't believe it, but they've never had it then." Vilma's left hand went to the hoop in that ear. "They told me he went there every Thursday."

Madison remained silent, hoping Vilma would talk herself into the realization Kevin Thorne wasn't as innocent as she wanted to believe.

"He liked to play with himself sometimes. Ya know, when he was stressed or overwhelmed. But another woman, nuh-uh. He'd never cheat on me." A hand went to her abdomen. "I'm two months pregnant."

Madison smiled at her.

"I can tell you found that out already. It was going to be such a happy event, but at least I'll have a bit of Kev with me forever." Her eyes misted and soaked her lashes.

"I have to ask you a question and it may be difficult to answer. Were you at Paradise Motel on the Thursday night he died?"

Vilma pinched the tip of her nose and let out a deep, jagged sigh. "Yes. I stopped by to say hi to Kev, but he liked his alone time sometimes."

"He wasn't happy to see you that night?"

A single tear slid down a cheek as she shook her head.

"Do you know why?"

"All I know is he told me he was expecting a guy from the office over. Said he was real bummed about losing his job and that he needed a release. He wanted me to leave before he got there."

Madison realized again how blind love could make people.

Sobs wrenched her body. "I...I know I should have told the other cop this, but I wanted Kev's death investigated. He never would have killed himself."

"When he told you he wanted you to leave, what did you do?"

"I left. I mean, what else was I supposed to do?"

"Where did you go?"

Vilma's bloodshot eyes looked into Madison's. "You think I did it."

"I'm not saying that at all."

"I just came home."

Madison nodded. "This guy from the office, do you know his name?"

She shook her head. "He didn't say."

"Did Kev have people from work over before?"

"Not that I know of, but we lived separately. We were waiting until we got married for that." More tears fell in silence. She continued. "I started questioning myself afterward, you know. Was he trying to tell me something? Was he reaching out to me by mentioning that he needed a release?"

"You wonder if he was trying to tell you something?"

"Yeah. If he did kill himself, it was almost like a coded message, looking back. You know, tying things together. He lost his job and the fact he needed a release." Vilma rose, pulled a tissue box from a kitchen counter, and brought it back with her to the table. "I thought he wanted to kick back and have a few drinks." She paused for a moment. "But I still can't accept that he killed himself. And drugs? No way. They say he had done some before he died. He wasn't a user."

"How did Kevin seem to you?"

Vilma's tears paused and there was a spark of happiness in her eyes. "Besides putting motives on his words, happy." She dabbed a tissue to her nose. "Definitely happy."

Madison picked up on the inconsistencies. He had told Vilma in e-mail, and in person, that he was feeling overwhelmed. Madison wasn't sure how that translated to happy. "Did you tell the detective this?"

"Yes. As I said, the last time I saw him he was happy, but I didn't admit to being at the motel that night."

"One more thing before we go." Madison reached into a pocket and pulled out a photograph of Lacy. She handed it to Vilma. "Do you recognize her?"

A fingertip traced the outline of Lacy's head, and then Vilma looked up. "She was a secretary at Kev's work. What does she have to do with this?"

He was expecting a guy from his office over. What if it was a woman?

"Did Kevin ever talk about her?"

"Was she the one you think he had sex with? No." Vilma shook her head. "He wouldn't do that to me." She paused; her eyes lit. "Did she kill him? If she was the last to be with him before he—"

Madison could tell by the reaction, the pretense of denial about an affair had diminished. Vilma knew. Vilma didn't want to accept it.

Chapter 34

Madison spent most of the night at her computer, imagining Hershey at her feet, but it was best he stay at the kennel until her hours balanced out somewhat.

A few e-mails had trickled in from the printers and she had a list started of companies that manufactured envelopes with the infinity symbol woven into the paper. She responded to them and requested a list of the companies that purchased these, specifically in the Stiles area. She presented herself as a business owner who wanted to contact these places directly to ask about their satisfaction with the product. She hoped that by handling it this way, there would be less resistance. There wasn't enough to obtain any sort of warrant for the lists.

In addition to her cold case, all the twisted motives of those surrounding Kevin Thorne played out repeatedly. Every time the killer was someone different.

Sovereign had called it wrong. Thorne's death was too suspicious to just rule it a suicide. On top of it, Sovereign had missed vital clues, such as the cars the motel employee had seen that night. He had questioned Vilma about whether she went that night but hadn't really pushed the inconsistencies when she had denied it. Again, if he had looked into the cars closer, he would have realized she had been there.

Vilma had opened up to Madison, but she had to wonder why. Why now? Was it because Vilma had something to hide?

Madison woke up about six in the morning, wiped the crusted sleep from her eyes, and got dressed for the day. She fanned her fingers through her short hair, teasing it with her fingertips.

Her eyes caught her attention in the mirror, and she touched beneath one and leaned in. Her age was starting to show. Only thirty-five, but all that she had witnessed in her life gave her a perspective many would never have. They were the fortunate ones that went about their lives, normally unaffected by the crime rate or the loss of loved ones to murder. She had decided to face this life head-on, but for the purpose of making a difference and bringing closure and justice to those left behind. She had opted to be the victim's last voice.

One last fanning of her hair and she headed out the door. En route to the station, the details of both Lacy's and Thorne's cases melded together. They had their connection now—at least Madison suspected they did. They both worked at the same place.

Madison wondered if this was where Hargrove had obtained a job for Lacy, and if so, why not mention it to start with? Why talk as if securing employment for her was a future hope? What was he hiding? Did he know about Thorne too? Did he have a reason to kill him?

CHAPTER 35

"Nice of you to show up." Terry sat at his desk, clenching onto a Starbucks cup like it was his savior.

She looked at the clock, ten to eight. "Come on, it's time to go."

"But you—"

"Come on."

Terry slurped back on the rest of his coffee and tossed the cup in the garbage can. "Coming, boss." He pulled his jacket from his chair and put it on in one fluid motion.

"Now, that's a better attitude." Madison laughed as she led the way to the lot to sign out a department car.

Today's plan had been laid out before they had parted ways last night. They would be going over to Modern Computers, where Thorne had worked.

"I came in early and went down to evidence lock-up to look over the interview notes in Thorne's file for his place of employment. Turns out Sovereign had interviewed both the owner, David Connor, and the General Manager, Christina Dunn. Neither of them knew of anyone who would want to harm Thorne. They also talked to coworkers," Terry said.

"Any note of Lacy Rose?"

"No comment on my initiative?"

"It's about time?" Madison laughed.

Terry shook his head. "And no, there wasn't mention of Lacy. You know, he basically told her he was having an affair. He said he was having a guy from the office over. Who rents a motel room to hang out with a guy?"

"Yeah, I picked up on that too. Sometimes love can blind you to people's faults."

She knew it well, the statement touched too close to her on a personal level. She switched her focus. "If Lacy was working there, I'm curious why Hargrove didn't say anything about it." She weaved through the morning commuter traffic at a good pace. "Based on what Trevor from the motel said, he worked there two months and Thorne and Lacy were regulars. Taking into consideration when Hargrove got the apartment for her she probably just started there. She and Thorne must have hit it off right away. The guy's stressed about his other obligations and he seeks comfort in another woman's arms. It wouldn't be the first time."

"True enough. Guess we'll find out."

MODERN COMPUTERS HAD REMAINED A viable business, despite the changing tides in e-commerce. Many people in the world still preferred to buy their electronics from someone they could have human interaction with and not just provide sixteen digits and a security number to.

The building was in a built-up part of the south end. It occupied a decent-sized storefront, which had curbside windows plastered with fluorescent-colored advertisements about the weekly deals and their in-house financing plan.

The door chimed twice when they walked in and a staff member, along with a few customers who were perusing the store, looked at them. Madison and Terry stepped to the side of the door.

His hands went straight to the keyboard of the weekly special. "Lightweight. Fast. Lethal."

"You all right?" Madison looked at him with a smirk on her face.

"All that could be done with one of these."

"It's a computer."

"It's not just a computer. Is a Ferrari just a car?"

Madison laughed. It drew the attention of the salesman again, who held up a finger and mouthed, *I'll be right there.*

The man he was helping noticed the motion, and Madison swore she registered jealousy over the clerk's attention to another customer. The man was gesturing with his hands, rapidly, and Madison picked up a few of his comments from where she and Terry stood.

"What are its graphic capabilities?"

"Does it have Wi-Fi? It needs to have Wi-Fi."

"Does it have a Blu-ray player and burner? Or only a player?"

Madison glanced at her partner, about to comment on the fact that modern technology was outdated the minute it left the manufacturer's warehouse, but she noticed his full attention was still on the laptop he coveted.

He slid a hand up the backside to feel the smooth shell of the computer and stopped when he must have noticed her watching him. "Just to think, they are so light and are capable of so much. Technology is incredible."

"That there is the best we have. It's a terrific value." The salesman who had raised his finger to her earlier came over and started listing off the features.

She looked past the salesman to the customer he had come from. He stood in front of a computer; his fingers touched the keys, his other hand caressed the back of the monitor, similar to what Terry had done to the laptop.

"You can do gaming on this puppy, and with all that storage you'll never run out of room."

"Sounds like a good deal. Too good." Terry smiled, his eyes lit like a young child on Christmas morning.

Madison lifted her badge out from under her coat. The movement caused the sales guy to step back a few feet.

She gave him the formal introductions and asked to speak with either the owner or the general manager.

"David's out. Christina is in, though."

"Thank you." Madison stuffed her badge back under the coat, yet ended up unzipping the jacket.

The sales guy looked over to the other customers in the store, as if making sure everyone was content for the time being, and then he turned back to Madison and Terry. "I can get her for you."

"Actually, before you go, do you know her?" Madison reached

into a pocket for the picture of Lacy and extended it to him.

He looked from the photo to Madison's eyes. "She used to work here. Is she okay?" He received the message and verbalized the answer before she had to. "She's not." The flat of his one hand flew to cover his gaping mouth. "Oh God! That's why...that's why she hasn't been in. We thought she up and quit."

His raised voice and dramatics had the other customers looking over at them. Terry waved a hand for them to go back to their shopping and perusal.

"People up and quit often from here?" Madison fought for eye contact.

After resting his focus on the photo for a few seconds, his eyes shot to Madison. He handed her the picture back. "The pay here—" He paused, looking over his shoulder to an office door that came off the back of the showroom. "The pay here isn't that great. It's minimum wage. But first Kevin kills himself and now this?"

"What did she do here?"

"Lacy? Everything? She hadn't been here long but had already proven herself an asset. She answered the phones, fielded customers' inquiries. Greeted walk-ins."

A woman of slight build approached them. Her light blonde hair was shoulder length. She wore a beige cardigan buttoned up to her neck paired with jeans.

"Is everything all right here?" Her question was directed to the salesman. Her voice carried the hint of a British accent.

"These are detectives. They're here about Lacy. They were actually looking to speak with you."

The woman's presence seemed to fade as if she wished to be a chameleon and blend into his side. "About Lacy?"

Madison noticed one couple had become more interested in them than the electronics lining the shelves. "Christina Dunn I assume?"

A slow nod.

"Do you have somewhere private we can talk?"

"Sure." The manager directed her employee to the customers in the store then led Madison and Terry toward the door at the back of the showroom. "Please excuse the mess." Dunn gestured to computers, monitors, and laptops from different eras that lined the perimeter inside the room. Even with those there, the office felt spacious. It was about twenty feet square and furnished sparingly.

Dunn sat behind a gray melamine desk and slid her keyboard tray in as she took a seat. She nodded toward the assortment on the floor. "We also offer service on computers. The sales guys seem to find it easier to drop it off here than to take it back to the warehouse. I don't really mind either because by doing this they are away from the front for less time." She gestured to the chair across from her. "I only have one."

Madison and Terry shared a look. Madison opted to stand then proceeded with their formal introductions. She told her Lacy was dead and Dunn's face fell.

"Major Crimes. I've heard that one too much recently. I knew you guys were out there, and I still wish that's all I knew. No offense."

"Understandable. And none was taken. What can you tell us about Lacy? How long did she work here?"

"Oh, not long at all. Maybe a month, but we haven't seen her in the same length of time."

"How did she come to work here?"

"She was a referral from a friend of mine. He said she needed a break in life."

Madison remembered Hargrove saying he was trying to find her a job and that she would be happy with anything. "Who is this friend of yours?"

Dunn's eyes hardened over. "Does that matter? I thought you wanted to talk about Lacy."

"We are, and this is part of the investigation."

"Peter Hargrove. He's a good man."

"Did he bring people like Lacy to you before?"

"People like Lacy?" She crossed her arms.

"People with prior drug addiction or hard pasts?"

"No. Lacy was a drug addict? Is that what killed her?"

"No."

An exhaled breath from Dunn lifted the edge of a sheet of paper in front of her. She put her hand on it to flatten it out. "What happened to her?"

"Before we tell you, we have a few more questions."

"So, I answer yours and you don't answer mine?"

"Sometimes that's how this works."

Dunn's jaw stiffened.

"How was Lacy as an employee? As a person?"

"She was hard working, for the brief time we had her." The corners of Dunn's eyes moistened. "Does Pete know? I'll have to tell him."

"We've already spoken with him—"

"Well, don't be thinking anything impure about the man."

Madison cocked her head. "Why would we?"

The two women remained in eye lock, neither of them saying a word.

Dunn broke the silence. "It's just you have a young girl, apparently vulnerable—"

"Peter never told you about her history?"

She shook her head. "No need. Pete vouched for her. I didn't even pay her wages. He said she needed experience and that he'd cover the tab."

Madison glanced at Terry. This man, by all accounts, truly fell from the sky as an angel to save mankind.

"Lacy didn't know. She thought she was being paid by us. I'd cut the checks out of Modern Computers and deposit Peter's money separately."

"Sounds like a good deal. Labor for free."

"After three months, if I loved her, I was to take over her wages. And I would have. She was that good of a worker. I could see it in the first couple of days."

"Did Peter offer to pay for her because Modern Computers was having money difficulties? We know Kevin Thorne was let go from his job just before—"

"It wasn't because of money issues, I assure you." Dunn sat back in her chair and tugged down on her sweater. "He was let go because of his attitude. He kept going on about his fiancée and how she was pregnant. How was he supposed to support her on minimum wage? I told him he knew the job when he took it. He asked about advancement." Dunn paused and gestured toward the showroom. "There's not much room. Even our lifers. Tom, who you were just speaking to, has been here for five years and only makes minimum plus the standard pay increase for living expenses."

"You're making it sound like Kevin Thorne quit now. The interview you had with Detective Sovereign has you on record as confirming he was terminated."

"He was." Her eyes focused on the space between them before settling on Madison. "He messed up bad. He sold a new model at the price of one from last year. It wasn't his first screw-up."

"He did this on purpose?"

"He said it was a mistake. Either way, it wasn't up to me. The owner wanted him gone."

"How did he react when he was fired?"

A shoulder rose to an ear, her brows shot upward. "Like anyone would, I suppose. Ranting, a little bit of begging, but it didn't last long. His human pride took over. He was sitting right where you are." She pointed to the chair Terry was sitting in. "He kept asking why."

"Did he seem depressed to you?"

"No, absolutely not. He was upset by how much things cost in life, but he didn't have highs and lows. He was, for the most part, a very balanced individual. I guess you never know what people are thinking."

"What about Lacy? When did you last see her?"

"The day Kevin was fired."

"How was her reaction to that news?"

"Oh, not good at all. She was more upset than he had been. She stormed out the door and we haven't seen her since." Dunn looked at Madison and then glanced at Terry. "What happened to her?"

"All I can say right now is her death is being investigated as suspicious."

"Which is another way of saying murdered?" Dunn jutted her

jaw forward.

"We're still looking into all the possibilities. What was her frame of mind here?"

"I thought she was happy. That's kind of why I was surprised she just up and left."

"You haven't seen her since Kevin Thorne was fired?"

Dunn shook her head.

"Do you have any reason to believe her old life caught up with her?"

"You tell me, Detective. She's dead." Fire singed Dunn's eyes. "Sorry, I didn't mean it like that. You're asking did anyone have a reason to kill her that I know of? No."

"How did you see her relationship with Kevin?"

"They got along fine. I noticed them laughing together on more than one occasion." Dunn fidgeted with the cuff of her sweater. "I found it odd she disappeared the same time as Kevin was let go. I assumed it was a coincidence, and now they're both dead."

"Likely unrelated." Madison lied. She had the feeling they were connected on a deep level, but Dunn didn't need to be witness to her suspicion. "To reiterate, Lacy didn't seem depressed to you at all?"

"Like I said, she seemed happy and I assumed it went beyond these walls."

"Okay, thank you for your time," Terry said and rose from the chair.

"Give me a call if you think of anything." Madison handed the woman her card.

CHAPTER 36

"I THINK THAT WOMAN KNEW about Lacy already." Madison did up the seatbelt and turned the key in the ignition.

"She was a good actress if she did."

"People only project what they want you to pick up on. It's the small things—"

"Yes, thank you. I did graduate the academy and make it to Detective." Terry glared at her.

"Don't be like that. I'm just saying, the fidgeting, the eye contact, the seemingly lost in space routine. Besides all of that, she was put together."

"She's a businesswoman. It comes with the territory."

Madison pulled the car from the lot and took a right, taking them in the opposite direction from the station. "Here's another thing, don't you find it odd that Hargrove mentioned trying to get Lacy a job? Meanwhile, Hargrove got Lacy one and was paying her wages. Why did he withhold that information?"

"Good question, but I'm not really sure where it gets us."

Madison pulled around a slow moving SUV. "And the other thing, Hargrove and she must be close. He and this Dunn lady. I think he told her about Lacy's past. She's not naive."

"She probably even called him to say the girl was AWOL."

"Yes, Terry. AWOL." Madison smirked. Her partner had a way with words.

MADISON PULLED THE CAR INTO the Paradise Motel parking lot. Three other cars were parked in front of rooms, no doubt rented out for

the purpose a *nooner* or afternoon romp. Motels like this made
the perfect nesting spot for cheating spouses who would duck out
during the work day or call it a day at noon. Their mates would
be none the wiser. It churned Madison's stomach if she gave it too
much thought.

For some reason, the thought of sex and love brought the faces
of two men to mind—two men she wanted to forget. One being
her colleague Sovereign and the other being Blake Golden, a
defense attorney—neither of whom she could ever get completely
away from.

Terry touched her forearm and pointed to the maid cart outside
of room fifteen.

"At least we know she's here."

The door was ajar and Madison knocked on the frame as she
pushed it farther open. "Ms. Bolton?"

She heard the hum of a vacuum cleaner and Madison stepped
into the room.

"Sheila Bolton?"

A woman of about sixty turned the upright off. Her silver hair
was cut in short, choppy layers. She dropped the cord to the carpet.
"Yes." Her voice was quaky and had Madison wondering if she
estimated her age incorrectly.

"We're detectives—"

Concern swept over her face; it fell and paled. "I already spoke
to a detective."

"Yes, we know you did, but we have some follow-up questions."
Madison continued with the formal introduction.

"He killed himself. I…I found him like that…in the tub." She
dropped on a corner of the made bed.

"I understand this may be difficult for you to talk about, but we
need you to run us through it again."

Bolton looked between Madison and Terry. "You think I missed
something the first time around?"

"I think it would have been a very traumatic thing to find
and that it would be easy for the mind to shut out some details."
Madison had noted in the file that Sovereign had visited Bolton a

couple weeks after Thorne was found. It was the last investigative thing he had done before the case was ruled.

"I don't know what else I can say. I want to help, but didn't the poor guy—" Her eyes communicated that she found it too hard to say the rest.

Madison could tell by the woman's drooping eyes that she was fatigued. She could also discern Bolton was still coming to grips with what she had seen.

"Run us through this again, one more time if you could. Maybe something will be clearer to you now. Or maybe you saw something you didn't even know you had."

A slow nod and a deep sigh, Bolton opened her mouth. "I showed up for my shift as normal." She looked at Madison for reassurance this amount of detail was required. Madison encouraged her with eye contact to continue.

"I got my cart ready to go, stocked up. The day was going good and I was making fast progress, until his room." Her eyes glazed over as if she were transported back to the discovery, everything clear in her mind, the dead body, and all that blood.

For a moment, Madison was happy Sovereign had been assigned the case. It was one thing to witness the amount of blood in crime scene photographs and quite another to be immersed in the scene with the smells and visual combination.

"I knocked on the door and no one answered. I let myself in and set my mind to finishing things up. I only had that room and one more before I could call it a day."

"When you went inside, what did you see?"

"The room was a mess. The comforter was on the floor. Clothes were on the floor. There was an alcohol bottle sitting on the nightstand. Empty." She looked at the detectives. "People do stupid things when they drink. And when it's not their place, why care about any mess they make."

"Did you notice any drug paraphernalia?"

A rapid shake of her head came to an abrupt stop. "There was a razor blade on the tub ledge and a bottle of—what was it now," her eyes pressed shut, "tequila on the nightstand, I think."

Madison gave her a small, reassuring smile. "The clothes on the floor, were they all men's clothes?" Madison knew how the file read; she wanted live testimony.

Bolton took a few seconds. "Yes. Boxers, socks, dress slacks, and a shirt."

"When you went into the room, did you call out?"

"Yes, as soon as I noticed the clothes. It's not uncommon for guests to leave their clothing on the floor, but there wasn't any luggage in the room. There was no answer to my calling out, but I started to notice a smell. It was metallic and very strong."

"You didn't notice this right away?"

"My nose isn't the best." Bolton's eyes misted as she continued with her recounting. "I followed the smell and found him there. In the tub. Blood was everywhere. I still have nightmares. Benefits here are a joke. I'd have to pay to see a shrink."

"Yet you're a strong woman. You came back to work."

Bolton's eyes went to Madison as if scolding her for the reassurance. "I need my paycheck. What choice do I have? Your PD set me up with a psychiatrist, but I can't afford that. And I'd probably come out with more problems than I went in with."

"Is there anything else you noticed in the bathroom?"

Bolton's eyes shut and tears soaked through her eyelashes. "I knew he was dead. His eyes were fixed open like he was staring at me, but the only thing is, he faced straight ahead. He faced the faucet of the tub. I screamed when I saw him and fell to the floor. It took me minutes to get myself together enough to call the police." Her eyes opened. "I called you on my cell phone. I watch those cop shows. I know better than to touch anything. It was bad enough I had lifted the comforter from the floor to the bed."

"You had no way of knowing what you were going to find." That piece of information had been recorded in the file and it hadn't come as a surprise to Madison. "Anything else you can remember?"

"No. That is all." Bolton stood up and straightened out the impression her weight had made on the bed, returning it to a condition ready to welcome new guests.

"Well, thank you for your time. If you think of anything else."

Madison extended her card to the woman, who took it and stuffed it into a pocket of her uniform without even looking at it.

"I won't, but I will." Bolton offered a weak smile.

CHAPTER 37

MADISON SLIPPED BEHIND THE WHEEL. Terry did up his seatbelt and looked over at her. "Nothing that we didn't already know there."

"Are you certain of that?"

Terry's brows furled and he rubbed the back of his neck. They had too few answers for his liking. "You pulled something from that? Something we didn't already know?"

"She said there was a razor blade on the tub ledge."

"We knew that. The surfaces in the room were also analyzed and nothing was found to indicate powdered drugs. The blade only had Thorne's prints on it."

Madison glanced at Terry. "Why a blade at all?"

"Not following."

"Well, if we're to believe he brought the blade to kill himself, why have company? And he wasn't a drug user."

"Maybe he was going to score some to help him take his life?"

Her partner's eyes darkened.

"What is it?" she asked.

"Crime Scene found a razor, but Richards found a spot between the toes where Thorne shot up. And if Thorne did it himself—"

"Where's the needle?" They said this together.

"Maybe he did it before reaching the motel?" Terry suggested.

"Vilma didn't mention he was high. Maybe she was in denial about that? Anyway, a man with no history of drug use shot up and drove safely may I add, to his destination only to down a full bottle of tequila and kill himself in the tub? Not to mention he somehow managed to get it up and have sex with a female."

"Blue pill?"

Madison rolled her eyes and smiled. "No evidence of that in his system."

"Maybe it reacted to the drugs and it wasn't able to be detected." Terry's cell phone rang. He glanced at the ID and answered. "Hey."

Madison could hear the person on the other end. It sounded like a woman. She spoke quickly and loud. She was panicked about something. Possibly Annabelle, Terry's wife. It would also explain the informal answer.

Madison split her attention between the road and passing looks at Terry.

"I'm sure everything will be okay...okay, what did he say...all right, well, let's not get worked up about it...I know, baby." Terry glanced at Madison but continued on with his phone call. "Do you need me to come home?" A few seconds' pause on Terry's end was accompanied by a flurry of talking from the other end. "All right... yeah, I'll be there as soon as I can." He went to put his phone away but lifted it back to his ear. "Love you."

Madison didn't look at him. She kept her attention on the road, even though she was dying to ask him what was going on. He told her before that she had a way of prying and asking too many personal questions at times. She knew she had let that weakness create a fracture in her relationship with Richards. She didn't want to do the same with her partner. Sometimes caring about someone at a distance was more acceptable than trying to worm in close to a situation.

"I've got to call it a day," Terry said.

"Sure." She kept driving, trying to keep her focus on the case and the afternoon traffic all around her.

"You're not even going to ask?"

Through her peripheral, she noticed him look at her.

"It's not any of my—"

"If you say not any of your business, I will punch you." She faced him. "Hey."

"Well, there are times it's okay to ask. Now is one of them." His one hand rubbed the back of his neck again.

She pulled the car into the department lot and parked it. With the car still running, she looked at her partner. His eyes were heavy with concern and cloudy with apprehension, yet there remained a glimmer of hope buried deep within them.

"Everything okay?" she asked as gently as she could, worried that something was wrong with the baby.

"I don't know." He exhaled deeply. "The doctor's saying her blood sugars are high."

Madison remembered her sister had gestational diabetes with her first daughter. "Is it—"

"Diabetes? Well, no, I don't… That's not what we're concerned about."

Madison gave him time to gather his thoughts.

"Anna's been doing some research and high sugar counts can cause all sorts of things to happen to the baby." He searched her eyes. She remained quiet and let him continue. "It's possible our baby could be deformed."

His last statement sank in the air, with the density of a heavy burden no parent should ever have to face—that of worrying about their child's health.

"He'll still be the luckiest kid—"

Terry half-laughed. "Maddy, you're not the best at the pep talks, but I appreciate your effort." He reached for the door handle.

Madison extended her hand and gripped his forearm. "I'm here for you, no matter what."

Terry nodded and got out of the car. He ducked his head back in. "I'll be in tomorrow." He tapped the roof of the car and was gone.

Madison remained behind the wheel, staring at the brick of the station. Her heart felt heavy for her partner, and with the uncertainty of not knowing the future. All Terry and his wife wanted was a beautiful, healthy baby. Would they get that?

CHAPTER 38

MADISON SPENT A FEW MORE hours back at the station, writing out reports on where the investigation was so far when it came to Lacy Rose. She also made a compilation of notes when it came to the suspicious death of Kevin Thorne. Somewhere between the two of them lay the truth.

Cynthia Baxter said they were still backed up in the lab. Even though it would be a fast check, she wouldn't have her comparison between Lacy and the vaginal fluids pulled from the motel sheets until the morning. Toxicology results on Lacy were still in the works, as was the final processing of evidence removed from Hennessey's apartment and the property.

Around six, Madison called it a night and headed home. She would pull in Hennessey and Bates for further interrogation come morning and push them about Kevin Thorne. Maybe he was the older man they knew about. Maybe they assumed he was the one who set her up with a condo and tried to free her from their lifestyle. Maybe they were the ones who took Thorne's life in their hands.

She picked up Hershey and then got a hamburger from a drive-thru. She justified the meal choice because she had hardly eaten all day, and she had been good most of the week. The fact that it was only Thursday didn't matter.

She dropped in her office chair and flicked on her computer monitor. As her e-mails downloaded, she unwrapped her dinner and ate. She swore she moaned as she bit off mouthfuls of the meat patty, cheese, and bacon.

"Damn, people food is good," she said, with a mouthful, to Hershey. She bit off more. "Looks so much better than that kibble of yours, my friend."

Four e-mails filtered in from printing companies. One insisted that she meet with them directly to discuss her business' needs. They attached a ten-page document providing her with testimonials. She skimmed through them and went back to the other e-mails.

The other companies were more forthcoming and she was reading through their e-mails when there was a knock on her door.

So much for a locked building.

She stuffed the rest of the burger in her mouth, wiped her hands on her pants, and went to answer it.

She looked through the peephole. "What are you doing here?"

"I wanted to talk to you."

"There's nothing for us to talk about."

"Please just open the door."

She took a deep breath and opened the door.

Toby Sovereign had both of his hands tucked into his jeans pockets. He wore a collared, black shirt with the top two buttons undone, under a leather coat that was unzipped.

He pushed past her into the apartment. As he did, his head turned, taking in everything. "Nothing much has changed."

The smell of his cologne hit her sinuses, threatening to rapture her to the past.

"Can you leave?" She stayed at the door and held it wide open.

"Hey, who's this?" Sovereign got down on his haunches and Hershey bounded toward him. He stopped a few feet shy and sat there barking. It caused Madison to laugh. Sovereign looked over his shoulder as he stood back up. "Even your dog hates me."

"We had a talk."

A grin lit his face. "About me?" He took off his jacket and slid it over the back of a dining chair.

"Get over yourself." Madison let out a deep sigh. *Why was he getting comfortable?*

It was evident that he wasn't leaving until he said what he came to say. She closed the door heavily. He didn't even seem to notice.

She picked up his coat and hung it on a hook before even realizing how she swooped in and did that. She pinched her eyes tight for a second. She felt a headache coming on.

"How did you—"

"Get up here? Easy, Maddy—"

She knew he kept talking, but hearing her first name come from his lips in such a casual manner, she was transported back in time. He used to always blend her first name with variations of nicknames he had for her, "pet names" he said. He could keep them. If she had to choose between Love Vixen and Maddy, the choice was obvious. She would prefer he called her Madison if he had to address her at all.

"So, a neighbor let you up. Which apartment?"

"Don't kill them."

"Huh." She cocked her head to the side.

He looked around the apartment. "Well, I can tell you're busy, so I won't keep you."

She didn't say anything but stared at him, through him, actually.

"Who is this little guy anyhow?" He bent down to pet Hershey again, but Hershey backed up and resumed barking.

Good dog.

Sovereign was smiling. "Is it just me, or does he hate men, in general, as his owner does?" He rose to full height, watching her as he did.

"I don't hate *all* men."

"Oh, that's right. Golden, right? The lawyer guy. Blake, that's his first name. How's that going?"

"What do you want?"

"Ah, none of my business, I get it. You like to keep your personal life private these days."

"It's none of your—"

"Yeah, like I said, private."

As he stood in front of her, she imagined many ways she could kill the man and get away with it.

"All right, I guess it's right down to business. I'm here because you're poking your nose around in my case." He dropped onto the sofa and picked up the television remote.

She went behind him and took the remote from his hand. "Are you worried I'll find something you didn't?"

"I'm worried you're wasting your time. I have it covered."

"Do you now? Did you know that Thorne's fiancée showed up at the motel the night he killed himself? Did you think about even hunting down another woman when she said she didn't stay and have sex with him?"

"Of course. It's obvious he was cheating."

"And answer this, why would a suicidal man long for company with someone else? They could stop him from going through with it." She was building up to the crescendo.

"A hooker, Knight. He's down, she makes him feel better."

"Did you confirm it was a hooker?" They held eye contact. "And why would Thorne long to feel better when he planned on killing himself?"

Silence passed for what seemed like sixty seconds, igniting the energy fields between them. She was the first to look away and step back.

"Explain why there wasn't a needle found. Thorne shot up, what happened to the needle?" She raised her voice.

"The girl came with it, she left with it. He killed himself after."

"Can you go now?"

"You think I did wrong by this case?"

Her jaw tightened. Words weren't needed.

"You think you can do so much better. At everything. There's no way in hell I could measure up to that." He brushed past her and grabbed his coat from the hook. The apartment door slammed behind him.

It took all the power she had not to hurl the remote across the room.

CHAPTER 39

DESPITE BEING SEETHING ANGRY BY the time her head hit the pillow two hours after Sovereign left, she slept through until her alarm. She wasn't going to let him get to her. It was time she buried her feelings for him in the past and move on. But sometimes when a wound cuts so deep, it scabs over many times. She had picked at it, allowed it to fester and scar over—a permanent reminder of her betrayal and something she decided to hold against all men.

Her confidence and determination in the new day carried with her as she dropped Hershey off at Canine Country Retreat Boarding, grabbed a Starbucks, and went into the station.

It lasted until she noticed Sovereign sitting on the edge of her desk, talking to his partner Lou Stanford.

She didn't have to say anything as she approached. Sovereign rose.

"You must be working part-time these days," he said.

She considered dropping in her chair and checking any voice mail that may have been waiting for her, but she kept walking.

"Maddy...Knight," Sovereign said.

She knew both Sovereign and Stanford followed her.

"Oh, she does hate you."

Madison stopped walking when she heard Sovereign's partner say this. The two men went around and stood to face her.

She looked straight at Sovereign. "To say I hate you—"

Sovereign pointed at his partner as if to say, *he said it.*

She addressed Stanford. "To hate someone would imply that I cared. I don't. Good day. I've got work to do."

"Please, just listen—"

"What Lou?"

Lou Stanford had a large build and dirty-blond hair. His dark eyes searched hers. She gave him nothing.

"Sovereign was thinking that maybe fresh eyes on the case may help."

"He didn't feel that way last night." Madison noticed the glance between the two men, Lou questioning what had happened. Madison moved between the men, heading to the interrogation room where Bates was being brought.

"Madison, please. You owe me that much," Sovereign said.

She stopped moving and turned around. "I don't owe you anything. Go do your jobs, and I'll do mine—"

"Knight."

She heard Sergeant Winston call her and saw him approach, but snuck in a quick look at the clock on the wall.

8:45 AM.

"Have a minute?" he asked.

"Sure." She read an uneasiness coming from him. "Is Terry all right?"

"He'll be fine."

"He *will* be?" She braced against the wall and laced her arms. "What aren't you telling me?"

"He's called in a personal day. He wants you to know he's fine otherwise."

She swallowed reflexively and nodded. She couldn't help but think if he was fine, why call in a personal day.

"You'll be all right working it solo today? If not, I can assign—"

"I'll be fine." The last thing she needed was someone else hanging over her.

"Where are we with the case so far?" Winston asked.

She could tell by the way he settled into his standing position, with legs positioned slightly apart, hips jutted forward, arms folded and resting on his paunch, he wasn't going to accept a few sentences and take the brush-off.

She filled him in on everything, from the recovery of the gun at Bates's apartment to their conversation with Vilma, Thorne's fiancée.

"So, it's a tangled mess."

"Yeah, pretty much, but I'll untangle it."

"I'm sure you will."

His tone of voice and his quick return toward his office had her questioning the sincerity of his statement. But that didn't hurt her. Terry should have called her to let her know everything. They were partners, but they were also close friends—at least she had thought so.

She entered the room with Bates. He sat there picking at the end of a dreadlock. He looked up when she tossed a photo of Kevin Thorne across the table. She sat down across from him.

"Is that the guy?"

Bates looked from her to the picture. He didn't reach for it. He barely glanced at it.

Madison's attention was fixed on Bates. He said nothing for at least forty seconds.

"The guy who?" He dragged out the word *who*.

"The older man."

"Didn't I tell you we never saw him?"

"We?" Madison looked around the room. "There's only you and me in here. We who?" She wasn't going to fill in any blanks, even if she knew to whom he referred.

His eyes flitted to the table.

She slammed the palm of a hand on the surface. "We who?"

"Me and Hennessey."

"Not really sure how he got involved with our conversation."

Bates shifted in his chair.

"I asked you if he was the older man Lacy had been seeing."

"Yeah and I told ya. Didn't see him."

"Actually, what you said was *we* didn't see him. How did he become a part of this conversation?"

"I dunno."

She held eye contact. "You do. You know what I think? I think you and Hennessey killed this man." She tossed a morgue photo of

Thorne on the table.

"No, uh, no! What? Why? We ain't never seen him."

"You're still holding to that?"

"It's the truth." He glanced at the photo.

"Are you sure about that?"

"Yeah."

"Then why do you keep looking at the picture?" It was fact that when a person knew someone in a picture, their eyes were more drawn to it.

"You put the picture in front of me."

"People don't normally stare at pictures of people they don't know or recognize. Why would they?"

"You're trying to play with my mind."

"I'm trying to get some truth out of you." She rose and paced the room. "You know what I think happened? You knew about him. You thought he was the man who set Lacy up in the condo."

Bates turned to face her.

She continued. "You followed them to the motel that night. You and Hennessey found her sleeping with him and decided to make it look like a suicide." She paused for a second and took a few more steps. "But where you went wrong was shooting him up. He never used a day in his life. Why would he start then?"

"There has to be a first time."

"Oh, I suppose." Madison stopped walking. "But what would make Thorne do it that night?"

"Maybe Lacy talked him into trying it. She still had a thing for it."

Madison smiled. The bait had worked. "You admit you knew Lacy was with this man?"

"Oh, man." Bates ran a hand over his mouth and pinched his lips.

"It really makes me wonder what else you're not telling me, Bates." She bent and put her arms on the table near him. "How are we supposed to establish a working relationship here if we don't have honesty?" She fought another smile from taking over her expression and pushed off the table to full height.

"The same man, or so you thought anyhow, who set her up with medical care and a condo, who tried to free her from her drug-filled life, decided to try them himself?" She was toying with Bates, trying to get as much as she could from his expressions. With his eyes, he followed every step she took. Even when she was behind him, he turned in his chair. "What aren't you telling me?"

"Your plan to harass me until I know something?"

She pointed at him. "So, there is something else you're not telling me."

His eyes left hers. "I ain't saying that."

She slipped into the chair opposite him again and clasped her hands on the table. "He was going to be a father."

"Lacy was—" He didn't finish the statement. His brow wrinkled up.

"You knew they were sleeping together?" Madison had referred to Vilma when she mentioned pregnancy but let him think it was Lacy.

He studied her eyes, seeming cautious of whether he should answer. "Yeah."

"You followed them to the motel?"

A slow bob of the head.

Madison's insides tingled. She could be close to proving Thorne didn't die from self-inflicted means.

"And then what did you do?"

"What do you mean what did I do? Nothing, a'ight. I'm not goin' back to prison."

"You're already wrong there. We know you helped bury Lacy's body. Charges are still pending as to whether you were involved in coercing her into pulling the trigger, or whether you actually did it."

"I told ya before. It was Hennessey. He just called me to get rid of—"

Madison made note of the painful inflection in Bates's voice.

His eyes misted with tears and his head bowed low.

"Did Hennessey kill this man?" She tapped a finger on the photograph of Thorne on the morgue slab.

Bates shook his head; his dreadlocks swayed with the motion. "Did you?"

He shook his head again.

There were only two people left, that Madison was aware of, who could have wanted Thorne's death to appear self-inflicted— the fiancée or Lacy.

"Did Lacy?"

"Where's my lawyer?"

Madison cemented eye contact with him and rose from the table. "I don't know all that happened there, but I will figure it out. You better prepare yourself to deal with that."

She left the room, and an officer came in her place, cuffed Bates and escorted him back to his cell. As they passed each other, her phone rang. She answered to Cynthia on the other end.

"I have the results from the cross-comparison. It was definitely your girl sleeping with Thorne in that motel room."

"I figured it must have been. One of the kids just confirmed she was there with him." She was still amused by how she got that confession.

"That's not all I have for you, though. Some results came back on the vic's—"

"Lacy's."

There was a deep exhale on the other end. "Her blood work showed she was pregnant."

"Pregnant? How far along?"

"Well, my guess is not very, or Richards would have caught it during the autopsy."

"Can we extract the fetus and test its DNA?"

"Already ordered for that." Cynthia laughed, and it gave way to a brief silence. "How are you doing these days anyway, my friend?"

Madison's thoughts whirled from the business to the personal. A montage of photos played through her mind, the break-up of her recent relationship, the surprise appearance by Sovereign last night, and, finally, the thought of Terry not calling her about his personal day.

"Everything's fine."

"I guess I'll let it go at that, but I don't believe you."

"You don't have to believe me. You have to accept it."

"Do I now?"

"What are you doing tonight?" Madison asked.

"Nothing much. What do you have in mind?"

"Dinner out. A nice, juicy steak, some red wine, and men bashing."

"Now you're talking."

Madison hung up the phone and was still smiling. The source of it coming from two places. First, news that Lacy had been pregnant. When they tracked down the father, she believed it would get them one step closer to the truth. And second, the thought of having a nice evening out felt like a welcome relief to her soul. She hoped the red wine and good company would silence the demons that haunted her.

CHAPTER 40

STILES STEAKHOUSE WAS LOCATED ON the main street. It had a sidewalk patio, which was open and full of patrons on any given summer evening. Tonight, however, the spring air was chilly and damp, possessing the ability to seep its way, through clothing and skin, to the bones. The patio would have another couple months to go before it saw the checkered tablecloths and pitchers of beer.

Cynthia met up with Madison at her apartment and they took a cab to the restaurant. Cynthia lived on the outskirts of Stiles while Madison lived a little closer to the action—not that there was usually much action in Stiles.

"Guess we're going all out tonight." Cynthia smiled at her as she got out of the cab.

"Dang right. It's been a long week."

"It's been a long few if you ask me."

Both women shared a laugh and made their way inside. Normally, they'd meet up for drinks at one of their places, preferring the solitude and privacy that came with it. There were times they'd go out on Friday night for two-dollar martinis at a bar called TJ's, but it had been months since they had done that.

"Yeah, we deserve this." Madison placed a hand on her friend's shoulder.

The restaurant hostess was slender with petite wrists and long fingers. They wrapped around the wax pencil she held for marking patrons on the seating chart, which sat beneath a pane of glass.

"Welcome to Stiles Steakhouse." She offered a sincere smile, passing a glance at both of them. "A table for two?"

"Yes, please," Cynthia said. She turned to Madison. "And tonight's going to be about fun, okay, not work. Can you promise me that?"

Madison hesitated. *Why make a promise she knew she couldn't keep?*

"Huh. I should have known." Cynthia smiled. "I guess if you left the job completely behind I wouldn't know I was with Maddy."

"I suppose I can drop talk about work, but can you go without a cigarette?" Madison laughed.

A waitress came and spoke to the hostess for a few minutes before directing them to follow her. She sat them in a booth large enough to comfortably sit four and handed them each a menu. "Your server will be with you shortly."

The tablecloth was red-and-white checkered and covered by a piece of brown craft paper. A small plastic cup held colored crayons. Madison reached for the red one.

"Seriously?" Cynthia laughed.

"You said it was about fun tonight." Madison took the crayon and scrawled an X.

"X marks the spot?"

Madison laughed. "It's the first thing that came to mind."

"You really have to learn to let go sometimes." Cynthia reached for the green one and drew short lines. She then reached for the brown one and drew a simplistic house made of a square and a triangle top.

"My name is Paul and I'll be your server this evening."

Both women looked up at the same time. Both of them laughed.

Paul was in his mid-twenties and had green eyes that seemed to see through to the mind. His blond hair was layered with his bangs slightly longer and curled over his brow. His cologne held woody overtures and made Madison think of Old Spice.

"We're just fooling around." Cynthia offered an explanation but didn't make a movement to put the crayon back.

Madison withdrew her hand that held the red one and put her arm under the table.

"That's what they're here for. May I bring you a drink while you look at the menu?"

Neither woman took their eyes off the server.

"Glass of red, Cyn?" Madison asked.

"Bottle."

Madison glanced at her friend, confirming the smile she had heard in her voice. She looked back to the server. "A bottle."

He smiled at her and she felt her heart tap.

Curse men. Curse good-looking men who smelled like that!

"Which one?" He opened a menu that sat on the edge of the table. "We have several reds. There." He pointed to the wine list, and Madison made the executive decision. But instead of verbalizing the choice, she pointed. Her finger brushed his.

"All right. It's coming right up, ladies."

With him out of earshot, Cynthia said, "What was that?"

"What was what?" Madison drew another X.

"That."

"Don't know what you're talking about."

"Like hell you don't."

"It's nothing."

"Maddy, it's me."

"Fine, so he's fine. Big deal. Let's move on."

"When was the last time you got—"

"You say that word, I will slap you here." Madison laughed and looked up from her drawing.

"He is good looking, and he smells good too." Cynthia adjusted her black-framed glasses.

"Yeah, he does."

"Huh." Cynthia pointed a finger at Madison.

"Hey, I'm not blind or dull of senses." She dropped the crayon in the plastic cup and pulled the menu over hoping to instigate a subject switch. "I already know what I have in mind anyhow."

"Oh, yeah, *beef.*" Cynthia winked and then bobbed her eyebrows.

Madison didn't say anything.

"What? What did I do now?" Cynthia splayed a hand on her chest. "Would I imply anything improper?"

"Yes, you would."

"So."

"So, that's why I luv ya, but if you tell anyone—"

"I know. You'll kill me."

"Yes, ma'am." Madison smiled.

"He is really good looking, though, don't you think?"

Madison shoved her foot against Cynthia's leg.

Cynthia put her hands up. "Fine."

"How are things going with you and whatshisname anyhow?"

"You mean Lou, Sovereign's partner? Fine." Cynthia buried her face in the menu.

"Cyn."

The menu slowly lowered. "Can I pull a line from you? I don't want to talk about it."

"What? Are you getting married and having kids?"

Cynthia coughed. "You trying to kill me? Seriously? Me? I don't think so."

"It is getting serious, though, isn't it? I can tell. Your eyes give you away. You also want to pawn the waiter off on me and not stake claim to him yourself."

Her friend leaned across the table, laying the open menu out in front of her. "Between us."

"Of course."

"I might care about him."

"Care about him? And you tell me I have issues in the romance department? You're just as bad."

"No, there's a difference between you and me."

The server returned and sat down two glasses in front of the women and displayed the bottle of wine, holding it at an angle as if pitching it for auction. He opened it and poured some in Cynthia's glass.

She took it to her lips, drained back a small mouthful, and nodded her approval.

He smiled at her. "Excellent." He poured her a half-glass and then put some in Madison's. "I'll give you ladies some more time, and then you can let me know what you decide," he said with his attention on Cynthia, only offering Madison a cursory glance before leaving the table.

"He likes you. They always like you."

"Don't be a hater." Cynthia laughed.

Madison took a drag on her wine. Her thoughts not so much on jealousy of the male attention her friend always garnered like metal shavings to a magnet, but envious of her frivolity. Cynthia possessed the ability to rein them in but was never serious about any of them. It seemed men were disposable to her, and despite their claims of love, Cynthia turned them all down—at least until now.

"So, Lou?"

Her friend took a few swallows of wine, and her eyes danced over other patrons, avoiding Madison.

"I'm your friend, Cyn. Tell me."

"Like I said, I care about him."

"Unprecedented."

"Yeah, especially if you're talking about caring for more than his ability to perform magic in bed."

Madison laughed. "Magic in bed."

"Hey, I'm trying to keep it PG here."

It was Madison who held up her hands now.

Cynthia took a deep breath. "I like him more than I should. The problem is we spent too much time talking. I see it in your face. Don't say a word. It's true, though. You spend too much time talking, you have things in common, and then this thing happens."

"This thing?" Madison's mouth formed the letter O.

"Yeah. Love. You can say it. It makes me sick actually." Cynthia reached for her wine again.

"I can't believe—"

"I know—happening to me? Who would have figured this? I trade men in like shoes. I told him we have to end it."

"Why would you—" Madison paused. Who was she to impart some great wisdom about love and relationships? She did her best to steer clear of them. She viewed the word *love* as an invention people made up to make themselves feel better, to make themselves feel as if they belonged.

"Yeah, I know it's deep. But now I'm hoping it's not over. Know what I mean?"

Madison nodded. She knew exactly. She hadn't felt much different too long ago. In the end, though, things didn't work out. She sometimes wondered if she were simply a self-fulfilled prophecy. She didn't believe in love, so she didn't have it.

"Oh, never mind all this. It's supposed to be fun tonight." Cynthia offered a weak smile to Madison, who returned it.

"We can talk about this—"

"No, thank you. I've already talked about it enough. Really." Cynthia held up her glass in a toast, and Madison raised hers to meet it. "To our independence."

The server arrived to take their orders and as they waited for the food to come, they passed the time talking about men and the complications of relationships.

About forty minutes after ordering, their meals were set in front them. Cynthia had a seafood pasta with lobster tails and scallops in a cream sauce. Madison had the steak she had come for. She picked up her fork and steak knife and sliced off a portion of the prime rib. Pink juices flowed from it and met with her side of garlic mashed potatoes.

"How's the diet going?" Cynthia asked with a mouthful of pasta.

Madison narrowed her eyes and put a forkful of beef in her mouth. She took time chewing it, savoring every morsel. She swallowed it and felt as if she were saying good-bye to heaven. "What diet?"

A couple hours later, and the same number of bottles of wine, they were back in a cab headed to Madison's apartment.

"Hope you don't mind if I spend the night."

"No, not at all." Madison felt at peace, a feeling she hadn't experienced in a while. With the sensation, however, came thoughts of the case, of Lacy, and of all the men in her life. "You know I was talking with Bates today."

"Oh no. Fun, remember?" Cynthia slapped Madison's arm.

"I've been good all night." Madison smiled.

"Okay, fine. By all means, continue." Cynthia rolled her hand,

and to Madison's wine-induced vision, it had motion swirls around it.

Madison's mind remained on Bates. "I think he knows who killed Thorne."

"That was the case ruled a suicide?"

Madison caught the cab driver's eyes glance up at them in the rearview mirror. "It was, but it isn't."

"You're sure of this?"

"Pretty much, yeah."

Cynthia settled back in the seat and rested her head. "Okay, so who do you think did it?"

"I'm wondering if it was Bates's friend, Hennessey. I really think he's the one who made Lacy pull the trigger on herself, or did it himself. He beat her. He was jealous of her. It would make sense, by extension, to kill the other guy."

"What does Terry think about all this?"

"He doesn't know about my most recent thoughts on this. I haven't even filled him in about Lacy's pregnancy yet."

Cynthia lifted her head and turned to Madison as if saying, *what do you mean.*

Madison told her about Terry, the situation with his wife and the baby, and his taking a personal day because of it.

"We spend the entire evening together and you don't say one word about this?" Cynthia asked.

"You said it was supposed to be fun."

"Yeah, fun, which meant not about work. Is he doing all right?"

Madison lifted a shoulder. "I don't know. I've tried reaching him a few times and left a message. Figured I'd update him once we connected."

"And he hasn't—"

Madison shook her head.

"Weird."

"That's what I thought. I can't make him talk to me."

"You're kidding, right? You can make a suspect sign a confession against their will. You can make Terry talk." Cynthia rolled her head, still resting against the back of the seat, and looked at

Madison. "What is it?"

Madison studied her friend's eyes. If anyone would understand, she would, but thinking about verbalizing her feelings made her feel stupid.

"I don't know what to say." She was honest. She wasn't good with the whole love and baby thing.

"You say 'Terry, how are you and Annabelle doing?' You take it from there."

"But what if they're not okay, what if they need—"

"Maddy." Cynthia reached out and rested her hand on Madison's forearm. "He's not expecting you to solve this. He knows who you are and knows what you're capable of. You can be a terrific listener. Just don't approach this as a case."

"I don't know anything about babies."

"And that's fine. Just be there for him. That's all you can do, and trust me, that's all he'll expect." Cynthia smiled at her. It lasted briefly as it gave way to fatigue.

"You're right."

"Yes, Maddy, I know I am." Cynthia laughed and faced forward. "And by the way, I'm definitely crashing at your place tonight."

Madison rolled her eyes and smiled. "I kind of figured that. Just remember, no smoking in the apartment."

CHAPTER 41

MADISON LET CYNTHIA HAVE HER bed, and she opted for the couch. Her mind, as normal, was racing with thoughts about the case, concern over Terry, and even the handsome server at the restaurant. She smiled when his face went through her mind.

She lay there staring at the ceiling and the city lights that danced across it. She thought she heard the knock, but it wasn't until it happened again that she realized someone was at the door.

She slipped out from under the single blanket she had draped over herself and got up. She glanced at the digital clock on the stove.

12:15 AM.

Who the hell?

She peeked through the peephole and let out a rush of air. "Go away."

"I need to talk to you."

She could tell by the way he stood there, and by the transference that projected through the wood barrier between them, he wasn't going away.

How did the man manage to get into a secured building at this time of night?

She undid the deadbolt and slid the chain. "What do you want?"

"I need to talk to you." Toby Sovereign wore the same leather jacket he had the night before, paired with blue jeans again. He brushed past her. His cologne caressed her senses.

"Keep it down—"

"You have a guy here?" he asked.

"It's not a guy. What do you want?" She shook her head. Why was she explaining herself to him? She wished she could tell him there was a man waiting for her. "I thought we talked last night."

He ran a hand through his hair and let it run down his face. "There's more I need to talk to you about." He came to her, arms extended, hands searching to touch her.

Her instinct was to step back, but her feet remained planted. Her head was still spinning from the wine, her logic not fully functioning between the alcohol and the lateness of the evening.

"I can't continue to go on like this," he said.

"Oh Lord." She raised her head heavenward. "This isn't about the case." She let out a slow, steady exhale.

"A lot of things in life aren't about a case." She heard him swallow. His hand touched her and she felt a familiar rush heat her core.

"You should go."

"Listen, I can't take back what I did. How badly I messed up, but we could have a future—"

"No. No way." She rapidly shook her head as she stepped back. He moved with her, his hand still on her arm. "Please let go of me."

A slew of emotions charged through her, ranging from disgust to betrayal, to the attraction she still felt for him despite her best efforts. She knew that just because he was the first man she fell in love with, it didn't mean she had to be strapped into the car of an emotional rollercoaster forever. She had her life in order now.

"Have you ever thought about where we'd be today if—"

"If you didn't fuck that girl?" She stared in his eyes.

He let go of her. "I've apologized for that so many times."

"You were only sorry you got caught."

In the limited light of the apartment, she swore his eyes misted. Silence sparked between them with a viable force.

"Please go."

He didn't move. "I still love you."

"Oh please."

"Really, I always have."

"How many girlfriends have you had since—"

"None of them was you, Maddy. Please, don't you see I'm

broken? I want you back in my life."

She caught the whiff of whiskey being carried on his breath, the warmth of his exhale blanketing her face. She didn't pull back. Her heart wanted to hear what he had to say. She'd suffered for nearly a decade having convinced herself she was the only causality of their broken engagement.

"I knew you wouldn't take me back. You're too strong. I've been trying to find you."

Her heart raced and she licked her lips. "I'm right here." *Damn wine.*

His eyes peered into hers.

She wiped a hand over her mouth. She had to try to reverse what she had said. "I didn't—"

"I've really missed you."

"Please, don't do this." Madison turned her head to look down the hallway to her bedroom. When she turned back to face him, his mouth pressed against hers.

This wasn't happening!

Warmth surged through her. Her hand reached out for him and wrapped around his head. She put her fingers in his hair as they kissed. Mouths both open. Hungry.

His taste, the whiskey, and her wine melded in perfection. Her pulse quickened. Her breath became uneven. They moved in sync as if they had never been separated—as if time, pain, and betrayal hadn't cast the ultimate wedge of divide between them.

She couldn't do this. She had to find the strength.

She surrendered to his passion, fusing it with her own until her mind wouldn't shut off all the glaring questions.

Why was he here?

What did he want with her now?

Why did he wait all this time?

The questions were followed by the flashing images of the past. The sheets strewed on the floor. The laughter she had heard as she made her way down the hallway. The woman's head lifting from beneath the sheets to look at her in the doorway.

Madison pulled back, and he moved with her until she placed a flat palm on his chest and moved out from his embrace.

"Please go."

He stared at her, as if in a trance. He barely nodded and headed for the door.

"Please don't come back here again." She felt the catch in her throat, and as she closed the apartment door, she braced against it.

She cradled her face with her hands. Her chest heaved and tears fell over a love that had broken her heart many years ago and that had returned to tear off the scab.

CHAPTER 42

AFTER HAVING A COUPLE VENTI Starbucks cappuccinos, the haze began to lift. Cynthia watched Madison as she drained the first cup with a blow and a swallow, a brief pause and multiple repeats.

"You all right?"

"Yeah, I'm fine." Madison offered her a smile, a good front to protect how she was really feeling.

They rose early enough to share their morning caffeine in the bistro. They talked little and observed people as the came and went.

"Normally it's me that feels the booze more." Cynthia lifted her second cup of coffee to her lips and took a slow draw. "I'm feeling rested. It must be your bed."

Madison let out a small laugh. "When I'm actually able to get in it, and am able to shut my mind off, it's not bad."

Madison's attention went to a woman dressed in a black suit, a young girl at her side. The girl's hair was long and blonde, like the adult version. The woman was striking, slim and above-average height with blue eyes that were stunning from a distance. Would the woman expect her daughter to grow up and be like her, wearing a suit, prepared to face the corporate world, or to be a wife and mother foremost?

"You look deep in thought," Cynthia said.

"It's nothing." Madison avoided eye contact with her friend, her thoughts still on the mother and her daughter.

What if she wanted to grow up to be a mechanic or didn't see any need to get married? Would her mother approve?

"What aren't you telling me?"

I never did the love and marriage thing. I'm a failure. It was probably my fault he cheated on me. My mother thinks it is.

"Maddy? Hello." Her friend waved a hand in front of her face.

"Oh, it's nothing. I'm just thinking about this case and Terry. I wonder how he's making out." She lied to Cynthia, and it didn't feel good, but she had to protect herself.

Cynthia nodded, pretending to buy the line, but Madison knew she didn't.

"What about the case?" Cynthia adjusted her glasses.

Madison knew she had to push aside the personal vortex last night's experience had churned. She had spent a few hours tossing on the couch afterward and the resultant headache from her pinched neck would be a reminder of it for most of the day. This would be two days in a row with a headache.

He had no right to show up like that.

Madison twirled her cup, watching the woman and the girl again. Cynthia turned to see where she was looking.

"What are—"

"Cynthia, do you ever feel like a huge disappointment?"

"Sometimes, but I don't allow myself to wallow in it."

"I feel like maybe I've made some wrong choices in life." Madison stalled there and raised a pointed finger. "If this conversation leaves this table, I will kill you."

Cynthia laughed. "You always threaten, but good luck pulling that off."

Madison's lips rose slightly, but the smile faded quickly.

"What's wrong, Maddy? You mention choices you regret. We all have them. We have to move on."

"Oh, it's stupid things. Like would everyone have been happier if I were married—"

"Whoa! Stop there. What train are you on? This isn't my Maddy." Cynthia put her cup back on the table, deciding against taking another sip. "What's bringing all this up? And who would be happier? Your mother on your case again?"

"Yes. No. It's just—"

"I'm missing something."

She put her fingers in his hair as they kissed. Mouths both open. Hungry.

"I blame it on the wine last night."

"Oh no, you're not getting off that easy."

Madison looked at her friend. Cynthia would be the only person who could understand the situation. She knew about Toby Sovereign and about how things had ended. She wasn't around then, but she knew the story. She knew that because of it, Madison couldn't trust another man and that she didn't believe in love and marriage and a happily ever after.

"After you were asleep last night, my past came by."

"Your past?" Her eyes got large. "Oh?"

"Yeah, oh." Madison took the last sip of her cappuccino.

Cynthia shifted in her seat. "We're talking about Toby here?"

"Unfortunately yes. He showed up two nights ago wanting to talk about the suicide case."

"The one you believe is a homicide."

Madison nodded. "Last night wasn't for business."

A devilish smirk lifted Cynthia's face. It faded when she read Madison's. "What happened?"

"A huge mistake."

"You had sex with him on the couch."

"It's not funny, Cyn. This man—"

"I know he ruined you for everyone."

"You make it sound so dramatic."

Cynthia adjusted her glasses again and bobbed her head.

"Fine, maybe when it's put that way." Madison's heart raced at the thought of telling Cynthia about the kiss. She would keep it basic, leave out the emotions, the resurfaced wounds. "He kissed me."

"Did you kiss him back?"

Madison slapped the table. "Shh." She wasn't even sure who would overhear or who would care. She couldn't keep the truth from the person that mattered most—herself.

"Well? Did you?"

"Maybe I did."

"Did you like it?"

Madison went to look back at the little girl and her mother, but they were gone. "I ended it. I'm not going down that path again. I can't do it."

"He wants to get back together?"

"I—" Madison's cell phone rang.

"Please don't leave me hanging."

Madison answered her cell. "Detective Knight."

Cynthia shook her head and started to smile. The expression was terminated when she pressed her mouth to the cup.

"I'll be right there." Madison hung up, clipped her phone in its holder and rose from the table.

"Where are you go—"

"Hennessey's other girlfriend, the one who showed up at the station waiting for her next fix. Well, she found it and she's being rushed in a bus to the hospital right now."

CHAPTER 43

MADISON CALLED TERRY AND GOT a hold of him on his cell. He'd meet her at the station and they'd head to the hospital together.

A young officer stood in the emergency waiting room, hands poised high on his hips and he rocked on the balls of his feet.

"They said she had shot up in her arm. She was unconscious when paramedics arrived on scene."

Madison fired a glare at him, and he stopped rocking. "Who found her?"

"Anonymous tip was called in."

"Son of a bitch!" Madison surveyed the emergency room. "Was the needle recovered at the scene?"

"Yes, and it's been taken in for evidence."

Madison picked up her phone and dialed Cynthia. "The needle Sahara Noel shot up with...good...I need you to get on analyzing it...I know...please." If they could connect what Noel took to what was in Thorne's system, it might end up providing some more answers. She closed her cell and addressed the officer. "What are the doctors saying?"

The officer continued. "They were trying to resuscitate her, but don't hold out much hope."

A door opened and a man in his late fifties came into the waiting area. His hair was the color of steel and his eyes were chestnut brown. He wore blue scrubs and wire-rimmed glasses with round lenses. His mustache was neatly groomed.

He walked toward them and gestured for them to join him at the side of the room. He pulled off his latex gloves and shook his head.

"She didn't make it."

Madison's legs felt unsure and her stomach tightened. What a waste of life.

"What do you think she was on?" Madison asked.

"She was experiencing symptoms, I'm sad to say, we've seen a lot of recently."

"Not your standard street drug?"

The doctor slowly shook his head. "It's a blend with a near hundred percent fatality rate. With most overdoses, they are the result of one drug, and it's relatively easy to give them another that can counteract the effects. With a cocktail like this, it's near impossible to treat from a medical standpoint."

"Am I too late?" Alex Commons, a narcotics detective, came toward them, and passed her a judgmental glance as he addressed the doctor. He didn't even look at Terry.

The doctor nodded his head. "Unfortunately."

"We're looking at the same thing?"

"Sad to say we are." The doctor excused himself and left the three detectives sizing each other up.

"What are you doing here?" Commons asked.

She had a run-in with Commons not long ago when a drug addict factored into a case. She wasn't inclined to answer his question. "A cocktail is going around killing kids longing for their next high. Know anything about it?"

"Coke, meth, and heroin. Its street name is Oz, also known as The Wizard's Cocktail. And like the fictional place, everything seems surreal to them and they experience a high like no other where no one, or nothing, can touch them. They are euphoric and untouchable."

"Until they're dead."

"Unfortunately."

"Why do you seem fascinated by its make-up?"

Commons's face turned somber. "You mistake my knowledge of it for excitement. There is nothing exciting about it. Twenty kids have already died because of it."

"Do you have any leads on this? How close are you to shutting this operation down?"

Commons let out a small laugh. "You leave us to do our jobs, you do yours."

Madison moved in close to his face. "You not doing your job, has interfered with mine."

"Who the f—"

Terry stepped between them. "She doesn't mean things the way they come across."

"It certainly seems she does." Commons's cheek held a pulse as he pulled down on his shirt and took a few steps back.

"We have a case," Terry said.

"And you're asking for my help?" Commons laughed.

"We are."

Madison felt uneasiness pulse through her. They needed to find out how Kevin Thorne got this cocktail in his system, a man who never used a drug in his life. She didn't like where her theories led. Lacy was supposedly the last to see him alive. She had a past littered with drug abuse. Did she bring it to the motel that night? And if so, why? She was trying to change her life around.

"We've narrowed it down to a dealer that goes by the street name Harvey," Commons offered.

Madison thought of the movie by the same name. The main character who was mentally ill could see an invisible rabbit.

"If you have him, go get him," Madison said. "Shut this shit down."

"It's not as simple as that. Harvey is the dealer, not the source. It would be like trying to take out Hitler by killing one of his men." He let his comparison sit there. "Meaningless and without effect. Many others would stand in his place. However, there is one thing in our favor. The blend makes it pricey, limiting its reach."

Madison thought of Lacy and Sahara Noel. Neither girl had unlimited funds, but both were beautiful, accustomed to life on the streets, and likely willing to do anything for their next high. But the thought with Lacy didn't fit. Bates said she refused to have sex with just anyone and about a month before meeting Thorne at that motel room, she wanted to turn her life around. Then the thought struck her, what if Hargrove gave cash to Lacy too? He set her up in a condo and with medical care; it wasn't a stretch for him to provide her with spending money also. And he did get her a job at the computer store. If she pocketed all her money, it was possible she could pick up the drug for Thorne.

"How much would a hit cost?" she asked.

"Closer to a hundred, which is quite high compared to twenty for a baggie of coke."

"How close are we to shutting this down?"

"We?" Commons laughed. "Narcotics is close, but not all the way there."

"We can help you."

"Why? Don't you have enough work to keep you busy?"

"We have questions that need answers."

"Share with me."

"We have a dead man who had this mix, a cocktail as you put it, in his system at the time of death, but he didn't die from that. Either himself or someone else, beat him to the nasty side effect of the drugs by slicing his wrists."

"Someone?"

If she wanted cooperation, she had to give some. "The ruling on the case was suicide, but there is some unresolved evidence in the case."

"And Winston is all right with you opening that all backup?"

"Winston knows of our interest. Do you want our help or not?"

MADISON AND TERRY HEADED BACK to the station.

"We need to find out who bought Oz around the time of Thorne's death," she said.

"I'm not liking where you're going with this. Somehow we have two homicides to solve now."

"Don't forget Sahara, now, so really three deaths. But I think we'll find her justice when we find out the truth about Lacy and Thorne. Lacy was supposedly the last to see Thorne alive, but there are questions there that begged for answers. The obvious one being what would make her kill him when she was turning her life around?"

"And she was pregnant."

Madison had filled him in on that fact on the way to the hospital.

"Exactly, and we still don't know who the father was."

She hadn't asked him what was going on in his life. She feared the answers, the conversation that would follow, the possibility she would have nothing to offer in the way of support, but she remembered Cynthia's encouragement to be there for him.

"How are you doing?"

"We're doing all right," Terry said.

"Good. I'm here you know, if you need—"

"I know you are, Maddy. Thank you. We did a lot of talking yesterday. There are a lot of ways things could go. Everything could be fine."

"Great news."

"But there is also the chance the baby won't be."

Madison didn't say anything. She didn't know what to say. She remembered him mentioning it could be deformed.

"We will love him no matter what and take great care of him. If it means Annabelle has to quit her job, that's what it means."

"You're going to make a great dad, Terry."

"Oh, don't get all soft on me."

She heard a smile in his voice, the hint of positivity. He would be all right—no matter the outcome they would find their way through and she would be there if they needed her.

CHAPTER 44

THEY WERE IN A PART OF the downtown core known for drug dealers and prostitutes. Most businesses had long shut their doors and the buildings remained, only serving as a reminder of what had once been a prosperous area.

The clock on the dash read 11:30 PM.

Madison killed the lights on the car and parked down the end of Second Street.

"If Commons finds out about this, he's going to kill us," Terry said.

"Do you really think I care about what he thinks? We'll get the answers we need and he'll get Harvey in exchange."

"He said it's the small picture."

"Small for him, not for us."

"What about all the other people who will die?"

Madison's heart sank. She had given it considerable thought. Her rationale concluded this was still a positive step in the right direction. Thorne and Sahara Noel deserved justice as Lacy did. Another thing clung close to her mind too. Had Lacy shot up just before her death and if she had, was it the same cocktail? Did she know what she was getting them into?

There were a few people across the street and down a ways. They hung in a cluster under a few streetlights.

Two guys and one girl. The girl wore a fitted jacket and a short skirt, paired with black boots that reached mid-thigh. Her blonde hair was pulled back into a tight ponytail.

The guys, pegged in their early to mid-twenties, shared laughter over something the girl didn't find the same amusement in. One guy had a shaved head and was of average height and a bit to the stocky side; the other had blond hair. The three of them turned and looked at another car that had parked across the street. The occupants stayed inside the car.

"Well, based on Marsh's description none of these guys are Harvey."

They had left Commons and Madison worked on Marsh for a description on Harvey. They were told that Harvey was a white guy in his twenties and typically wore a black puffy coat. He had dark hair and eyes. He would be seen on occasion with a tall and "super skinny" white man in his forties.

Madison reached over Terry and opened the glove box. She pulled out a Hershey's bar and peeled back the wrapper.

"You're eating a chocolate bar? Right now?"

She answered with a mouthful. "Yeah, why not?"

"And I'm not sure why we're parked so close. Harvey's not going to come around if he thinks we're cops."

The girl walked away from the group of guys. She glanced at Madison and Terry, her eyes half-mast and darkened. She was seeking a fix, but she must have sensed their presence.

"The female has some brains," Madison said.

"I think we may have saved her this time. She may not be so lucky next time." Terry tapped his fingers on the dash, slowly at first and then picked up speed. He got a rhythm going as if he were playing the drums.

"Seriously?" Madison laughed.

"You eat chocolate, I'll play music."

The two guys watched the girl walk away. One hit the other in the arm and they both laughed.

"Guys can be such pigs." Madison stuffed the rest of the bar in her mouth and crumpled up the wrapper.

Terry passed a look from the guys to her full mouth, to the wrapper in her hand.

"Shut up." Madison laughed.

"We're not going to accomplish anything by sitting here. You think Harvey's just going to walk up to us and say—"

"Terry." She eyed the image in the rearview mirror. He was walking down a cross street. "Marsh said dark hair and a black puffy jacket."

"Yes."

She got out of the car. She heard Terry's steps behind her as they hit the pavement and he closed in on her.

She moved quickly, yet in a calm manner. She didn't need Harvey making a run for it. Despite watching what she ate a little better than normal, the exercise routine hadn't exactly made it into a permanent spot in her daily schedule. She didn't need this to turn into a chase.

Harvey didn't seem to notice them as he kept his pace consistent. There wasn't anyone with him.

They followed him around the corner where he entered a sports memorabilia place. It had been there for decades and it didn't seem to matter what transpired around it, it was a constant feature.

"We're going to handle this calmly," Madison directed Terry.

"You're telling me to be calm. Normally it's me giving you a variation of that speech."

She narrowed her eyes. "We're going in. Pretend to be interested in baseball cards or something."

"I'd prefer hockey."

"You would."

"What's that supposed to mean?"

"Doesn't matter. Let's go."

"No, what did you mean by that?" Terry stopped on the sidewalk.

"Don't worry about it."

He stared at her.

"I'm just joking around, Terry. Let's go." She headed toward the store.

"You know hockey is a huge sport."

"I know it's popular with Canadians."

"Oh, so it's a bash about my having a Canadian mother now?"

"I didn't say that."

"Maddy, if I didn't like you—"

"What, Terry?"

"Never mind."

"Good, let's get to work."

The door chimed when they entered. No one was behind the counter. In fact, no one was in the store. Madison was starting to understand why the business stayed despite the crumbling economics of the neighborhood. It was a front that catered to the drug crowd after hours.

The space was crammed with sports memorabilia. Jerseys tattooed with different sports teams hung from the ceiling, suspended over racks of baseball caps and novelty items such as license plates and hockey pucks. Pennant flags were tacked along the top of the displays. Clothing and posters were set out in an organized fashion. Each sport had a section of the store. Behind the long counter that was on the left, there was a shelving system with clear plastic trays full of collector cards.

A guy came from the back. There was no sign of Harvey.

"We're closed." His teeth were stained yellow from tobacco, but otherwise he was groomed nicely. He wore an NASCAR sweater, paired with blue jeans. He towered over Terry in height, about seven inches, placing him at six foot seven. He was all of six inches deep when he turned on the side. He fit the description of the second guy.

"We're just looking," Terry said.

"I said we're closed."

"Hubby here really likes hockey." Madison passed Terry a smile.

"I'm not sure what part of closed you don't understand."

Madison rifled through some T-shirts on the rack.

"Go. Get out."

Harvey had walked out of a back room. "Good doing business with you as al—" He stopped when he saw Madison and Terry. He knew they were cops. There was something in those eyes.

"Maybe I can make an exception," the skinny guy said as Harvey headed to the door.

"Hold it there." Madison directed Harvey to stop. He didn't turn around but started into a run. "Ah, shit!"

"I got him." Terry went after him. "Stiles PD! Stop!"

Madison turned to the clerk who had made a run for the back of the store. She did her best to maneuver through the sales displays. She nearly went headlong after her foot caught the base of a rack, but she came out ahead of him. She stuck a leg out and the guy fell flat on the floor.

"Holy shit! Bitch!" He moaned as he went to stand up. "Fuck."

Madison put a foot on his lower back. "Don't even think about it." She bent over, wrenched his arms back, and secured cuffs on his wrists.

"What the—"

"You have the right to remain silent. Anything you say or do can and will be held against…" Madison listed off the Miranda rights as she lifted him to his feet. With her grip firmly on his cuffed hands, she said, "Things could have gone a lot differently."

He exercised his right to keep quiet.

Madison directed him toward the door. It opened to a thrashing Harvey, who struggled against Terry's grip.

"Let's go downtown, boys." Madison smiled at Terry.

If they got lucky, maybe they would shed light on the death of Kevin Thorne.

CHAPTER 45

"I'M NOT REALLY SURE WHAT you guys are up to with this." Sergeant Winston had called them in as soon as they got both guys situated in an interrogation room.

"We're doing our jobs. We're following a lead."

"On what case exactly?" Winston stretched out his arms across his desk. "Isn't your case, officially, a dead girl pulled from a garden?"

Madison counted to ten in her mind, to slow back what she really wanted to say. "You put that nicely."

As much as Terry often wondered about her desire to keep her job, she couldn't imagine life without it.

She continued. "You had mentioned we could look into the death—suspicious may I add—of Kevin Thorne."

"Yes, poke around, but not reopen it and take it over, Knight."

"They are both one and the same to me. You should know that. If there's something that can tie all of these incidents together— Lacy's death, Thorne's apparent suicide, and the overdose of a young girl—"

"You work in narcotics now?" Winston looked between the two of them.

Terry slowly shook his head.

"You're in Major Crimes for a reason."

"The same reason we're following all the leads we can." Madison slumped back into the chair. "We know Lacy and Thorne were connected. DNA has confirmed they were lovers the night he died. She was one of the last people to see him alive."

"Ever think she may have been the killer in this apparent suicide?" His question wasn't a sincere inquiry but enclosed mockery.

"Boss, I need you to give me a little air on this one."

Seconds ticked off waiting for the man to acknowledge her statement.

"Don't let me down," he said.

"Wouldn't think of it." Madison pressed on a smile and left the room with Terry.

"One day things aren't going to go your way," Terry said.

"You think that went my way? I steered the direction of that conversation, Terry. And the sarge wouldn't have let me if he didn't see any merit in this."

HARVEY'S LEGAL NAME WAS HARVARD Coleman. With the potential that came with being named after an Ivy League school, he had turned had destroyed any chance of a good life when he hit his teen years. His rap sheet was entries long, with everything from childhood bullying causing hospitalization to drug possession and B&E charges by the age of sixteen.

They obtained the identity on the slender sport-memorabilia clerk—Allan Burgess. His record was legally spotless but contained interesting information nonetheless.

Madison sat across from Burgess. "Shows here your father owns the store."

"That's right. Is that enough to arrest someone these days?"

"We didn't bring you in about that."

His eyelids fell slowly and opened as if to say, *let's get this the hell over with.*

"You're friends with Harvard Coleman."

"Who? Harvey? Is that a crime now?"

"We have reason to believe you're business partners." Madison didn't refer to the store.

"Business partners? Yeah, we are." Burgess laughed and laid a flattened palm on the table.

"I'm not talking about sports memorabilia."

"You can't put me away on a rumor. You would need to catch me in the act."

Madison gestured between Terry and her. "We're not narcotics."

"What do you—"

"We're Major Crimes." Madison watched for a telltale expression, but his never changed. "Homicide."

His eyes enlarged. "Oh no, I never killed anybody."

"Your drugs do every day, even if it's little by little."

"You have no proof."

"It's a fact of life. Drugs kill."

"No, you can't prove it. You have to prove it if you're going to charge me."

Madison ignored his rant. "This is where you're going to help us." Madison pressed the tip of a finger onto the file folder on the table. "That is if you want to keep this clean."

A slow nod.

"All right then, we need a sample."

Burgess laughed. "You want me to sell you some coke?"

"Oz." Madison held eye contact with him.

"Oh no. I don't know—"

Madison rose from the table and addressed Terry. "Waste of our time. We should book him and finalize the search warrant on the store."

"I might know where to get it."

Madison ran her tongue over her teeth to stifle a smile. Too easy. She sat back down. "We're listening."

Burgess took a deep breath. "Can we deal?"

"You really don't want to play this game with me." She put a picture of Sahara Noel on the table. "Recognize her?"

Burgess extended his arm across the table, tapped once on the surface with an index finger and pulled it back. "I'm not saying."

She put a photo of Lacy Rose beside Sahara. "What about her?"

"Ain't never seen her."

"Lie."

"What? How the hell—"

"Your facial reaction. You never saw the first girl, but the second one, you know her. Why? Did you sell drugs to her?"

"Hell no. Are you kidding? She's RH's girl, isn't she?"

Madison played the silent role.

Burgess shifted in his chair. "RH has his own people who back up him up. Suppliers. We try not to cross paths."

"Like I said we need your help."

"To get you some drugs?" Burgess laughed. "A little unethical for a cop, don't you think?"

"You help us, we help you."

"Uh, no, don't think so. You find out my blend killed someone, my lily-white ass will be in a cell—for life."

"So, you admit to dealing a special blend?"

"Fuck!" His face scrunched up and he pointed a finger at her. "You tricked me!"

"There are two ways we can go about this. You hand it over willingly or we seize it." Madison turned to Terry. "Sound about right?"

"Sure does." Terry slipped his hands into his pockets and jingled the change there.

Burgess leaned back in his chair and stretched out his legs. He crossed them at the ankles. "So, damned if I don't, damned if I do."

"Poor life choices, but it doesn't have to be that way forever."

Burgess stared at the wall behind them. Eventually, he nodded his head.

She didn't disclose the fact that he was simply on borrowed time. As soon as Commons heard about their bringing in Burgess and Coleman, the place would be torn apart. She was surprised he wasn't here yet.

CHAPTER 46

"Your friend's cooperating with us, Harvard." Madison flipped open his file on the table.

"For what? We haven't done anything."

"At least you're admitting to a relationship there."

Harvard Coleman, known on the street as Harvey, took a deep breath.

She tossed a photo of Sahara Noel across the table. "You recognize her?"

"Maybe, maybe not."

"Waste of time." Terry walked to the table and paced behind Harvard.

"What? No, man, I swear."

"Playing stupid only hurts you. We know you do. You sold to her in the last few days." Madison refrained from naming Oz specifically; she didn't need him clamming up.

His eyes lifted and looked into hers. "I—"

"No point in denying it. Your friend told us."

"That little fuck—"

"Now there's no need for that kind of talk," Terry said.

Harvard glanced at him, eyes narrowed, jaw tight. "He ratted me out. I can't believe it." He looked Terry in the eyes. "Fuck—"

Terry slammed his fist on the table beside Coleman.

He looked at Terry with eyes full of fire. It would take more than dramatics to break him. "Is she dead or something?"

"Or something." Madison studied his reaction—nothing. "Did she come to you often?"

"Maybe."

"Listen, kid, we know who you are, what you do," Terry said.

"Whatever."

Madison slapped a photo of Lacy on the table. "What about her? You recognize her?"

Coleman shifted in his seat and pressed fingers to his forehead for a second.

"I'll take that as a yes." Madison smiled at Terry and rolled her eyes.

"I'll deny that I do."

"Why? Who are you afraid of?"

He looked in her eyes. "I ain't afraid of no one."

"You seem to be. When did you last see her?"

"Nuh-uh. No way."

"Detective Grant, why don't you go bring in RH? He can join us." She used Ralph Hennessey's handle from the street.

Terry moved toward the door.

"No, stop. Okay, I'll talk."

"Go ahead."

"She'd come to me." He pointed to the photograph of Lacy. "Hennessey can't know. He'd kill me."

"Because she was his customer?"

"Because she was his girl."

"When did you see her last?"

"Three months ago, maybe more."

"Three months or more?"

"Yeah."

That didn't fit with the timeline. In Madison's theory, Lacy bought the drugs the night Thorne died. Three months ago, Lacy and Thorne wouldn't even have known each other.

"Any time more recently? Say about one month ago."

His eyes drifted about the room. "No."

"What aren't you telling us?"

"I'll need protection."

"Let's hear what you have to say first."

"RH came to me."

Madison sat up straighter. "He went to you. Why?"

"He wanted in on a new product line."

"Oz?"

His eyes snapped to hers. She had her answer—no words were necessary.

"Did he ever get any off you?"

A slow nod. "Please protect me. That guy will kill me."

"That guy is behind bars and already facing charges for drug possession." She didn't mention that he was also a murder suspect. "When did he last buy from you?"

"About a month ago."

CHAPTER 47

OUTSIDE OF THE INTERROGATION ROOM, Madison and Terry weighed the information they were given.

"About a month ago corresponds with the night of Thorne's death. If the drugs in his system come back a match, we have an idea how Thorne came into contact with them," she said.

"Do you think that Hennessey killed Thorne?"

"Yeah, or the alternative is Lacy. But it doesn't go with her turning her life around."

"Maybe Hennessey gave her the drug? Thorne expressed he was stressed out and Lacy offered it to him without knowing the consequences?"

"It begs for an answer to the question of how he managed to slit his wrists. How could this be missed? Even Richards mentioned he had a lot of drugs in his system."

"Doesn't mean he wouldn't be capable of cutting his wrists."

"Suppose so. But what if Hennessey slit Thorne's wrists? Maybe he even knew Lacy would give the drugs to Thorne."

Terry rubbed the back of his neck. "Possible. But there were no prints found on the razor other than Thorne's."

"Easy enough. He wore gloves."

Terry conceded with a nod. "Okay, possible. But he wasn't smart enough not to wear gloves when he touched the gun? Let's say he did kill Thorne because of jealousy, why not kill Lacy at the same time? Why leave her alive? She didn't die until a week after that."

"Well, that's an estimated timeline, not an established fact. We're definitely missing something, and either way she didn't die in the motel room." Madison paused. "I've mentioned it before, but what if Lacy killed—"

"But why? She loved him."

"Did she? Or maybe she did, but he wasn't too thrilled when he found out she was pregnant too." Madison raised her brows. "Two women, two babies on the way. He could have sided with his fiancée and told Lacy to hit the road. She might not have taken that too well."

"You're saying the girl killed him?"

"Yeah. Hate to say it, but it's a possibility. She was trying to put her dark past behind her, but further rejection could have caused her to snap."

"So, they fool around, he shoots up, probably with a little help from Lacy. She tells him about the baby and he flips."

"Okay, how did she get him from the bed to the bathtub?"

"That's the easy part. She probably talked him into a bath afterward."

"He would have really been riding high. First time taking drugs. You'd think the last thing he'd want to do is have a bath. Why not stay in the bed?"

"Good point actually. Lacy would have known how the guy would be feeling, using for the first time. If she loved him, she wouldn't want him drowning in the—" Madison's eyes enlarged. "Wait a minute, there wasn't any water in the tub."

"So she didn't talk him into having a bath."

Madison thought for a moment. "I remember from the file that the blood hadn't been diluted by water, so it wasn't drained."

"Could be suicide. He went in there so there wasn't as much mess. Maybe there was an altercation, Lacy got angry and left. With everything going on, Thorne couldn't take it. Maybe he was suicidal going into the motel room that night?"

"But the clerk said they rendezvoused every Thursday night. Thorne would have expected her to show up. Why answer the door? Most suicidal people don't want to be talked out of it."

"Okay, back to that. What if he wasn't suicidal? She shot him up to weaken him. I don't know. It seems like there's a lot of speculation.

We don't even know if she was carrying his baby," Terry said.

"For that matter it could be Peter Hargrove's."

"You're still barking up that tree?"

Madison rolled her eyes at the cliché. "I still can't buy the fact that the guy is that nice, for no reason other than to just be—" Madison's phone rang. "Knight." She established eye contact with Terry. "All right, we'll be right there."

"Let me guess. We know whose baby it is."

"No, but the full toxicology panel is back on Lacy." Madison saw Commons headed straight for them. "Time to go," she said.

CHAPTER 48

JENNIFER ADAMS WORKED IN THE lab with Cynthia and specialized in serology and toxicology—basically she knew her bodily fluids and how to analyze them. She was only a couple of years younger than Madison, but the two of them had never bonded outside of work. Jennifer was particular in that she preferred to be called by the full version of her name. Abbreviations were not acceptable.

Jennifer sat in front of a computer when they walked into the lab. Her posture straight, as always, shoulders back, everything at her station set up ergonomically correct. She turned to Madison and Terry as they walked toward her.

Jennifer's blonde hair was ironed straight and parted with the hair flipped to the right to frame her round face. Her chestnut eyes were deep pools and were usually hard to read.

"The vic's results show she was high at the time of her death. Stomach contents didn't reveal anything special."

Cynthia had told Madison a while ago Jennifer was engaged. Madison looked to Jennifer's finger and noticed the gold band there with a single diamond—nothing more than a simple setting would be expected.

Jennifer continued. "Other results came back and indicated that the vic had given up drugs for a while. But she was definitely laced with drugs when she died."

"Was a profile run on the drugs found in her system?" Madison asked.

"Yes. It was a cocktail of cocaine, meth, and heroin. We were also able to pull some residue from the needle puncture between her toes. When I looked closer at the parameters in the database, it looks like it was also the results on a man who died a month—"

"Kevin Thorne," Madison finished her sentence.

Jennifer nodded.

Madison turned to Terry. "If Lacy was going to give up drugs, as Peter Hargrove told us she was going to, what would make her shoot up? She did have defensive wounds."

"Hennessey forced the drugs on her," Terry concluded Madison's thought.

"When she was high, he made her pull the trigger?"

"It would have been easier to."

"Or he did it himself. To me, that possibility hasn't been completely ruled out. He could have played on her low self-esteem. For one, she had a father who didn't want her. Hennessey not only physically abused her, he likely did mentally as well. He could have told her that she killed her lover when it was in fact him, and possibly Bates, who did," Madison continued.

Jennifer cleared her throat, causing both Madison and Terry to turn to her.

"As you know she was pregnant at the time of death. The results are still being processed to see if we can get a DNA match to those of highest interest—Hennessey, Bates, and Thorne." She swiveled the chair to face the monitor.

Madison glanced at Terry and thought, *conversation over?*

"Thanks, Jenn. Jennifer," Madison corrected with a laugh.

"Why is it so hard for people to get it?" Jennifer spun around to face them again.

Madison remained quiet.

"My name is Jennifer, just as yours is Madison."

"And people call me Maddy all the time. It doesn't bother me at all."

"I guess it's what makes each of us unique. My mother put it into my mind not to abbreviate names."

There wasn't any doubt to Madison why they had never connected outside of work. Jennifer was too serious.

"Let me know as soon as the DNA results come back on the

fetus."

"Will do." Jennifer's tone held an irritation as she swiveled back around to her computer.

CHAPTER 49

"I THINK WE SHOULD GO see Peter Hargrove again to see if he was aware Lacy was pregnant," Madison said. "See, that's another thing that doesn't fit. Lacy was cleaning up her life, she was pregnant, possibly wanting to make a go of things with Thorne. The defensive wounds were from her fighting off Hennessey. He killed her."

"We assume she fought off Hennessey. Was any epithelial pulled from her wounds?" Terry asked.

"From my understanding, there was."

Terry was already on his cell inquiring about the results. He hung up a few minutes later. "Still on their to-do list."

"To-do list? It could be a direct link to her killer."

"Ours isn't the only case, Maddy, and a case isn't fully solved by forensics."

"Still doesn't make me happy."

"Well, what are you going to do? That's life."

She disregarded his correction. "We've also got to speak with Hennessey and Bates again, starting with the latter. He's the weaker one. If we confront him about Thorne and Lacy, maybe he'll roll on Hennessey."

"Off to see Hargrove first then. He's not going to be pleased to see us." Terry took a deep breath.

"You didn't become a cop to please people I hope, or you'll be sadly disappointed." Madison kept the full thought to herself. They risked their lives and received very little, if any, respect for it.

ONE WOMAN SAT BEHIND THE front desk at Solarpanel Energy and she wasn't one of the two who had been there on their first visit. Her skin was the color of mocha and her eyes near black. Her brown hair tousled over her shoulders.

She offered a sincere smile. "May I help you?"

Madison flashed her badge and made the formal introductions. "We're here to see Peter Hargrove."

"Certainly, but he's not in. His partner, Mr. Kendal, is in."

"He's returned from his holidays?"

Madison turned to Terry. "We could talk to him."

Back to the receptionist. "Please get him for us."

"Of course." She pressed some buttons on the phone. "Mr. Kendal, I have two detectives here to see you...yes, okay. I will do." She hung up and spoke to them. "He will be up just shortly."

Less than a minute later, Kendal rounded a bend of partitions.

"I'm not sure what we would have to talk about." His body language said it all, *I talked to you at my house and there is nothing left to say.*

"How was your holiday?" Madison asked, feigning interest.

"Surely you didn't come here for that." Kendal led them to a conference room. He pressed a hand against his suit jacket as he took a seat. "I am more than willing to help you in whatever way I can, but I don't see how I can be of any."

"Peter Hargrove was helping Lacy out. Did you know this?"

"Of course I knew. He's my business partner, and it's my business to know what he's doing."

"Even with his own money."

"With things that concern me."

"How did his use of personal money affect you?"

"In business, over half of the generated revenue is reliant upon the reputation of its owners." A hand gestured to the right. "The other half, upon product and service. Peter didn't understand that."

"It really bothered you that he helped her."

"There wasn't a need for it." Kendal straightened his jacket and adjusted his necktie. "He always does this, though."

"Does what?"

"He sees a charity case and goes for it. He claims it's good for people to see that side of him."

"Do you think that's all Lacy was to him? A charity?"

Kendal's eyes studied Madison. "She was a good-looking girl. If, and I mean if, she was my daughter, for that I would be proud. But the girl was messed up, broken. She showed up at my place high. She went on about how her boyfriend was abusive and she needed to make changes right away."

"Results showed that Lacy hadn't taken drugs for some time before she died."

"She was on something when she came to my place, I tell you."

"Is that why you sent her away?" Madison played along. This man was lying to them.

"I told her if she was mine, her mother was a cheap whore. I had my house assistant show her to the door."

This man was truly calloused and in love with two things—himself and his money.

"Did you know she was pregnant?" Madison asked.

Kendal cleared his throat. "She didn't mention that." He straightened his tie. "I remember her touching her stomach when she was pleading for help."

"How did she react to being shown out?"

He snuffed out air from his nostrils, his jaw shifting askew. "She got hysterical. Pete ran in from my home office—where we were discussing business matters when she interrupted our evening—and I knew the minute he saw her he'd be a lost cause."

"Because she was beautiful?"

"That, and desperate."

"Peter have a thing for pretty and desperate women?"

"Oh, does he."

"Does his wife know?"

"God no. If she knew, she'd divorce him instantly and take him for everything."

"This is why his actions bother you. You're afraid she'll touch the business." Madison noticed Terry glance at her for her forthrightness.

"Damn straight. And I can tell by the way that you're looking at me with those judgmental eyes, you think less of me for it. Well, I don't really care."

"So, did Peter ever mention her to you after that?"

"No way. He knew better. It has been a constant source of conflict between us."

"The fact he helps desperate women?"

"Yeah. One day he's gonna get caught with that hand of his in the cookie jar and I'm gonna have to pay for it."

"Do you think he slept with Lacy?"

"He set her up with healthcare, a condo, and a job. Yeah, I know about everything. Do you really think he did it out of the kindness of his heart? Even Pete's not that generous."

"It's interesting you brought up the condo and the job. Did you know that Peter set her up with those things about a month prior to the day she came to your house and met you?"

"What? No. How would I have any way of knowing that?"

"Thought it was your business to know." Madison stood and tossed her card on the desk. "Call us if you think of anything else."

CHAPTER 50

"THAT GUY IS A LYING SACK OF—" Madison looked over at Terry in the passenger seat.

"Thank you for not finishing that."

"You notice too?"

"Oh yeah. First he knows nothing and then he knows everything."

"It makes me wonder what his motives are. Why lie about when he met Lacy? Why say she was high when he knows that's something we could disprove? Do you really buy his line about not knowing she was pregnant?"

"Not fully, no."

"And then his comments about Hargrove. Was he still lying or telling the truth? He said he had a thing for young, beautiful women. You must be the only faithful one out there." She glanced at him and asked the rhetorical. "Tell me you're faithful."

"Maddy, I'm either with you or my wife. You both keep me busy. When would I have the time to?"

"So it's a matter of time?"

"Let me start again."

"No, it's okay. I get it. Men are easily attracted to loose women." She shifted her position so she was angled more toward Terry. "If a woman threw herself at you, what would you do?"

"Run." Terry laughed. "No, seriously. Annabelle would kill me. I would be a dead man. Forget being taken for all I'm worth, I'm not worth much anyway, but I'd be dead."

Madison turned to look out the front windshield, her thoughts on Hargrove's wife. "Do you think she knows about her husband's affairs?"

"Doubt it."

"See, I think a woman always knows. But she's taken care of, so why upset things? I couldn't live like that."

She thought back to Sovereign—their recent kissing session and their past. She finally believed she was strong enough to let it go now. She didn't need him. She did fine on her own.

She lifted her cell phone and dialed the Hargrove residence. Beverly answered after four rings. Madison announced herself and asked to speak with Peter. She was advised he was at work. Madison slowly put the phone down.

"According to the missus, Hargrove's at work today." She squeezed the steering wheel and didn't look at her partner. "I told you, didn't I? I told you he wouldn't do all that for Lacy without sex being involved."

"You're assuming—"

"Come on, Terry. The man has a history of helping women out."

"Says his business partner."

"Yeah, a man who makes it his business to be involved in Hargrove's life. Remember when we first went to Kendal's house. He told Hargrove, that's what you get with a ten-dollar whore."

"He could have meant it about himself. Besides we've already proven the man is a liar." Terry lifted his brows. "Besides not every man on the planet is guilty of being unfaithful, or even capable of it."

"What about Christina Dunn, the woman from the computer store? She knows Hargrove, he convinced her to hire Lacy."

"So, you think they had an intimate relationship?" Terry laughed.

"I'm being serious here. We have to think of it from every angle." She dialed another number then said to her partner, "I just have a feeling." Back into the phone after it was answered, "Is Christina Dunn in?" When she received her answer, she smiled and hung up. "The dirty bastard."

"Maddy?"

"I called Modern Computers and Dunn isn't in today either. Coincidence?"

"Quite possible."

Madison reached over and jabbed his shoulder. "Seriously? This is how you're going to play it?"

"Well. It could be."

Madison rested against the headrest. "Where would I go if—" She lifted her hand. "I got it. He's at the condo." She changed directions. "I'll give you one more chance to change your bet. Peter was sleeping with Lacy."

"You said he factored into her death."

"And I stand by that."

"Good because once it's said, it's done. No reneging."

"Reneging?" Madison laughed.

CHRISTINA DUNN WAS COMING OUT of the Luxor Apartments when Madison and Terry reached the front door.

"Detectives?" She wore a fitted, beige trench coat that was the length of mid-thigh. Beneath it, she wore black dress pants. A gold chain with bulky links dangled around her neck and was paired with diamond-studded hoop earrings.

"You live here?" Madison asked.

"No, I was just here visiting a friend. I really must be going." She offered a weak smile.

Madison stepped out of her path.

"Good day to both of you," Dunn said.

Stepping inside the building, Madison held out an opened palm to Terry. "Would you like to pay up now, or later with interest?"

"Not yet. And you are just assuming her friend is Hargrove."

"My assumptions are usually right."

Terry laughed. "Don't think so."

"What are the chances?"

"How many units in this building?"

Madison jabbed his shoulder.

He rubbed it. "You've got to stop doing that."

"Why, you like it? You miss it when I don't do in a while. I'm being thoughtful. I don't want you to have to miss it."

"I see." He continued to massage his shoulder as they headed for the elevators.

They stood outside the condo door and knocked.

"He might not even—"

The door opened.

"Hello?" Hargrove's single word arched with an enclosed question as to what they were doing there.

"We thought we might find you here," Madison said.

His eyes fluttered. "Am I missing something? I've been very cooperative with you—"

Madison brushed past him into the condo. "Can we come in?"

Hargrove raised his arms in the air. "Seeing as you're already inside, why not?" He latched the door shut behind them.

She spun on her heels. "We ran into Christina Dunn on our way in."

"I'm not sure—"

"She said she was here seeing a friend. You're friends, aren't you?"

"Yes."

"Yeah, she mentioned you got Lacy a job working at the company she manages."

"That's right."

It was obvious he wasn't going to offer up why he hadn't said anything about it earlier.

"Does your wife know about your affair?"

"Excuse me?" He raised his voice and shared eye contact with the both of them. "You have a lot of nerve coming in here—"

Madison glanced at Terry. "He's really defensive."

"I'm defensive because every time I turn around you're accusing me of a wrongdoing."

"But I shouldn't be because you've done nothing wrong?"

"Yes. Exactly."

"Huh." Madison paced a few steps.

"What's that supposed to mean?"

"How you got Lacy a job and held that back from us. You had known about her before she showed up at Kendal's. That's been proven between when you got this apartment and secured her job."

"I didn't think it mattered."

"Avoided truths create doubt. Doubts can foster deceit, and deceit, to me, equals a lie."

"I didn't think it mattered," he repeated himself.

"You convinced her to approach Kendal, didn't you?"

Hargrove's eyes filled with sorrow. "I didn't expect him to reject her. She was getting her life together. I felt horrible."

Madison needed more to feel empathy for the man. She thought on Kendal's advice to Hargrove when they had first met the two men at the house.

"Do you go see women other than your wife? Kendal mentioned that's what you get for fooling around with a ten-dollar whore."

Hargrove looked to Terry, his eyes coated with a defensive spirit. "Yeah, in reference to himself!" Hargrove gestured a hand between him and Madison. "You might get a better response from people if you asked them questions and believed their answers."

"People lie all the time."

"I'm not sure what Maurice told you, but he doesn't know me either."

"He thinks he does."

"Well, that's all it is. He doesn't know me."

"Still stuck on why he would say that. You said he meant it in reference to himself?"

His expression hardened.

"Your wife doesn't have any idea does she?"

"You can both leave now." He made a movement toward the door. Madison stood in front of him.

"Lacy was pregnant."

Hargrove's brow compressed and his eyes misted. His legs buckled under him, but he regained his composure before falling or losing his balance. "I had no—" He shook his head and stopped talking.

"Is there something you should be telling us before we find out?"

Hargrove stood there.

"Did she threaten to go to your wife?"

He still didn't say anything.

"You loved her? Were you going to be there for her and the baby?"

"I'm not saying it again."

"Did you know that Lacy also had another guy? She met up with him all the time at a motel on the east end. She met him where you got her the job."

"I didn't kill her." His voice was weak. He headed for the couch and dropped into it.

Madison and Terry followed him but remained standing.

"Did you kill him?" Madison asked.

"Who?" He lifted his head to look at Madison.

"Lacy's lover is also dead. He died around the same time Lacy did. It must have made you angry, though, after all you did for her. And then she takes your baby into the bed of another man."

"It's not my baby." He rose to his feet.

"How can you be so certain of that?"

"I told you it wasn't like that with me and Lacy. I keep telling you that, but you're not hearing it."

"Are you willing to provide DNA to prove that?"

He studied Madison's face. "Whatever it takes to make this go away."

"Just one more question. When Lacy showed up at Kendal's house, was she high?"

"No, absolutely not."

CHAPTER 51

MADISON AND TERRY HEADED TO the lab after seeing Hargrove through the process of having his DNA collected.

In the lab, Jennifer was standing over a table peering into a microscope. She didn't look at them when they came in.

"Have any updates for us? Where's Cyn?"

"Out having a smoke."

Cynthia walked into the lab as if on cue and everyone turned to her. "I was missed, I see."

Madison walked over to her, scrunched up her face, and waved a hand in front of her nose. "And you smell."

Cynthia stuck her tongue out at Madison.

"When are you going to stop smoking? You know it's not good for you."

"When are you going to stop acting like my mother?" Both women locked eyes. Cynthia smiled first.

Madison gave way. "Fine. Die of lung cancer."

"Nice. You could have left it at fine, but nope, just one more dig. Bitch."

Both women shared a laugh. It came to an end when they both sensed the other two pairs of eyes on them. Jennifer looked all serious, and her eyes questioned if now was a good time to be fooling around. Terry's jaw was slightly open as if in shock Madison was all right with being called a bitch.

"It's okay, Terry. You should know by now. I'm allowed, you're not," Cynthia said. She must have picked up on the same thing as Madison.

"Just as she's really all right with me reciprocating and bossing her like a mother," Madison added.

"The bitch thing, okay, but the mother thing," Cynthia was smiling, "that's pushing it a little." The light switched in Cynthia's eyes. "What are you guys looking for anyway?"

"Results."

"Well, you're about to have a bunch of them and I'll be giving them to you all at once. I will share this news with you, though. The abrasions on Lacy Rose's knuckles didn't have any epithelial, however, the finger that the landlord first dug up." Cynthia paused to smile. "It did."

"And?"

"And I don't have the results for you yet."

"Come on."

"Your case isn't—"

"I know it's not the only case, but I need something."

"I've done my best to rush some things through for you, but I can't do it with everything or no one else would get results."

"Okay, what about the shovel? I'm sure it's been analyzed. You said you have results for us but want to hand it all over at once? Give me this. Were there any fingerprints lifted from it? Were any a match?"

"I actually just got to the shovel today." She must have noticed Madison's look. "Don't even start."

"Seriously?"

"Yeah, I know. Hang on and I'll compare them to your two key suspects right now."

"Not even so much suspects in this aspect. They pretty much confessed to burying her. Proof is a lovely thing, though."

Madison leaned against a table while the computer analyzed and cross-compared the prints from Hennessey and Bates with those pulled from the shovel. The computer chimed.

"All right. Here's your proof."

Madison read the screen. "Bates."

"Yes, ma'am."

"Hennessey's story was he came home and found Lacy dead.

Bates's story is she was already dead when Hennessey called him down to help get rid of the body. Based on the prints, he was the only one who buried Lacy. And we already have the results on the gun we got from Bates's apartment. Hennessey's prints were on there. They were in on this together. Has it been confirmed if that's the gun that killed Lacy yet?"

Cynthia glanced at Terry. "She has no patience, does she?" Back to Madison. "Sam's got it. She's probably firing rounds into Jell-O now." She smiled at them due to her loose terminology.

The "Jell-O" she referred to was a product scientifically designed to be a close match in density and consistency to that of muscle tissue.

They left the lab and headed to see Samantha—Sam, as she preferred to be called. Madison found it ironic how one girl in the lab was set against having her name abbreviated and the other one preferred it.

"The gun we pulled from Bates's apartment had Hennessey's prints along with Lacy's," Madison said, recapping what they knew to brainstorm with Terry. "Okay, what are you thinking?"

"I'm thinking that Bates may be telling the truth. He helped to get rid of Lacy's body. Now that's been confirmed with his prints on the shovel."

"My thinking is why was he smart enough to wear gloves and keep his prints off the gun, but not enough to do so when it came to the shovel."

"Nerves?"

"Exactly. He is telling the truth. He wasn't there when Lacy, or Hennessey, pulled the trigger. He had time to think and prepare mentally when it came to hiding the gun. The burial of Lacy's body was last minute, thrown upon him. He would have been emotional and irrational."

"Yes, nervous."

"Yes, Terry." Madison smiled at him.

They stepped into the room and saw Sam with the gun pressed into the opening of a testing chamber. The inside was full of the material designed to simulate the reaction of human flesh.

Sam wore earmuffs to stifle the noise. She called out that she was going to fire and eased back on the trigger. A bullet lodged into the composite.

Sam was all of four-ten in height, and her nest of brown curls reached her shoulders. She pulled the muffs off when she noticed them and set the gun down.

"I take it that it's too soon to ask if the bullet striations are a match," Madison said.

Sam glanced at the chamber and laughed. "A little, but I am getting closer. We know that the casing found at the apartment is a match to this model of handgun. I still need to verify that it belongs to this specific gun."

"All right, well the minute you know, call me."

"Will do."

Madison and Terry left Sam and headed to the interrogation room where they would be questioning Bates some more.

Outside the room, Madison said, "We've got to work this guy hard this time. He knows more than he's telling us."

"We've got his prints on the shovel. Wonder what he'll think about that."

They opened the door. Bates picked at the end of one of his dreadlocks; he let it go when they came in.

"I've told you everyt'ing." He looked through them. "I don't know what more yous want from me."

"The truth." Madison sat across from him. Terry walked behind him. "You told us Hennessey found her dead and wanted your help to bury Lacy's body."

"That's the truth, man."

"We have proof of that."

His eyes lit. "Then I can't be charged with murder."

Madison let his comment go. "We have proof that you buried Lacy. Your prints were on the shovel."

She tossed a morgue photo of Lacy on the table. She would withhold the fact Hennessey's prints were on the gun. There was more here to uncover, possibly including an explanation for Thorne's death.

Omitting some truths, she continued. "There is no sign of Hennessey anywhere. Nothing connecting him to this except for the fact that he lived in the house with her."

Bates shifted straighter in the chair. "No, you have it wrong. He—"

"He what? Did he kill her and then ask for your help to get rid of the *evidence*?" It hurt Madison to refer to a once-living individual as evidence.

"It's not like that."

"The fact of the matter is that's exactly what it looks like. Drugs were forced on her. Did you know that?" Madison ran with her gut feelings.

"No. No." His head shook, sweeping his dreadlocks across his face in the motion.

"She didn't want to do drugs anymore did she? You didn't like that fact." Madison settled into the chair and flung her arm over the back of it. "We're thinking Hennessey did come home to find Lacy dead."

His eyes lit and read, *you believe me.*

"We believe you killed her and left her there. I mean it would explain why you came running to help him out."

"It's not like that—"

"Why not call nine-one-one?"

"We were scared."

Madison laughed. "You're a drug dealer and you were scared?"

"No, we were. Scared. And I don't deal drugs anymore."

"Hennessey did, though, didn't he? We have a witness who is willing to testify to his buying drugs the day that she and her lover died."

"Don't know—"

"Please don't say you don't know what she's talking about," Terry said into Bates's ear.

Bates turned his head to the side to look at Terry. "I don't, man."

"Oz. The Wizard's Cocktail. Hear of this?" Madison reined her interview back.

"You think he killed her with drugs? I thought she was shot?"

"She was shot, but by whom is still a mystery."

"Hennessey said he found her like that."

"We think you know more than you're telling us. Hennessey bought Oz, two vials. We have two dead people in his circle. Coincidence? Do you want to go down with him?"

Bates went silent. His facial expression relaxed.

"You let him hide the gun in your home." She studied his response. "There were no prints on the gun other than Lacy's and Hennessey's. We know a dead girl never walked it upstairs to your apartment."

"I never touched it." Bates lifted his shoulders and let out a deep breath.

"We know you're telling us the truth about helping bury her, but why did you do it? Why not turn on Hennessey?"

His eyes glazed over.

"It makes me wonder what you're hiding from us. Did he have something even larger on you? Something he could hold over your head? What was it?" Madison softened her approach at the end hoping to draw him out. There was truth in this mess, but Madison couldn't see it clearly yet.

His two hands covered his face.

"If you talk to us, we can help you. If you don't—"

"None of it went according to plan." Bates looked at her, but Madison didn't say anything. "He came home, a'ight. Found her dead."

"It doesn't explain the struggle."

Bates now avoided eye contact.

"Lacy struggled with someone. We believe it was to avoid being shot up with a drug known on the street as Oz. She hadn't used for weeks prior to that."

"You know about—"

Madison cocked her head.

Tears filled Bates's eyes. "I loved her. Hennessey, he used her. Thought she was a good ticket item. When he found out about her rich boyfriend, the condo, the job she got, he held it over her. Told her she didn't deserve any of it." He wiped tears from his cheeks.

"There was a spark of life startin' in her. Hennessey hated the freedom she reached for. I think he hated it more so because she was having success with it. I loved seeing her happy." Bates sniffled. "But she got into drugs again. She had told me the day before she died that she didn't deserve life."

Madison thought about their theory of the killer manipulating Lacy into pulling the trigger, bringing her down with thoughts that she wasn't worthy of a second chance. She still wasn't fully buying what Bates's was saying, but she would play along.

"Did she say why?"

"Yeah, she listed off several reasons." His eyes met Madison's and sparked with sarcasm.

"Mind sharing one?"

"Her baby."

So, he knew about that. "Why would that make her feel unworthy?"

"She thought of it as a gift but didn't think she deserved it."

This was the first time they heard about this. Everyone they had asked told them she seemed happy. "Okay, so do you know why she went from determined to change to feeling unworthy?"

He slowly shook his head.

"When you got downstairs to help dispose of Lacy, what was Hennessey like?"

"He was freaking out. Said he never expected it to be like this."

"To be like this?"

Bates looked at her and Madison knew from his eyes there was so much more that he wasn't saying.

"What aren't you telling us?"

"I don't know." Two hands lifted in surrender. "That's what he said."

"And you didn't ask what he meant by that?"

"Lacy was dead. In front of me."

"Where was the gun when you came into Hennessey's apartment?"

"It was on the floor beside her."

Madison thought about the scenario. If Lacy had shot herself, the hand that had held the gun would have dropped down to her lap and the gun would have slid to the floor. But that would be easy for Hennessey to figure out and stage for Bates's benefit.

"Did he say anything else to you?"

"Just that she was high—"

"She wasn't dead when he came home."

Caught in a lie, his eyes deadlocked with Madison's.

"You said that Lacy was dead when he came home. If she was, how did he know she was high?"

Bates sat there, blinking rapidly.

Terry slammed his hands on the table. "Answer the question."

Bates jumped. "It doesn't really matter what I say now, does it? I'm going to prison."

Madison nodded. Bates visibly swallowed.

Terry walked around the table and stood beside Madison.

"Do you believe Hennessey found her dead?" Madison asked.

Bates shook his head. "Someone was going to pay us to kill her. And before you ask, I don't know his name."

She thought back to what Hennessey had said to Bates. It wasn't supposed to be like that. Maybe he never expected to feel any remorse, or it could be because of the mess it made.

"You have no idea who paid you?"

"He paid us cash. He left it in an envelope in the mailbox. A few hundred up front, a grand upon completion."

For a mere thirteen hundred they were willing to kill Lacy, a woman Bates professed to care for. It was disgusting.

"Why did this man want her dead?"

"Don't know. Don't care."

Madison slammed a fist on the table. "You want anything to work in your favor, get talking."

Bates rolled his eyes. "He said that she needed to go."

"How did he communicate with you?"

"E-mail."

"We'll need to see it."

"Can't."

Madison exhaled loudly. "What do you mean can't?"

Silence.

"You better start talking."

"He contacted us through a video game."

"A video game?"

"Yeah. Online you can set up friends and have private rooms. You can communicate via messaging."

"Which game and what's the guy's name on there?"

Bates sucked in on his bottom lip. "I want to talk a deal."

Madison scoffed laughter and looked to Terry. "He wants to talk a deal." She faced Bates. "Guess it depends on what you have for us."

"You need to have played a round with 'em or be live friends."

"Live friends?"

"Xbox." He stared through them as if they were ancient not to know about it.

"Okay. Name?"

"His handle is Slayer1962."

"WE'VE GOT TO GET A hold of a gaming system and find this guy. There has to be some way for them to trace back usernames to billing addresses."

"There is—" Terry's words froze when Madison stared at him. "What? I like to play sometimes."

"You play video games?"

"Yes, I do." He seemed proud of that fact. "It's nothing to be ashamed of."

"Terry, you're thirty-one years old."

"I fail to see your point."

Madison laughed. "Who's going to be the biggest kid in the house, the new baby, or you?"

"Hey."

He trailed her as she headed back to their desks. They sat down across from each other.

"What if the altercation between Hennessey and Lacy wasn't the result of him forcing drugs on her? What if it was a struggle for the gun?" Madison asked.

Terry's eyes sparked with the revelation she had. "Hennessey wanted to be the one to pull the trigger—"

"We could be looking at this the wrong way. Maybe in her altered mind, she did choose to kill herself."

"Remember Hennessey's prints on the gun."

"Still strange, though. If you were going to kill someone, why do it in your house? Why not somewhere that has no connection?"

"You know who we're dealing with here."

"Suppose you're right. Remember when we went and saw Peter Hargrove's wife?"

"His nephew was there."

"He was playing a video game."

"You think this will tie back to Hargrove? Why would he want her dead?"

"Going back to my original theory, maybe Lacy was going to cross the line and cost him everything." Madison went quiet, mulling over the different angles. "We can't just go running back to Hargrove though."

"A fourth time is too much?"

She narrowed her eyes. "He willingly gave us his DNA. It was almost too easy to get it. But first things first. Since you're all savvy on the gaming thing," Madison whirled her hand in a circulation motion, "see if you can track the player down to a real name and address. I'll go update the sarge before he smells the leads in the case and accuses me of not communicating."

"It's a good thing I'm sitting down or I'd fall down."

She smiled at him, knowing that his comment had to do with the fact she usually did all she could to avoid status updates.

"Don't you have phone calls to make?"

Terry laughed. "It shouldn't be too hard to get the information we need anyway. Every live account—that means connected to the Internet for live gameplay—requires a credit card and home billing address."

She came back thirty minutes later and she could tell by Terry's face that he already had his answer.

"The address for the account is twenty-one thirty Barber Avenue.

That's Peter Hargrove's—"

Madison was already on the move.

THEY PULLED TO A STOP out front of the Hargrove residence. Three squad cars with five officers came as back-up.

Madison directed four officers. "Two of you go around back. The other two of you watch the front." She turned to the fifth officer. "You come with us." She rapped her knuckles on the door.

"Stiles PD. Open up!" She knocked again and repeated the request. "One last chance! Stiles PD!"

She stepped aside, freeing the way for the officer to forcibly enter.

"Stiles PD! We're coming in!" She motioned to the officer.

The door opened just before the officer lunged at it.

"Whoa!" Peter Hargrove stood there looking at all of them as if they had gone mad.

She handed him the warrant to search his premises.

"What's this?"

"Put your hands behind your back!" Madison yelled at him. "Now!"

Hargrove tossed the warrant to a nearby hall table, turned, and placed his hands behind his back.

Terry moved past him toward the television area where the boy had been playing before. He opened cabinet doors until he found the gaming console. He turned on the television and the console and found the right input.

"What is this about?" Hargrove protested.

"Are we looking good?" Madison asked Terry.

A window opened on the screen, saying *"Sign into Xbox Live."*

Terry said, "Oh yeah, we're good. His account name is Slayer1962."

CHAPTER 52

"YOU THINK HE PAID THE kids to kill the girl?" Sergeant Winston stood with his hands on his hips, his paunch tugging on the fabric of his shirt.

"The account links back to his house," Madison said.

They had fully updated the Sergeant on how the Xbox account that hired Hennessey and Bates to kill Lacy traced back to Hargrove. He had approved the request for them to obtain a search warrant, but he wanted to discuss things further.

"Still, can you prove he's the one that propositioned these kids? Could anyone log on under his handle? What's the man's motive?"

"Lacy was pregnant—"

"From what I understand, we still don't know who the father is."

"No, but it's being worked on. But even if he wasn't the father, he put everything on the line for her. He set her up with healthcare and a condo. He finds out she's hooking up with this other guy, Kevin Thorne. Maybe he got jealous when she didn't return his affection and thought he'd take care of it. He didn't care if Hennessey and Bates went away. They were part of Lacy's downfall."

"And if he is the father of her baby, she could have threatened to go to the wife." The Sergeant finished the line of thought.

Madison nodded. "A possibility we've also considered. Even if she never slept with Hargrove, say if the baby isn't his, she could have threatened him and tried to bribe him somehow."

"Only one way to find out." Winston gestured through the glass toward Hargrove inside the interrogation room.

"Maddy, before we go in there…"

Madison stopped outside the door. "What is it, Terry?"

"The sarge brought up an interesting point. He said how do we know if it's Hargrove?"

Her foot started tapping. "I'm listening."

"Anyone could have logged on as Slayer1962."

"What do you mean? And you're bringing this up now?"

"Just thought of it, but all anyone needs is the handle and the password that goes with it."

"Ah shit. Now where does this leave us?"

"Still looking for more proof."

"YOU THINK I KILLED HER?" Hargrove asked when they came into the room.

Madison took a seat, and Terry jingled the change in his pocket, walking behind Hargrove.

Madison opened a file folder on the table. She pulled out a morgue picture of Lacy.

"Get that away from me." His voice cracked. "She was a wonderful girl."

"A wonderful girl who slept around, did drugs and bribed you—"

"You've lost your mind. Have you gotten the results back on my DNA?"

"Did she threaten to go to your wife about the two of you?"

"There's no point talking to you about this."

"You're looking good for conspiracy to commit murder."

"What are you talking about?"

"You play video games online correct?"

"Yes. What does this have to—"

"You go by the online name of Slayer1962?"

"Yes." His eyes searched hers.

"Do you know these people?" She tossed photos of Hennessey and Bates across the table.

He picked each of them up.

"Do you know them?" She repeated her question.

His eyes slowly lifted from the photos. "Yes."

"Did you approach them to kill Lacy?"

"Who is telling you this? Are you getting it from him?" Hargrove pressed a finger onto the photo of Hennessey. "He was no good for her. He hooked her on drugs in the first place. He beat on her."

"Our concern right now, is did you approach them to kill her?"

"I'd have no reason to want her dead."

"Your Xbox handle."

"What are you talking about?"

"Slayer1962 paid two people to kill Lacy."

"I didn't."

Madison thought on Terry's words—basically anyone could log on to a handle name with access to the password. The truth of it cast darkness over her suspicions.

"Anyone else play under your handle?"

"My ten-year-old nephew uses the console but come to think of it, he doesn't log online. His mother, my sister, doesn't think it's good for kids to be exposed to the online world."

"If it wasn't you, who else had access to your—"

A knock came on the door.

Terry answered to Cynthia and turned to Madison.

Madison spoke to Hargrove. "One minute."

"Sure."

She stepped into the hallway.

"I have your results on the fetus in Lacy's womb, but I guarantee you that they're not what you were expecting." Cynthia handed the folder to Madison.

She read the results and passed them to Terry.

"Are you sure about this?" Madison searched her friend's eyes.

Cynthia nodded. "It's the science, Maddy. It doesn't lie."

CHAPTER 53

MADISON WENT BACK IN WITH Hargrove while Terry stayed in the observation room. She didn't say a word but paced, her focus steady on Hargrove.

"What is it you want from me?" He laid both hands flat on the table in front of him.

"Earlier you identified Hennessey and Bates. How?"

"I met them."

"Elaborate." She remembered both Hennessey and Bates had said they didn't know what Hargrove looked like. If they did, it was likely they would have pointed their finger at him for Lacy's death by now.

"I followed Lacy home one night."

"Why did you follow her?"

"I was curious what this guy looked like—especially this Hennessey who beat on her. I also wanted to know where to point the cops if anything happened to her."

"And something did." Madison dropped into a chair. "Who has access to your gaming password?"

"Well, I guess only me and my wife."

"No one else?"

"Not that I can think of."

"Did you notice a change in Lacy?" Madison's thoughts were on what Bates had said about her being withdrawn and sad. He was the only person who mentioned that about her.

Hargrove nodded. "She called me about a month ago."

"That's when we placed her time of death. Why bring this up

now?"

"I know I should have said something earlier, but I didn't want to taint her memory. She was high."

"Do you remember the time of day and what day of the week?"

"Thursday night I think. It was really late."

"She said she did something."

The timeline would fit with the day of the week Thorne died.

"What did she do?"

"She wouldn't tell me. She just kept saying sorry. I assumed it was because she was using again." He analyzed Madison's expression. "Is there more to this? What did she do?"

Madison didn't answer his question but rose from the table.

In the observation room, Terry said, "You didn't tell him the results."

"He doesn't need to know right now."

"Maddy?"

"I think Lacy killed Thorne."

"Come again."

"I think she killed him. Maybe he didn't want anything to do with her. Maybe she gave him the drugs to cheer him up because he lost his job, and he went unconscious. This makes a little more sense now."

"What are you thinking? I know when you get that look."

"Lacy could have thought he was dead."

"She could have panicked and slit his wrists to make it look like a suicide," Terry continued with her line of reasoning.

"We might never know for certain. We'd have to put the razor in her hand." Madison let out a sigh. Her thoughts were on the fact that she wouldn't have satisfying answers to provide Vilma, except for the fact her fiancé likely didn't leave this world willingly. She continued. "Lacy could have realized afterward what she had done. Maybe he came to when she cut him, but it was too late. There was no turning back or undoing what she had done. She didn't know there was a good chance the drugs would have killed him anyway."

"Oh God." Terry rubbed the back of his neck as if a genie in the bottle would magically appear and provide answers.

Seconds passed. Madison sifted her fingers through her hair.

"If Hargrove didn't proposition Hennessey and Bates to kill Lacy, who did?"

"He said only his wife and nephew had access to the gaming console."

"And only the wife was apparently able to go online."

"The kid wasn't." Terry finished the thought.

"The wife knew Lacy, but she didn't understand her husband's need to help her to the extent that he was. It would make her suspicious of an affair."

"Suspicious enough to kill?"

"Why not? People have killed for a lot less. Who had the most to lose?" As their eyes met, Madison saw a fire in her partner's eyes. "I think you're thinking what I'm thinking."

CHAPTER 54

MADISON SLIPPED INTO THE CHAIR across from Hargrove. Terry stood by the door, hands in his pockets but not jingling change.

"Why do you keep leaving the room?" Hargrove searched her eyes.

"You said only your wife and nephew were on the Xbox?"

"My wife wouldn't do what you're talking about."

"But you're certain no one else had access to your gaming information?" She couldn't feed him the name in her mind. She wanted him to say it.

Hargrove shook his head briefly, and his forehead compressed as if he had a migraine. "Maurice? Maybe?"

"He would know your password?" Madison remembered clearly how the man felt it was his responsibility to take care of Hargrove, how he felt everything the other man did would reflect on and affect him.

"We'd play sometimes."

Ironically, Madison never saw Maurice Kendal as the type to sit down and play a video game.

"I can see it on your face. We didn't play often. But there's always work to do. Sometimes you have to let go and unwind."

"Was he at your place when you played?"

Hargrove nodded.

"Is there any way he could have logged on as you?"

"There was one time I went to log on, come to think of it, and it said the account was in use. I chalked it up to a technology error. A few minutes later, I was able to get in. You think he did this? He wanted to kill Lacy?"

"You tell us. He thought you were sleeping with her."

"With Lacy? I don't know why he'd—"

"He said you sleep around on your wife regularly."

"Me? No. I haven't been unfaithful a day in my life. I haven't even looked at another woman since my wife."

"Christina Dunn from Modern Computers, she just came by to visit."

"I told you that. She wanted to talk about Lacy." Hargrove looked between Madison and Terry. "Not every man is a cheater."

Madison felt Terry's judgmental stare from the back of her head.

"Is it possible Maurice Kendal logged on as you without you knowing about it?"

"I suppose so, but why would he?" His skin went pale. "He set me up for this? I can't believe he'd do this."

"He thought you would ruin your marriage, your wife would come after your money and the business."

"It would be better for me to go to prison?"

"They say even bad publicity is good publicity."

Hargrove looked like a man who had his beliefs in life shattered. His eyes were misted and unfocused.

"I don't think he even intended for you to take the fall, but if one of you were going to, it wasn't going to be him. Kendal may have thought Lacy would ruin everything somehow. We still have to prove this." Madison felt her voice getting weaker as she approached the truth as to the DNA results. "We have the results back on Lacy's baby."

His face birthed a smile, and he balled his hands into fists. "Then you know I never slept with her."

"It might be really hard to hear what I have to say next."

His expression turned somber.

"The results showed that your DNA is a familial match to Lacy. You were her father."

"I what? I was her—" His face fractured into hard edges and tears pooled in his eyes.

"We imagine this is a lot for you to process."

He looked at her. "I never cheated on my wife." His plea fell in contrast to the evidenced truth. "I don't know how this could have happened."

"It would explain why you had such a draw to help Lacy, such compassion."

Tears fell down his cheeks. He bit his bottom lip. "My wife, she would be devastated if she…she can't find out…oh my God, what have I done?"

"Lacy was confused. She thought Maurice was her father, but you were. Both of you shared her mother one night."

His jaw slid askew.

"When we were there at Maurice's house, the first time we met you, he said that's why you stay away from ten-dollar whores."

"Oh God." Hargrove massaged his forehead with one hand. The tears had stopped falling, but he truly appeared before them a broken man. "We were celebrating this new contract we got. It was Maurice's idea. There was a lot of scotch involved." He looked up from the table to Madison. "I woke up the next morning beside this woman. I didn't even remember her name. We were both naked. I don't know how he did it, looking back, but Maurice had convinced me it wasn't what it looked like, that I didn't sleep with her. What a mess." His voice petered off and he stared past them. "What am I going to tell my wife?"

"Just tell her the truth," Madison said.

"Did you ever find the necklace?"

"No, I'm sorry we didn't."

"I CAN'T EVEN IMAGINE WHAT he's going through," Terry said outside in the hallway.

"We've got to set Kendal up and make him pay for this. Until we do, Hargrove has to sit tight."

"How do you propose we do that?"

"We need to log in as Bates. See if a message is already there. If not we'll fire one off to Slayer1962."

"What makes you think he's going to respond? He knows she's dead. Wouldn't he want to back away from it completely at this point?"

Madison shook her head. "Kendal's all about the money, not just the results. If he paid for Hennessey and Bates to kill Lacy, he'd expect them to be responsible, to be able to prove it."

"So, just show up at their place. He must know who they are."

"And risk us finding everything out? No way. The papers have been terming Lacy's death as suspicious. Kendal knows we've been investigating the case. He probably believes he owes them the balance of the promised money. Hush money at this point."

"How do we know he didn't already drop the cash?"

"Guess we don't, but we don't have a choice. Bates told us about the proposal and the handle name; he would have told us the rest. Besides, he seemed afraid that the fact Lacy killed herself would get out."

"Are you going to tell Bates?" Terry asked.

"What? Tell him he buried his child? Not yet."

AT LEAST TERRY HAD KNOWLEDGE of the gaming console. They obtained the one from Bates's apartment, not for evidence, but the department was on a budget and they needed an Xbox. Terry wasn't willing to part with his. He logged on under Bates's profile and went to the messages.

"Nothing there."

Madison's cell rang. "Knight…yes…okay." She tried to flag Terry's attention from the system. "Thanks, Sam." She hung up. "You're on the job, you know that. No gameplay at work." Madison laughed.

"Life is so unfair."

"You're telling me? The results are back on the gun. The bullet that killed Lacy was definitely fired from the gun we found in Bates's apartment."

"Okay, we figured it would come back that way." Terry's eyes never left the screen. "I'm going to message him and see if we can get him out of hiding. Until we hear back from—"

The screen blipped and an oval came up in the top right-hand corner with the message, SLAYER1962 IS ONLINE.

Terry looked at Madison. "He didn't waste any time."

"He was waiting on Bates to log on."

Another blip and an oval that read YOU HAVE A MESSAGE.

"Open it. What does it say?"

Terry turned to her.

"Come on."

He shook his head and smiled. "You have no patience."

"I was born that way. Terry?"

"You said parents blamed their kids for everything. It seems it works both ways."

She jabbed his arm.

"Here we go." Terry clicked the envelope icon.

"Perfect, he wants to meet."

CHAPTER 55

THE DROP-OFF LOCATION WASN'T anything exciting like leaving a lunch bag full of money in a garbage can of a busy intersection. Slayer1962 wanted to meet where he had left the first installment—the kid's apartment. While the first time had been a drop only, this time he wanted to meet face to face.

"You mess this up, you'll never see daylight," Madison said glancing in the rearview mirror to Hennessey, who was cuffed in the backseat.

They had pulled Hennessey because the meeting was to be at his apartment.

"You're going to do this exactly as we instructed you."

"You said we'd deal."

Madison didn't respond to him but thought of Alex Commons. He hated it when she swooped in and made deals with drug dealers, although the fact she and Terry helped stop the distribution of Oz earned her some respect. After they had got the sample of the cocktail, Commons had pushed Coleman and Burgess into flipping on their supplier and the producer of the drug. A deal had been made and Oz was officially off the streets.

There was one thing still bothering her. How had Kendal gotten a hold of Bates's online profile to connect in the first place? But they would get that information.

Terry sat beside her in the passenger seat. Hennessey was loaded up with surveillance equipment on his body. A small microphone taped to his chest would feed back to a recording device. It would transfer back to the van that trailed the department car Madison and Terry were in, as well as come over the earbuds they wore.

"No improvising. Stick to the plan," Madison reiterated the directions to Hennessey.

They didn't think Kendal held any threat to him, but they would be nearby should that change. Madison and Terry were going to hide in the bedroom where Lacy had been shot. They were arriving an hour before the scheduled meet to get inside undetected.

Madison parked the car two blocks away.

"One wrong move, my partner will blow you away." Terry uncuffed the kid.

Hennessey passed Madison a glare that only tempted her to pull the trigger. They walked behind him, at a small distance, toward the apartment.

They were in position in the bedroom, which was at the front of the building, and now all they had to do was wait. Madison looked at her watch. There were ten minutes to go when she heard movement outside on the front walk.

She strained to hear. Feet were definitely shuffling along the paved sidewalk to the back of the house.

Terry was near the front window and peeked through two horizontal blind slats. "They went by already. Didn't catch a—"

A knock came on the back door.

"Game time," Terry whispered. Madison silenced him with a finger to her lips and mouthed, *shh*.

"You have the money?" Hennessey asked.

"You do the job, or did she take care of it herself? The papers weren't too clear."

Madison turned to Terry. The voice sounded familiar, but it wasn't Maurice Kendal's. It was female.

"Bullet's in her head. I buried her. You said the rest of the money on completion."

Silence fell between them.

"Do you have the money or not? You paid me to kill her. I did," Hennessey said.

Footsteps came toward the door and made the wood flooring groan.

"Where are you go—" Hennessey started but was cut off.

"Where's your friend? Why isn't he here? You were in on it together." The footsteps stopped. "Where have you been?"

"Around." Hennessey played it light and added a small chuckle in there. "You wanted her dead. We did it." He laughed. "We got away with it."

"Where is your friend?" The woman repeated her question.

"He's at work," Hennessey lied.

Everything went quiet again and Madison felt the woman debated whether to believe Hennessey.

"Let me see the picture."

Madison mouthed, *the picture?* Terry looked as confused as she was.

"Come on, I haven't got all day," the woman demanded.

More floorboards creaked as a heavier weight moved toward the bedroom. The footsteps stopped outside, and the person, likely Hennessey this time, cast a shadow beneath the door.

Another door opened and touched the back of the bedroom one. It would have belonged to the hallway closet.

"Is this necessary? You know she's dead. It's in the papers," Hennessey said.

"I want to see it for myself."

"Yeah, I guess they don't show dead bodies in the papers."

Madison's stomach tossed for a couple reasons. They had taken pictures of Lacy after she was shot, holding onto them like trophies to collect on a death. Another churning sensation stemmed from the fact they had searched the apartment and came up empty. Maybe they had shuffled the photos like they had the gun that killed Lacy?

"Oh man, he must have moved it. The cops have been all over us."

"Hush! Something doesn't feel right about this."

"Whoa, don't get like that." The closet door shut and Hennessey thumped against the bedroom door. "We killed her like you asked. You paid us to kill her—"

"I paid you to succeed. That means no one going to prison for it."

There was the definite click of a gun.

"Gun! Please don't shoot me!"

Madison and Terry drew their weapons. They had one shot at this. Hennessey was pressed against the other side of the door. From the sound of it, the woman was just beyond that. They would have to be very careful about how they handled the situation or they could all end up with a bullet in them.

"Gun!" Hennessey repeated.

"Who are you talking to? Did you set me up?" Footsteps came nearer to the doorway.

"I didn't—"

"Are there cops in that room?"

Madison motioned to Terry, and on the count of two, he pulled the door open. Hennessey fell in, toppling backward onto the floor.

Christina Dunn stood in front of them, gun raised high, ready to shoot. Her control wavered and the gun swerved in a small, uneven circle. She laughed. "I didn't do anything. You heard him. They killed her."

Madison knew she continued to talk but was focused on the gun, on her demeanor.

Madison was in front of Hennessey; Terry packed tightly to her right.

"Christina, we're going to need you to put the gun down." As Madison studied her, assessing and trying to calculate her next move, her thought went to motive. What would push her to this point?

The woman, whose hands and neck had been adorned with jewelry the last time they had seen her, wore nothing but a simple gold chain. Her makeup was modestly applied. Her painted eyes sagged downward like a hound contesting for a treat.

"Go away!"

"No one needs to get hurt. Put down the gun."

"I didn't do anything."

"We just want to talk."

The woman mocked laughter, a tinge of insanity swept over her face. "Then you put your gun down."

Madison held out a hand in surrender and replaced her gun to her holster. She noticed Terry flinch and hoped the brief hesitation wouldn't cost them their lives.

"And him." The woman waved the gun from Madison to Terry.

"Until you put yours down, his stays," Madison said.

The woman shot a fiery glare at Madison.

"This doesn't have to end badly." Madison kept both hands up, palms toward Dunn. Swirling through her mind were the possibilities for a motive. The picture wasn't completing itself.

"You have no idea what's it's like." Tears streamed down the woman's cheeks with anger as the seed. Her cheeks were a bright red, her lined brows arched downward like pointed arrows, and her eyes were like fiery pistons. "He loved her."

He loved her? The words repeated in Madison's mind as a question. "Peter loved her?"

"Yes." The *s* came out as a hiss. "She was a whore, a druggie. He loved her, adored her, spent his money on her."

Madison softened her voice. She would play this from the viewpoint of a woman, an equal. "Love isn't always fair. We don't always get what we want." Flashes of her kissing Toby Sovereign layered in a bombardment of images.

"But I'd have had everything if I had him."

"We can't help who we fall in love with, Christina. I know."

The gun faltered, shifting downward slightly.

Am I about to make a confession to get the situation under control?

"How would you know? You're a cop, you've got everything together," she said through clenched teeth.

Madison wanted to glance at Terry because she felt his energy shift, but she knew better. You always kept your eyes on the subject.

"I'm also a woman," Madison said.

Dunn wailed. She brushed her one cheek with the hand that held the gun. She was quick to bring it down. Her eyes threatened Terry, *one move and I'll blow your head off.*

"We all want to make it out of this. It's up to you how it ends."

"You say you know about love. How?" The single-worded question hurled from Dunn's mouth as a bullet from a gun—the impact as severe to Madison.

She swallowed hard. "I've been hurt before."

Detection of a faint smile. "You still love him."

"What you feel for Peter, it can't be helped. He's a great guy, generous, and giving."

The woman studied Madison's face.

"He gives from his heart," Madison added.

"And other places! But he didn't want me! The whore would do!" The situation was escalating again.

Madison couldn't risk countering with the truth right now. The woman would perceive it as a lie to obtain the upper hand.

"I know what it's like to be you." Madison felt the strain in her voice as she attempted to verbalize her experience. "To love someone so completely that they can destroy your world, and your future, in a single instance, it's not fair." Madison hoped she had pacified her enough, but her eyes disclosed she wanted a continuation. "I was engaged to the…" *Love of my life* is what Madison wanted to say, but pride hindered her from saying the words out loud. "Anyway, he broke my heart, my belief in other people."

"You still love him?"

Madison wished Terry wasn't in the room so that he wouldn't be able to witness this weaker side of her. She hesitated to nod but eventually did. "But it doesn't matter now."

"How can you turn it off like that?" Dunn's question fell, impacting the room like a stone tossed into the river—ripples amplifying in its wake.

"You have to." Madison's heart raced; her stomach lurched. She noticed the woman's shoulders sag.

"Please put down your gun. We can take you to talk to him."

Dunn's eyes went to the gun she held and then to them. "Okay." Her voice fractured as her spirit was broken.

CHAPTER 56

"ANOTHER CASE SOLVED," Terry said.

"We still don't know how Dunn knew Hargrove's log-on information for Xbox, how she connected with Bates and Hennessey, or even how she knew of them."

Madison watched Dunn through the window of the observation room. She truly was a woman wrecked by love, a love she would never see reciprocated.

"Some answers you don't get."

"I can't live like that," Terry said.

"I know."

Madison brushed past him into the room. She sat across from Dunn.

"How did you do it? How did you know Hargrove's log-on name for Xbox?"

Dunn's eyes lifted from where they had been fixed to the table surface. They revealed a conflicted mess of thoughts, webbed behind the color of blue.

"Peter's house."

"From Peter's house?"

A slow nod. "I've been over there before. I know his wife."

With her words, and the cover of darkness that shifted in over her eyes like a clouded veil, Madison knew there was still much to uncover.

"We were friends." A sickly smile showcased. "She trusted me."

It had been established that she had first met Peter Hargrove at a meeting for local entrepreneurs. Even though Dunn only managed

Modern Computers, she had some business ideas. After that first meeting, they ran into each other in a bar, the same bar where Hargrove ended up hooking up with Lacy's mother. Dunn had been carrying a love for Hargrove since their second sighting.

"They had me over for dinner. She took a shine to me." Sadness reflected in Dunn's eyes. "She liked me more than her husband did."

"You played games on Peter's console?" Madison tried to redirect the conversation back on course.

"Yes."

"So you knew his name, but how did you know the password?"

She laughed. "Now that's the best part. You probably think he makes regular use of a password? Well, he does. He runs proposals past me before approaching his partner. He always said his partner undervalued him. And he did, you know."

Madison searched inside for patience.

Dunn's attention weaned from Madison back to the table. Her fingertips caressed the surface as the touch of a lover on skin. She lifted her eyes. "I jacked his account. Not too hard to do if you know what you're doing. The Internet is a terrific resource."

"You set up the man you love for murder?"

"Is he in prison? I think not. Charges never would have stuck to him, but he needed to be taught a lesson. May I see him now?"

Madison disregarded her question. "How did you hook up with Bates and Hennessey?"

"They were online friends of Peter's. People talk too much, run off at the mouth, thinking they can hide behind a fake name and a gaming console. People can be found. Easy."

"Still doesn't answer why you'd approach them, how you would even know they were connected with Lacy."

Her eyes lifted from the table, her fingers stopped moving.

Madison waited out the silence. She knew how much Maurice hated the idea of Hargrove helping Lacy and how he was concerned about the *bottom line* when it came to the business. "Was someone else involved? Was it Maurice Kendal?"

All movement stopped.

"Did he put you in touch with the kids?" Madison remembered they had told her they never met Dunn in person. She sensed this had been a lie.

"I followed her home from work one night."

"Lacy?"

"Yes." She looked up from the table. "She went to some motel."

"Do you remember when this was?"

"Not long after she started. I wanted to know what was so special to have Peter going out of his way to help her. She met up with someone there."

"And you don't know who?"

Her eyes glazed over, and her fingers pinched as if feeling the textile of fabric, yet nothing was in her hands. "I thought the one vehicle looked like Kevin's."

"That must have bothered you."

Her hand balled into a fist. "She had the man I loved and was screwing around on him."

"I take it you waited things out."

"A few hours later, she came out and got on a bus. I followed her until she got off. It wasn't the condo. I watched the place for the next few days and worked up the nerve to knock on the back door." She stopped there as if her story were complete.

"This is when you met Hennessey and Bates?" They had left this part out.

"You cops always call people by their last names?" Dunn paused. "But yes."

"And you thought the best way was to communicate over Xbox?"

"It's secure, private, different."

Madison nodded.

"When can I speak with him?"

When Madison and Terry had told Hargrove that Dunn had set out to orchestrate the death of Lacy, his face hardened, as an ice block.

"We told him."

Dunn straightened, hopeful expectation tattooed on her expression.

"He didn't want to talk to you." Madison had softened the blow in translation. Hargrove's words had been that he hoped Dunn would die in prison.

Tears fell down Dunn's cheeks, which were a bright hue of red. "I was doing this for us."

Madison felt sorry for Dunn. She had loved a man and she would never see that love reciprocated. Maybe Madison should have kept her mouth shut, but she felt compelled to let this woman know, to possibly help give her some closure, some understanding.

"Peter was never sleeping with Lacy."

"I don't be—"

"She was his daughter."

"His daughter?" She mulled over the statement—the implication and where this left her. Her face lit into a large smile. "He cheated on his wife at some point. I will get him. I will win his love."

Chapter 57

"SHE'S DELUSIONAL AND NEEDS THERAPY," Madison said. "She thinks she can win over a man who is in love with his wife."

"Well, she'll have a lot of time to think about it. Twenty-five to life for conspiracy to commit murder," Terry said.

"See where love gets you." Madison smiled, but the expression was wisped away without acknowledgment from Terry.

Silence fell between them and Madison sensed Terry wanted to ask what exactly had happened back at the house, but he refrained.

"Despite trying to orchestrate Lacy's death, the girl may have beat her to it. Crazy case."

"And Lacy, by all accounts, appears to have killed Kevin Thorne. That's not going to be a fun one to get resolved."

"It's not like you can sentence a dead person."

"We have to be very careful what we rule suicide or homicide. There has to be more accountability." Madison's eyes searched Terry's.

"But, Maddy, nobody is perfect either."

"People look to us, Terry. We provide answers. We are to bring justice to those who have been affected by crime."

"Then it's a good thing we have you." Terry put a hand on her shoulder and squeezed.

She smiled at him and turned away. They had found the photographs of Lacy's dead body tucked away in Bates's apartment, and when they had told him he was the father of Lacy's baby, he had cried. Madison didn't think even with all the time he faced behind bars that his pain would ever heal. She hadn't informed

Vilma about her fiancé yet, but she knew the woman deserved final closure. The case was officially reopened and would be amended.

Her cell phone rang and it was Cynthia.

"You want all your results now? Come get them."

"You wait until we have this wrapped up?"

"Trust me. I'm sure you'll still want to hear what I have to say." A smile of victory carried over the line.

"We'll be right there."

"HAVE A SEAT, GUYS. This will take a while." Cynthia opened a file folder on the table and took a seat. Madison and Terry followed her direction.

"As I said, all of the results are back from this case."

"Please don't keep us waiting any longer," Madison said.

"Lacy didn't pull the trigger on herself. We covered Hennessey's entire apartment including the exterior door handle. Particulates came back a match to GSR, specifically lead, barium, and antimony. Now, while it's true that transfer can happen easily, we also obtained prints on the knob which were a match to Hennessey."

"That part makes sense, as it was his apartment."

"It's the GSR I find interesting."

"But couldn't that transfer simply have been made when Hennessey picked up the gun to hide it?"

"Evidence is stacking against him. Didn't he say he found her that way?"

Madison nodded.

"So, if he picked up the gun off the floor, the concentration of GSR wouldn't be in the quantities pulled from the door handle. It is my expert opinion that he fired the gun." She shifted through papers in the folder and pulled one to the front. "There was also a fiber found on Lacy's body."

"I don't remember hearing about the fiber before now."

"Can you imagine how impatient you may have been then?" Cynthia laughed and Madison narrowed her eyes. "Anyhow, a sweater found in the dryer at the condo was a match to the color of the fiber. We sent it to an outside expert along with the exemplar and extensive testing proved it came from that sweater. We know Hennessey was living at the condo."

"All right, that proves he helped bury her, or in the least was around."

"Oh, here's the best part. The sweater was tested for GSR as well. Well, we didn't get too far with that because it had been washed, and who knows how many times before we collected it from the dryer. But we were able to pull blood trace that was a match to Lacy. Hennessey's story was he came home to find Lacy dead, well, that's all it was—a story."

"So, even though it had been a month—"

Cynthia nodded. "Blood never lies."

"What about the bullet casing? Did you ever get the results back?"

"Yes, ma'am, and prints on it were a match to Hennessey. He has at least the three things against him. The GSR, the blood, and the casing."

"Looks like we have all the evidence we need. He did kill her," Terry said. "Just how does Bates factor in?"

"Oh." Cynthia smiled. "You remember his prints were on the shovel? Well, his epithelial was a match to what was pulled from Lacy's fingernail."

"You are amazing!" Madison stood. "This is enough evidence to get them all behind bars."

"Maddy, this isn't everything either. Sit down. Kevin Thorne, the man whose death was concluded a suicide? I have proof it wasn't. You remember that Lacy had blood on her shirt."

Madison nodded. "We all assumed it was hers."

"Well, I'm paid to do more than assume." Cynthia paused to smile. "I ran extensive testing on it and found microscopic blood droplets. It came back to Thorne."

Madison looked at Terry. "She called Hargrove and told him she was sorry."

"She must have given him Oz not knowing what it was, panicked, thinking she had killed him…when she cut him, she probably realized he wasn't dead from the drugs," Terry said.

"Then she shot up with the other vial. That's why she was high when she called Hargrove. Makes more sense too, because I couldn't figure out how she would have been competent enough to slit his wrists while high."

"Hennessey and Bates must have shown up and helped cover part of the mess. But they didn't want Lacy dying that way or they'd never see their money."

"They dragged her back to the apartment, where they killed her." Madison's heart fell heavy, burdened with the guilt of a young, dead woman who had tried to turn her life around, who had wanted to be found innocent—what an ironic tragedy.

Cynthia closed the folder. "Sounds to me like you two have it all figured out now."

"Yeah. One hell of a case, well, two really. Wow. Complicated." Madison looked at Terry. "I guess we also have the drug dealer to hold accountable for Sahara Noel as well. I only wish we had proof to hold Kendal responsible for his part in all this."

"Well, from the look of things, if he was involved on any level, he hid his path well."

"Yeah, son of a bitch."

"SEEMS THERE'S A BUNCH OF paperwork we'll have to finish up," Madison said as she slipped into her chair, Terry across from her at his desk.

"Yeah, and you're not leaving me with all of it this time. And you owe me twenty. You said Hargrove was involved. He wasn't."

"Fair enough." She pulled out the bill and handed it to him.

"Good job on the case."

Madison looked up to Toby Sovereign, who held his hand extended to Terry.

Madison searched her mind for an excuse to leave, but Terry had just warned her not to stick him with the paperwork.

"I'm going to grab a coffee." Terry gestured to the bullpen, got up and left.

Madison narrowed her eyes at the back of her partner's head. She felt a touch on her shoulder and looked up at Sovereign. "What do you want?" She asked, anger rising within her. She hated how his touch made her weak and vulnerable, how it retraced the past and yanked it into the present. But she couldn't continue to fall victim to him anymore.

He lifted his hand. "I can't go on like this, Maddy."

Her heart raced and her stomach tightened.

"You look through me. You won't talk to me."

"There's nothing to talk about."

"Are you sure about that?" His question hung there as he searched her eyes. "The other night? It was amazing. It was like old times."

He couldn't be doing this. How could he think he could come back after all this time, after hurting her the way he had. No, she had to be strong.

He continued. "If you can look me in the eye and tell me you don't love me anymore, I'll never bother you again."

She felt sick. As she gazed into his eyes, her throat went dry.

Epilogue

Sometimes the answers are in the past, and if that's what it took, then that's where Madison was going.

She pulled her car to a stop across the street from Homeland Logistics, one of many fronts for the Russian Mafia. The sun was starting to set and waves lapped against the shore, combining with the sounds of the gulls to make a peaceful evening—if she were anyone else.

Her plans were anything but peaceful. She had answers to gather and it started here. She had waited too many years for all her hard work to equate to nothing. It would be resolved today.

She pulled the letter from her passenger seat and studied it. In Dimitre Petrov's own handwriting, she read his message. She had resolved from the start she wouldn't give any credit to a man who had killed his own parents and who was responsible for the deaths of so many. He didn't deserve to be heard.

He had been heard, however, and his days in court saw him serving twenty-five to life for a single murder. But accounting for one sin wasn't enough to erase the bloodstains left in his wake.

Madison pulled her visor down and studied her eyes in the mirror. She knew what she contemplated doing was stupid, reckless, extremely dangerous even, but what choice did she have. One man whose life was cut short at a young age deserved vindication. The voice of his soul begged for justice. She would see that he got it.

She ran fingers through her hair with one hand and tossed the letter back to the seat with the other. If Terry had any idea what that letter contained, he would tell her to walk away, to finally admit this case was a cold one. But she couldn't do that. This was personal.

She turned the car off and walked across the street. A huge crane hoisted a container from a platform onto a ship. She watched it as she contemplated each footstep. She would go right in their front door and demand answers. She made it to the property of Homeland Logistics, and her hand went to her holster. She confirmed her gun was there—again.

The door chimed when she opened it and a young woman sat behind a wood-laminate desk. Her eyes were dark and her structure thin. Her black hair was cut short, exposing a long, slender neck.

"Can I help you?"

"Tell Sergey that Madison Knight is here."

The woman's eyes went to the gun on Madison's hip.

"Hurry. It's urgent that I talk to him."

She got up from the desk, walked to the door, and flipped over the open sign so it would read closed to the outside.

"Shift's over." She left.

Madison heard banging out back and headed to its source. *What would make the girl leave?* Madison's heart thumped, bouncing off her rib cage like a scared bird. She pulled her gun.

She went through the door that came off the front room, her gun at the ready. She conducted a sweep and stepped through.

Two men with hammers looked up at her and raised their hands.

"Get to work!"

The voice caused her to turn. The banging started up again.

"I could say how nice it is to see you again, Detective Knight." Sergey took the stairs down from an upper landing. He and Anatolli were Dimitre Petrov's right-hand men.

Sergey offered a sincere smile, the kind that sent shivers down her spine. "I see you came here to start a war." He pointed to her raised gun and looked behind her. "Yet you came by yourself."

"I need answers." She kept her gun held up but could feel her hand shaking.

Focus on what you came here for.

"Why did you kill the lawyer?"

"Kill the lawyer? Ah, we're still worried about that." He rubbed his hands together and came to a stop in front of her. "You and me. We spend some quality time together first." He walked until the barrel of her gun pressed into his chest. "You are not a killer, Knight. You are blue. Blue-blooded. Now, let's put that away so we can talk like two regular people."

His Russian accent would haunt her nightmares if she made it out of here alive. She just needed the answers. She was tired of running around looking for them only to be in another dead end. Resolution was proving to be as elusive as smoke.

"Stop there." She would shoot him. She pressed the barrel harder against him.

He held up a hand and took two steps back. "You want to talk, you do it our way."

The end of a gun barrel pushed against the back of her head. Madison's breath froze.

"Come, Anatolli. You come with us." Sergey smiled at him. "It seems our day has arrived."

Madison knew what that meant. They were going to kill her. Everything flashed through her mind, but she was determined not to succumb to the negative thoughts groping at her.

"First, let me take this away from you." Sergey yanked on Madison's gun.

If she let him have it, she was dead.

If she shot him, she was dead.

She took a deep breath and squeezed back on the trigger.

At that moment, she was gifted with clarity. She thought back to the testimonial list provided from the one printing company. She had only briefly looked at the list but recognized one of the businesses, Knockturnl. Now she knew why.

With the revelation, Dimitre's letter came to the forefront: *"It wasn't me who killed the lawyer."*

Note to Readers

If you've enjoyed this novel, please tell your friends and family about it. If you have time to write a brief, honest review on the retailer site where you purchased this book that, too, is appreciated.

Carolyn loves to hear from her readers. You can reach her at carolyn@carolynarnold.net.

Upon receipt of your e-mail, you will be added to her newsletter mailing unless you express your desire otherwise.

Keep on reading for a sample of *Just Cause*, book 5 in the Detective Madison Knight series.

Do you, or have you, worked in law enforcement?

If so, Carolyn would love to know how you thought she did when it came to the police procedure in this story. Her goal is to provide the most realistic and entertaining police procedural novels in the marketplace. Your feedback would be much appreciated. Please e-mail her at the address noted above.

Read on for an exciting preview of Carolyn Arnold's next thrilling novel featuring Madison Knight

JUST CAUSE

CHAPTER 1

THE BULLET MEANT FOR HER head ricocheted off a stair. The thunderous ping of metal against metal rang in Madison's ears, reassuring her, along with the shooting pain in her legs, that she was still alive. But alive for how long was the question.

When the guns had fired, she dropped to the ground, slamming her knees onto the concrete.

She willed her eyes to open, despite the searing agony that made it easier to keep them closed, and she was forced to face reality.

Her bullet had found purchase in Sergey's side, and he sat on one of the steps, a hand to his wound, staring at her blankly. His eyes were clouded over and distant.

She surmised he was experiencing the same euphoric feelings as she. Her heart beat adrenaline through her system, its pulse drumming in her ears.

She was alive but was she shot?

She looked down at her body and couldn't see any blood.

Having faced a fifty/fifty chance of survival, she had come out the other end.

Anatolli pulled up on her short hair, his fingers digging into her scalp. "Get up!" He thrust the barrel of a gun to her face with enough force it skewed her jaw and her teeth bit the inside of her cheek.

A warm metallic flavoring coated her tongue and she spit out blood, the pressure of the gun was unrelenting.

"Get up! Or you die!"

Her legs were unsteady and her head spun. She couldn't go out like this. She had fought too hard for her life to end this way.

"Go to hell, you son of a bitch!" She slammed the heel of her shoe into his instep and moved to the side.

Anatolli yelped out in pain, but she heard him cock the hammer on the gun.

A revolver. Six bullets. Six opportunities to die.

The barrel was pushed against her skull.

She pinched her eyes shut and images of her life played out, interspersed with meaningless thoughts. How would Sergeant Winston spin this to the media? Would he miss her beyond their regular confrontations, for which she knew he thrived on, or would he be able to move on quickly?

Her grandmother entered her vision and spoke from beyond the grave, telling her it wasn't her time yet.

Anatolli applied more force behind the weapon. "You are going to die."

"Stop!" Sergey eased himself off the step he had been perched on.

Swallowing hard, she knew the delay in killing her meant only one thing—they would make her suffer until a bullet to the head seemed like a welcome escape.

The haze cleared. Where was her gun? She had pulled the trigger and ducked out of the way to avoid the one aimed at her head. If she could find her weapon, she'd have a chance...

As Sergey inched toward her, with gritted teeth, he swore in Russian. He resembled a rushing bull setting out after a waving red cape.

Her only chance was to reach her weapon, but the odds were stacked against her. If she were to make a bet with Terry, they'd likely both wager she'd leave in a body bag.

The gun came away from her head, but she still sensed that Anatolli held it aimed at her.

She looked around, taking in the space.

She was in the warehouse of the Russians' main business front, Homeland Logistics. Men were around when she first came in, but now all seemed silent, except for her and her two Russian opponents.

She remembered pulling the trigger and catapulting herself to the ground.

The left side of her hand tapped a pulse. She lifted it, but it fell limp, as blinding shivers of pain raced through her arm. But with the throbbing came clarity. She had banged her hand on the metal step as she fell.

She fought the urge to cradle her wrist to her chest. She had to remain strong.

Her eyes fell to the floor just beyond the staircase, where her gun lay, at least four feet away. There was no way for her to reach it before they killed her.

She lifted her arms in surrender.

"Get to your feet." Sergey spat in her face.

Instead of humiliating her, it fueled the anger raging beneath the surface. She would see their entire operation come down— even if she did so single-handedly.

She rose to her feet, keeping her arms above her as she moved.

"Do you want me to kill her, boss?" Anatolli pushed the barrel into her lower back. "Or we could watch her flop around like a fish."

"*Hvatit!*"

Anatolli lowered his gun.

Sergey spoke more words in Russian and Anatolli linked her arms behind, in his hands. Pain from her left wrist made her want to vomit, but it hardly deterred the man. He adjusted his grip and pulled her back into his chest.

"You are going to pay." Spittle from his mouth sprayed her cheek in a fine mist.

Anatolli pushed her up the stairs while Sergey led the way and struggled with each step.

They went into a large office, the size of the chief's, but, unlike his, they didn't accessorize to impress. Their focus was on necessity and usability.

The floor was a dark hardwood and contrasted with the lighter oak of the executive desk that stood at the one end. A flat-screen monitor sat on its top, to the right, and a desk calendar was in the middle. There were hand-written scribbles all over its surface in a variety of colors.

Next to the desk, numerous filing cabinets lined the wall. The room was devoid of artwork, except for a framed map of the world on the wall behind the desk and three clocks, set to different time zones, on the facing wall.

What had Madison's real attention was the doorway that came off the back of the room. This is where they were taking her.

Anatolli shoved her into the darkness and she momentarily lost her footing.

"Sit!" he barked.

At the same time, Sergey switched on a light. Its brightness momentarily blinded her as Anatolli pushed her toward a chair in the middle of the room. Chains were attached to the arms and legs of it, and there was a collar that would secure around their victim's neck while they worked out their sadistic pleasure on them. The floor was concrete and stained with splotches of dark crimson.

Blood.

More bile rose from her throat and mingled with the copper taste in her mouth.

Madison felt this sensation at a murder scene, and she felt it here, too. Lost souls cried out to her. Her mortality knew, beyond the sight before her, that lives had been brought to an end in this room, and that this particular road to hell had been paved with pain.

Anatolli thrust her into the chair.

"You're never going to get away with this."

Both Russians laughed.

"You are nothing special. Besides we have waited way too long." Sergey gestured for Anatolli to continue.

Anatolli secured her wrists, but when he bent to tie the shackles at her feet, she instinctively lifted her leg, connecting her knee with the cartilage of his nose.

"Bitch!"

His hand swiped across her face and torqued her neck to the

side. She wanted to fight back, but her eyes faded to black.

CHAPTER 2

SHE MUST HAVE BAILED ON him again. She seemed to have an aversion to paperwork and had crafted her avoidance of it down to a fine art.

"See Madison yet today?" Terry asked Ranson at the front desk.

Ranson shook her head. "I haven't. You check with the sarge? Maybe she called in sick."

Terry laughed. The thought of calling in over the stomach flu wouldn't even occur to Madison. She'd come in and puke in the garbage can before she'd succumb to a bug. Besides, he believed most infections and bacteria were afraid of her.

He pulled out his phone and dialed her cell. It rang several times before putting him to voice mail. "Where are you? I'm not doing all the reports." He hung up but had a hard time dismissing the feeling in his gut. Something was wrong. When she had ditched him in the past, she was upfront about it.

He tried her again and this time it rang straight to voice mail. He dialed her house and got her machine. He was left with one person—Cynthia. She was head of the crime lab and friends with Madison. She answered on the third ring.

"Have you heard from Maddy?" he asked.

"No, should I have?"

"She hasn't come in. It's not unlike her to be late, but not this late. Add to that, I can't—"

"You can't reach her?"

He hated it when people finished his sentences for him. Madison did it periodically, and his wife, but outside of those two women, it really wasn't acceptable.

"Like you said, she can be late. Maybe she just slept in. She's done that before."

Maybe he was being paranoid, but the fact he couldn't reach her nagged at him.

Then, as if Cynthia could read his mind, she said, "She's a tough girl. She can take care of herself."

"I just have a feeling something isn't right."

"She's rubbing off on you."

He detected Cynthia's smile over the phone. "Not sure if it's for the better."

"Maddy? Definitely."

"No answer on her cell or at her home."

"All right, that is weird."

"What's she up to?" The tone of Cynthia's voice had tipped him off, causing him to ask the question. She was withholding something due to her friendship with Madison. "Is she digging into that cold case of hers again?"

Chills went through him as his thoughts turned dark. Had Madison's vendetta with the Russian Mafia gone too far? The hairs rose on the back of his neck. "Tell me everything you know."

"Do you think she's okay? Now, you're getting me worked up, and I'm typically a balanced individual."

"Cynthia, I need you to focus. What was the most recent thing she had you look into?"

"Well, it was a bit ago now. Months even. But she had a…"

"Had a what?"

"If you would have let me finish." Irritation laced each of her words. "She had an envelope she wanted run against the piece found in the attorney's driveway."

"All right, I remember her mentioning it, but she's nuts. She's after them because of a stationary match?"

"I don't know for sure, but that part doesn't matter. We've got to find her—but what makes you think they're the reason she's not in?"

"I've gotta go." Terry hung up and made a few phone calls. He checked in with the kennel that took care of Hershey during the day. They said she didn't come in last night to pick him up and never called.

He stormed into the sergeant's office. "Madison's missing."

Winston pried his attention from his paperwork as if it were more riveting than his detective's latest drama. "Missing?"

"I believe so, yes. She's not answering her phone, either her mobile or home number. Her dog was left at the kennel overnight without her so much as making a call to them to explain."

Winston watched him intently. "That's not like her."

"No, it's not. She lives for this job. If she's not here, it's because she can't be. I've got a bad feeling."

"Go by her apartment. I'll get out an APB on her car."

LIGHTS FLASHING, Terry tore through the city to Madison's apartment building. He tried her intercom button and imagined her answering. He hoped that he had fabricated nothing into something. But there was no answer.

He pushed random buttons until he got someone. It was an elderly lady, based on her fragile voice.

"Who's there?"

"Stiles PD. I need access to the building."

"No way, creep. I know what you want. You have a granny fetish, you sick bastard. Go away or I'll call the police."

Terry rolled his eyes, tried another button, and received a more favorable reply. The door buzzed and unlocked for him. He was in.

He pounded on Madison's apartment door loud enough it could have roused the dead.

The last two words replayed in his head. *The dead.* What if something happened to Madison and he was too late?

He fell back against the door. The moment he made contact with it, he had his answer.

How could he have been so blind?

It took him thirty minutes to reach the harbor when it should have taken at least forty-five. He saw her Mazda across the street and his heart sank.

He parked the department-issued sedan a block away and

hoofed it to her car. He confirmed the plates and called it in. He would need backup.

Chapter 3

THE DOOR OPENED AND THEN slammed shut. It would have been enough to jar her if she hadn't been awake. She knew night had passed and morning had come along. Her hand maintained a steady, thrumming heartbeat and she wondered if it were broken.

"They're going to come looking for me." The words slit from her throat, her tongue and mouth were so dry.

"We're planning on it." The voice came from the shadows, but she recognized it as Anatolli's.

The light came on and he moved closer.

"They've been calling all morning." He held up her cell phone and tossed it into her lap. It fell off and landed on the floor at her feet.

"Let me go and we can work out a deal."

He didn't say anything but moved closer to her. He pulled out a cigarette and lit it. Taking a deep drag, he exhaled the smoke into her face.

She coughed on reflex.

"You shot my friend." He scowled.

As Madison's eyes adjusted, she observed the wildfire in his gaze and feared for her life.

He grabbed a handful of her hair. White flashes of pain limited her vision.

"Listen, we can make a deal if you let me go now." Her sentence came out fragmented, carried on bursts of breath. Maybe if she could somehow appeal to him. She had always considered Anatolli the weaker of the two.

"You are in no position to make deal." His Russian accent cut the air and his warm breath cascaded over her face, delivering the stench of nicotine.

What if she died here? This could be the last thing she remembered before she left this world.

Her cell phone rang again, vibrating across the floor.

"What will all of your friends think when you're dead and they were too late to save you?"

The way he was talking, she wondered if Sergey hadn't made it, but the door opened again and Sergey came through, walking with a gimp and favoring his right stride.

"You can't kill the devil." Sergey lifted his shirt and showed her the sutures that sealed up the bullet wound.

"Next time I'll be sure to finish the job," she said with more confidence than she felt.

Sergey's teeth clenched so tight, his jaw bones protruded in sharp, jagged lines. He nodded his head toward Anatolli, who released his hold on her hair, but drew his gun and put its barrel to her forehead.

She went to move to the side but found her motion limited. They had placed the collar around her neck. Panic stole her breath.

"But we won't kill you right away." Sergey gestured to the revolver in Anatolli's hand. "You like to gamble with your life, so how about we play a game?"

Her breathing stalled, her heart splintered in her chest, and her stomach tightened and heaved, tossing bile up the back of her throat.

"We simply call it roulette when we play. The Russian part would be redundant." Sergey paced the room and Madison didn't miss the flicker in the man's eyes.

"Anatolli's going to pull the trigger. If you live, we will take our time with you. If you die," he shrugged, "well, I suppose, game over."

Both men laughed, sending chills through her.

Her entire life didn't flash before her eyes, but moments of it did. Images of kissing Toby Sovereign haunted her, dredging up the feelings she harbored for him, but if she got out of here, could she look beyond the past to a future with him? He had challenged her to say she didn't love him anymore and to look into his eyes while she did so.

A deep breath escaped her lungs.

Cynthia. Would she understand? Cynthia knew how much solving this case meant to her. She had been supportive, but would she understand why she risked her life?

Her mother would never see her happily married with children, and their relationship would never be mended. She could envision her father grieving as if she were already gone. Tears fell over a daughter who was always just out of reach.

She wouldn't have a chance to say good-bye to them or to her sister, Chelsea. She wouldn't see her nieces grow up.

Terry would be disappointed in her and she would never meet his baby, his son, as he was so certain it would be.

The ache knotted in her chest with the realization that she'd devoted her life to the job to the point of isolation. She had one best friend, a partner who was like family, and a dog. Hershey. Who would look after the chocolate lab when she was gone?

For an instant, she imagined her fingers caressing the soft velvet of his ears. She witnessed the spark of life and a dancing reflection of love in his irises.

These thoughts occurred to her in fractions of seconds.

If she had a chance, she would do things differently.

Tears hit her cheeks and a part of her soul submitted to the inevitable. She was going to die in this room with no one by her side but the two Russians who would carry out her murder. Her only hope was that fate would intervene before her death became a reality.

Also available from
International Best-selling Author
Carolyn Arnold

JUST CAUSE
Book 5 in the Detective Madison Knight series

Sometimes cold cases are deadly...

The past threatens the future and puts Detective Madison Knight's life in danger.

A cold case pits Madison against the Russian Mafia, but things take a swift turn when the unthinkable happens—a new threat arises and has Madison hunting down an unknown killer.

While trying to make sense of the clues, bodies are piling up, and the brass is hungry for explanations. In addition, Madison must balance all of this while nursing an injury, talking out her emotions with a therapist—a bureaucratic necessity—answering to an eager journalist, and facing an internal affairs investigation.

As the answers come together, Madison narrows in on a possible link between the Russian Mafia and someone within the Stiles PD.

Will she have the courage to confront the person she believes is playing both sides, even though they hold a position of great power?

Things are about to be shaken up, and, for Madison, that means she just might have to let go of the past to embrace her future.

Available from popular book retailers or
at carolynarnold.net

CAROLYN ARNOLD is the international best-selling and award-winning author of the Madison Knight, Brandon Fisher, and McKinley Mystery series. She is the only author with POLICE PROCEDURALS RESPECTED BY LAW ENFORCEMENT.™

Carolyn was born in a small town, but that doesn't keep her from dreaming big. And on par with her large dreams is her overactive imagination that conjures up killers and cases to solve. She currently lives in a city near Toronto with her husband and two beagles, Max and Chelsea. She is also a member of Crime Writers of Canada.

CONNECT ONLINE
carolynarnold.net
facebook.com/authorcarolynarnold
twitter.com/carolyn_arnold

And don't forget to sign up for her newsletter for up-to-date information on release and special offers at carolynarnold.net/newsletters.

Made in the USA
San Bernardino, CA
27 April 2018